THE OUTFIT: OUTLAWED!

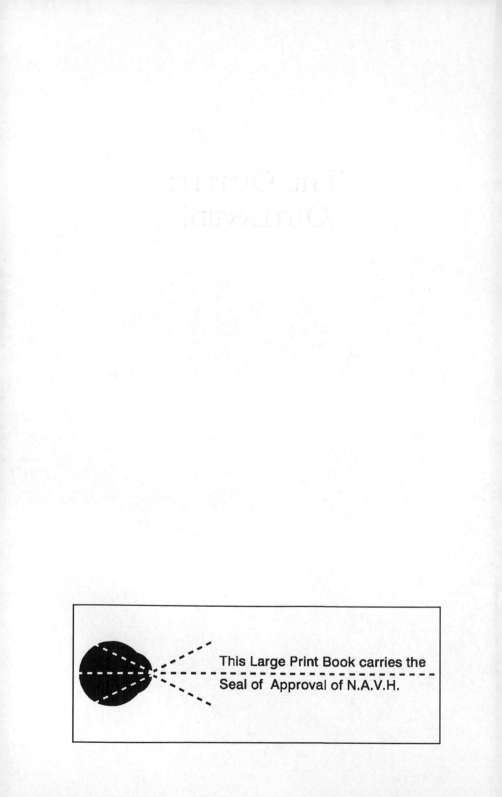

This Large Print Book carries the
Seal of Approval of N.A.V.H.

THE OUTFIT SERIES, BOOK 3

THE OUTFIT: OUTLAWED!

MATTHEW P. MAYO

THORNDIKE PRESS
A part of Gale, a Cengage Company

Farmington Hills, Mich • San Francisco • New York • Waterville, Maine
Meriden, Conn • Mason, Ohio • Chicago

Thorndike Press® Large Print Western.
The text of this Large Print edition is unabridged.
Other aspects of the book may vary from the original edition.
Set in 16 pt. Plantin.

LIBRARY OF CONGRESS CIP DATA ON FILE.
CATALOGUING IN PUBLICATION FOR THIS BOOK
IS AVAILABLE FROM THE LIBRARY OF CONGRESS

ISBN-13: 978-1-4328-4923-8 (hardcover alk. paper)

Published in 2019 by arrangement with Cherry Weiner Literary Agency

Printed in Mexico
1 2 3 4 5 6 7 23 22 21 20 19

To friends . . . old, new, and yet to be.

"Never contract friendship with a man that is not better than thyself."

— Confucius

OUT·FIT (noun): A group of people engaged in the same occupation or belonging to the same organization, occasionally with the implication of being unconventional or slightly disreputable; a collective of cowboys employed by a cattle ranch.

CHAPTER ONE:
CASH IS KING

Talbot Timmons climbed aboard the west-bound train thirty minutes before it pulled out of the station at Santa Fe. He smiled, puffed with pride at his life's recent twists. Not only was he warden of Yuma Territorial Prison, but after the War of Northern Aggression, he'd managed to revive and ride point on the Brotherhood of the Phoenix, the mightiest group of die-hard Confederates the world had yet seen. *And soon,* he thought, *soon I will be a governor, then a senator, then — and why the hell not? — President of the United States.*

And then, by God, we'll see who dares to stop the Brotherhood from rising to its rightful place. A quick thought twitched his smile. It was true his powerful covert group had foundered in recent months, but Timmons was dedicated to reviving its waning cause. "The South," he whispered, "shall rise again, reborn from the ashes!"

He chuckled at the promise of the phrase as he stowed his leather suitcase of clothing and toiletries on the top luggage shelf at the end of the car. He didn't buy into the Confederate cause like the other members of the Brotherhood did, never really had, if he were honest with himself. He did believe wholeheartedly in attaining ever-greater positions of power over others. And with that, he knew that his personal fortune would continue to amass, as it had steadily since long before the war.

The Brotherhood of the Phoenix was little more than a convenience, a way to exploit the Rebel-fevered minds of wealthy southern men, so Timmons stroked their feathers and endured their foolish rants, even when they let him down. *I should be knotted in anger,* he thought. After all, he'd been let down right here in Santa Fe by one of the junior members, one Colonel Turlington the Second, sloppy, bloated offspring of the original Colonel Turlington.

Rufus Turlington the younger had been entrusted with overseeing the Brotherhood's big fundraising opportunity in town, the poker tournament, the Tournament of Kings. Yet instead of seizing the opportunity to impress the senior members of the Brotherhood, the oaf had embezzled the group's invested funds.

He had been caught in the act, given a second chance, then limped through the event, only to botch what was to have been the crowning moment of the Brotherhood's rebirth: the public lynching of President U.S. Grant, flanked by two former slaves. The spectacle was supposed to have shown the world that the Confederacy was far from dead and buried. Indeed, it was to have been the Brotherhood's finest hour. Then that foul Rafe Barr and his chums burst in on the situation like the yipping, yapping pack of curs they are. He'd heard they were calling themselves The Outfit, or some such silliness. More like outlaws . . .

Timmons sighed, shaking his head at the memory of the squandered opportunity. And yet, he wasn't angry. He was grinning like a circus clown, couldn't help it as his gaze drifted down once more toward his boots, to the bulging carpetbag groaning with cash.

Its dead weight pressed with reassurance against his leg. Its contents had been stuffed tight, testing the seams and toggle buttons atop. Timmons snugged the bag on the floor between his boots. *Reborn from the ashes,* he thought of the Brotherhood once more

13

with a wry grin, *but only for as long as I need it to be.*

He sat down, one hand still gripping the satchel's long loop handles, and lifted off his bowler. He fanned himself briefly before resting the hat on his right knee. Through the window, the depot looked small and tired in the sun. Passengers walked toward the ticket office; others eyed the train as if deciding on a purchase.

Timmons tensed as he felt someone sit down in the seat facing his. He did not turn from the window, but sighed. The little zing of happiness he'd felt moments before withered. "I daresay," he said. "There are plenty of other seats available. No need to crowd each other now, is there?" He turned, a tight smile pasted on his face. It slid away as soon as he saw who'd joined him.

"Turk Mincher," said Talbot Timmons in a low voice. "What in the hell do you want?" Sudden worry shined in the warden's eyes. "You aren't taking the train west, are you?"

The man said nothing.

Timmons looked back out the window, his cheek muscles bunching. "As I recall, we are done with each other. You were paid in full for . . ." he looked around in case anyone else happened to be about. "For your efforts," he said in a lowered voice.

14

The man who'd joined him was clad in the only clothes the warden had ever seen the killer-for-hire wear — spotless black on black, but with a blood red shirt that appeared to be silk seeming to glow on the swarthy killer's torso. Mincher rolled a matchstick back and forth between his lips. "Now, now, Warden Timmons. You ought to know that once I become acquainted with a man I sort of see him as a friend, not someone I can leave hanging, so to speak."

The reference to the botched lynchings was not lost on Timmons. He regarded the man a long moment. "What is it you want, Mincher?"

"Want?" The man in black laid a hand across his chest, eyebrows rising in shock. "Whatever makes you think I want something, Warden?"

"Because your kind always wants something."

Mincher leaned back, arms stretched along the back of the seat. "Now is that any way to talk to your old friend Turk?"

"We are not friends, Mincher. Never have been, never will." He regarded the man a moment longer, his hand tightening on the satchel's handles.

Mincher's eyes flicked downward once toward the bag, then back to Timmons's

15

face. Neither man spoke. Finally, the warden's face softened.

"You've thought of something. I knew it, you can't live without ol' Turk."

"That is an exaggeration. But, yes, something did occur to me. It seems you are intent on playing the part of a sniffing coyote, so I'll give you something to sniff into."

"Favors I don't need, Warden. If I hire on to do a thing for a man, it has to be worth my time."

"Oh, it'll be worth your time." The warden plopped his hat back on his head and leaned against the window, one hand still holding the satchel handles. "You recall a certain daughter of a certain governor?"

"Hmm," Mincher drummed a finger on his square chin, at the spot where the two long pink scars that ran along his jawbone nearly met. "You mean the one who was held prisoner in Deadwood by that foul creature, Al Swearengen? The spoiled little girl you should have sent me to retrieve in the first place? The one you instead sent Rafe Barr to rescue some time ago? The same Rafe Barr who was locked up for life in your prison for murdering his wife and son? The girl he did rescue and then failed to turn over to you? Is that the one?"

16

The warden sighed. "What happened was regrettable. But, fortunately for you, I find I have a renewed interest in her procurement."

"How fortuitous for the both of us — how's that for a three-dollar word? Why, imagine if I hadn't wandered into your train car."

The warden leaned forward, doing his best to look steadily into Mincher's cold, snake eyes without glancing away. He worked to keep his voice steady. "Don't toy with me, Turk. I don't like you, you don't like me. But we each have something the other man wants."

"I have skills you need, that is true. But you, Warden Talbot Timmons, don't have a thing I need."

"I beg to differ, Mincher. You see, I happen to know you are a bloodthirsty bastard and what's more, you don't much like it when an opportunity is snatched from you, something you feel you deserved. Am I correct?"

For the first time in their unpleasant conversation, Turk Mincher's carefree smile slipped into a grim slit. His dark eyes settled on the warden. "It'll cost you, Timmons." He stretched a leg out into the aisle. "But then again, I don't reckon money is much of a concern to you now, is it?"

"What do you mean by that, Mincher?"

The man in black smiled once more, then jerked his chin toward the bulging carpetbag between Timmons's feet, its handles gripped tighter in his hand.

"A little birdy told me someone who looks an awful lot like you was seen scooping up, shall we call them, neglected piles of cash following that poker tournament that turned into a holy mess right here in Santa Fe. I hear tell the bag this mystery man used looks a whole lot like that one yonder, at your feet."

His voice rose as he spoke until it felt to Timmons as if Mincher was shouting for the entire town to hear. "Keep your voice down, for God's sake, man!"

"What's the matter, Warden? You afraid somebody's going to figure out that the entire kitty, even the cash in the hotel safe, somehow made its way into your satchel?"

Timmons gazed through narrowed eyes out the window. A scrim of dark cloud in the distance streaked the sky. It could mean a storm was coming, but that was a rare event in these parts. More likely it was an illusion, heat rising off the dry earth. "You appear to be particularly well informed."

"Then you don't deny it."

"Why should I, Mincher? If you think I'm going to be bullied and pushed around by someone like you, then . . ." he shrugged.

"Perhaps you are correct. To a point." Timmons made a show of sliding a cigar from his inner coat pocket. He did not offer one to Mincher. Timmons sniffed it, clipped the end, and lit it. He enjoyed the first pull, then expelled the smoke in a blue-gray cloud.

"Is this little pantomime of yours supposed to leave me weak in the knees and scare me off, Warden? Strikes me people will soon learn a whole lot about the protector and upholder of the law who, in their midst, stooped to such foul levels as thievery and deceit."

The warden smiled. "Yes, you think you know all about the Brotherhood of the Phoenix. You think you know how I came to be carrying a satchel stuffed with what you perceive to be cash money. Ill-gotten, if I am to believe your probing ways. But make no mistake, Mr. Mincher. You cross me in future dealings and I will see to it that you are not killed, that would be far too simple. No, I will see to it that you are . . . hmm . . . What's the worst thing that could possibly happen to a man of your reputation, your skills?" The warden smiled and puffed his cigar.

"You are not capable of that, Timmons."

"Watch me. In fact, I have a particular cell at Yuma Territorial Prison for a man of your estimable talents. Not surprisingly, it was last occupied — in a long-term stay, I assure you — by none other than the man who bested you in obtaining this job. Yes, I refer to Mr. Rafe Barr. So, in a way, you'll be playing second fiddle to him for the rest of your days." He puffed the cigar, pluming smoke at the wooden ribs of the ceiling.

Passengers began clumping up the steps and entering the long car. "Oh, don't fix me with that sneer, Turk. It will all work out, I assure you."

"Tell me what you know of the girl's whereabouts." Mincher's scowl was a dark thing, replacing the usual smiling sneer on his face.

Timmons drew on the cigar, held the smoke, then pushed it out. "If I knew that, why on earth would I hire you, Turk?"

Mincher rose, the scowl still in place. "It will cost you, Timmons." He nodded at the bag at the warden's feet. "In fact, I expect it will cost much of that haul. Elsewise . . . well, you know."

As he left the car, Turk Mincher touched

the brim of his black, flat-crown hat, and once more there was that confident smile.

Warden Talbot Timmons fancied he saw something else there, too. Something he'd not seen on the killer-for-hire's face before. Perhaps it was uncertainty. Or fear.

CHAPTER TWO:
OLD DEBTS, NEW FRIENDS

With every minute that passed, the window-less storage space, a lean-to off the little adobe cottage's kitchen, felt less safe to Cookie McGee. But he could hardly complain; as hideouts went, it was a decent place to hole up. With the help of the girl, they'd arranged an old star-pattern quilt and two moth-chewed gray-wool blankets on a low-slung rope. Anyone glancing through the door would see a sloppy stack of junk, and nearby a small, tidy stack of chopped firewood for the cookfire. Other items piled in the space looked to be of little use — a round table with three legs, one of which was half-missing, old brooms, ristras of chiles, and a jumble of dust-covered wooden chairs and stools locked together in a tangle of wood.

Marietta had told him what was now her home had once been her father's cantina. All that was left was her mother's cookstove, and the remaining bits of furniture. In hard times, she had taken to breaking up the furnishings to burn for heat. Cookie reckoned she had enough left to survive one week in a cold spell. Then she would be out of luck, and out of heat.

He shook his head at the memory of how he'd met her — talk about a stroke of good fortune, though he'd come to find out it wasn't due to luck.

He'd been dragging Rafe to safety and had neared the mouth of the alley when something hissed from the shadows. Cookie had spun, clawing for his revolver. All he saw was a pile of rags. Then that slowly stood and became a bent old Mexican man. It had shuffled closer, parted the close cloth of a hood, and that's when he noticed the rag-wrapped hand looked to be that of a woman, long fingers thick from work.

He'd been about to ask her to explain herself when she bent close to Rafe. She pushed the hood off her head and Cookie saw her profile, a stunning young woman with crow-black hair, a solid chin, and a thin nose with a slight bend, as if it had been broken long ago. In that slight glimpse of her face in the late light of the fading day, he'd been gripped by her beauty. The moment passed with finger-snap speed, and all his thoughts returned to helping Rafe.

Cookie bent down next to her. He had no choice — he had to trust her. "Ma'am, you know English? I need a doctor for my friend. He's alive but in a bad way. Please, I need to get him to a doctor, you understand?"

"Sí, sí," she nodded, her voice little more than a whisper. "I speak English fine. I know a man who can help. But don't drag him anymore. You'll harm him worse."

Rafe groaned.

"Oh, God," said Cookie. "I have to get him to help."

"Sí, I'll go fetch him. And a door."

"Door? Ma'am, I don't know what game you're —"

She stood, holding up a hand before Cookie's face. "To carry him on. I have a room where we can hide him — and you — until he is well."

"Hide? You know who we are, then?"

She nodded. "I know. But later, time for this later. Stay here, in shadows. I'll be back." With that, she was gone.

"Hang in there, pard," said Cookie, tugging as gently as he could on Rafe, dragging him over a few more inches into the dark. If the girl knew about him and Rafe, then the whole town might know they're wanted.

He'd hoped that him, Rafe, and the gang saving President Grant's life might have smoothed over the rough edges of their outlaw status. At least long enough to get on out of town, maybe back to the ranch. But it looked like someone had changed his mind, or was not aware — or worse, didn't care — of the favor they'd done for the president. Oh, what a mess.

"Rafe, pal," Cookie whispered, "you have to get well. I don't know exactly what happened to you, but you don't look good. We get a doc to look at you, then we'll know better. Might be it's a mere scratch."

Cookie paused, bending close to his friend's face, but he detected no response, no fluttered eyelid, no twitched mouth corner.

"You remember that time I set off too hot a charge, nearly kilt myself?" Cookie whispered. "Oh, I know what you're thinking, I do that all the time. I can hear you now, saying, 'Cook,' — you know you're the only one I let call me that. Others have to call me Cookie. Anyways, I can hear you saying, 'Cook, you have to be more specific — which time that you set off a hot charge and nearly killed yourself did you mean?' "

Cookie shook his head and continued with his whispered tale. "Why, it was that time, after the war, before you, ah, settled down at the ranch with Maria. We was hunting those rebel train robbers, tracked them to that old tobacco plantation down Arkansas, or might be it was Missouri way. Anyway, I slid clear across that old barn on my backside, only thing stopped me was that wall. I managed to crack a few ribs and boards in the barn wall, too! Knocked myself clean out. I come to with you leaning over me, one of them godawful cigars of yours stinking up the place." The old rooster of a man smiled at the memory. He was brought back to the present with a low moan from the unconscious Rafe.

True to her word, the girl returned, a wool blanket draped over a shoulder and carrying one end of a plank door that looked to be two feet shorter than Rafe's north-of-six-foot height. The other end was lugged by a squat, plump man wearing a straw hat that looked as if its brim had been sacrificed to a swarm of rats, so ragged and gnawed did it appear.

"You a doctor?" said Cookie in a low voice.

"Sí, sí," said the portly little fellow. He spoke low to the girl in Spanish, instructing, from the looks of it. They laid the door beside Rafe on the ground and the fat man

26

nudged the brim of the hat back to reveal a florid, sweating face. He nodded at Rafe. "He's a beeg man, eh?"

"Yeah, yeah, okay," said Cookie. "If you two are going to help me, we best get to it."

The man said something to the girl and she turned to Cookie. "You and Ricardo lift your friend here," she pointed at Rafe's shoulder. "And here." Rafe's hip. "I will slide the door under him. Then we ease him onto it and then we cover him with this."

She dropped the blanket she'd been carrying, and bent to the edge of the door. "Okay, now," she said, nodding at the two men.

Rafe groaned long and low. By the time they had him situated roughly in the center of the plank door, his groaning had tapered off to a wheeze.

Cookie looked close at his face. "Rafe? You . . . you okay? Still with me, pard?"

Cookie felt a hand on his shoulder. It was Ricardo. "He has asleep." At Cookie's confused glance, he looked to the girl for help with the word.

"Passed out," she said.

Ricardo nodded, "Sí, sí. We go now while he is passed asleep."

The girl covered Rafe's body with the blanket, then tugged it over his face as well.

Cookie said, "Now see here, he ain't but sleeping, as Ricardo says."

"I know," said the girl, "but if we are seen, it will look like we carry a dead man. No one wants to look at a dead man, sí?"

Cookie nodded, but tried not to look down at Rafe covered up like that. "Ain't right," he muttered.

The girl helped Ricardo heft his end of the door. Rafe's legs bounced nearly at the knee, hanging off the end.

Cookie carried the end with Rafe's head. "You damn big bastard," he muttered, stifling a sob. "I've a good mind to drop you, show you how worked up I am." Then Cookie decided that shutting his mouth would give him more stamina.

They'd been shuffling along, cutting across streets and between buildings, when a voice barked, "Hold up there!"

Ricardo stopped, but in a low tone Cookie said, "No, dammit! Keep going. Might be he wasn't talking to us." He kept hefting.

The voice called out again, "I said hold! You folks toting the body!"

Cookie groaned and sighed as they stopped.

A tall shape walked toward them.

Cookie's arms trembled from holding Rafe. "Got to put him down," he said to the girl. They lowered the door, resting it on their boot toes as the man walked closer. He was a soldier from Fort Marcy. Cookie knew they'd been scouring the city looking for someone, now he wondered if it was him and Rafe. Cookie tugged his hat brim lower.

The soldier had come within fifteen feet when Cookie held up a hand. "Don't come no closer!"

The man stopped, a hand working to unfasten the flap on his sidearm's holster. "What's going on here?"

"This man," Cookie pointed at Rafe's covered form. "He's passed on, but he's still contagious. We're all exposed to it. Heading to a quarantine house now, over yonder."

The declaration had the effect Cookie hoped for. The soldier's eyebrows rose and he paused in his groping for the gun. "What . . . what was wrong with him?" he said as he stepped backward.

Cookie leaned low toward him, face still shrouded in hat-brim shadow, as if they were sharing a secret. "Nobody knows yet. But they're not ruling out the pox." Cookie nodded.

"The . . . the pox?" The soldier backed another two steps, held up his hands, and said, "Oh, lord, no, not the pox!" He spun and ran, crunching gravel down the road.

"Pox?" said Ricardo, looking from Cookie to the girl.

The girl almost smiled and shook her head at Cookie. "Let's go before he returns . . . with friends."

It turned out the woman lived two lanes over from the alley where he'd found Rafe. They made it to the little adobe structure with a leaning ramada out front. Cookie saw a black gap where the front door should be. She'd taken down her own door to help Rafe. What manner of girl was this?

They eased Rafe, angled up slightly on one side, through the open doorway.

"Keep going, straight back," she said.

They passed through a low, wide arch hung with cloth that parted in the middle as Cookie edged through.

"More, to the back wall," said the girl, nodding at a spot behind Cookie.

They were in a kitchen. Cookie saw a small cast-iron cookstove at one end, a table and cupboards and a dry sink along another wall of the small space.

They stopped once more while Cookie, on her orders, thumbed the wooden latch on yet another door. As if reading his mind, the girl said, "This room is for storage. There is a cot, but we have to clear away a few things first. Get him in there, set him on the floor."

Cookie helped her shift dust-covered junk from the cot. It was strung with rope and, to his relief, the rope, though obvious it had been unused for some time, felt solid. She laid a thick straw-ticked mattress on top of the ropes and it barely sagged in the middle, it was decent enough to hold up Rafe. They laid him on it and the girl covered him.

"Hurry, help me with the door before we are seen by anyone else. The gringo soldier might have second thoughts about the pox story. He could be searching for the dead body he saw."

The door's leather strap hinges proved no challenge and soon enough it swung as it should. As it clunked closed, Cookie heard horses walking at the far end of the street. It was nearly dark and he backed toward the room with Rafe at the girl's insistence. "We won't light the lamp until they've gone."

They spent the next few minutes tense, waiting for the sound of soldiers to arrive, relieved to hear none.

She shrugged. "It might have been somebody I know. This is a busy part of town."

They helped slice off Rafe's shirt. Ricardo muttered and the girl left the little dark room, returning right away with a black doctor's bag and an oil lamp.

Cookie nodded at the bag. "You wasn't kidding. This fella is a doctor, ain't he?"

The girl fumbled with a match, squinting at the lamp. "Sí, I told you so."

She closed the door and held the lamp, wick turned low, over Rafe. In the dark, tight space, Cookie, the girl, and Ricardo leaned over the big man. They saw his chest slowly rise and fall. They also saw much dried blood that looked to be from two wounds, one up high on his left side, below where the heart sits, and the other, lower on his right side. Each of the punctures was no wider than an inch, perhaps less.

"Stabbed," said Cookie through tight teeth. "Doc, you do anything for him?"

"Sí," said Ricardo, "but go away. I need room to work."

"But he's my friend. I'm staying, no ifs or buts, buddy."

The girl laid a hand on Cookie's arm. "Come," said the girl. "Leave him to work. I will make tea."

Cookie looked at Rafe another long moment, then nodded and followed her into the kitchen. He turned away, dragging his oversized old bandanna under his nose. "You got anything stronger, I'd be obliged."

She nodded and opened a cupboard, then

brought down a jug wrapped in woven fronds.

"He's my pard," said Cookie. "I can't stand to see him this way."

"I know. I can tell."

Cookie and the girl each sipped mezcal from chipped stoneware mugs. He was about to ask her a question when she said, "I have watched you, all of you, from the first."

"What?" he thought for a moment she was having trouble with the language, but no, she spoke English better than he did.

Again, she almost smiled, then the look was gone. "I met your friend, the black man, the fancy gambler with the cane. The night before the gambling tournament. He saved me from getting beat up, in a bar in town."

"Jack? You know Jack?" Cookie smiled, sipping the mezcal. "Doesn't surprise me."

Her brows clouded. "What does that mean?"

"Now, don't take no offense. I only meant that he's, well the man has good taste. Maybe not in clothing — he wears the damnedest togs — but he can sure spot a pretty lady, all right." Cookie felt his face heat up and he sipped, looking around the kitchen.

"Where is he now, this Jack?"

"He's . . . he's off at the ranch, healing up."

The girl said nothing, but stared at him.

"Now, look, I can't take you there, why, word was to get out I was doling out free directions on the map to everybody, I might as well turn myself in to the blasted authorities and be done with it."

She sipped, looking away. "I was not asking about your ranch. I only want to know if he is hurt badly. I was too far away to help. By the time I made it to where he was about to be hung by that fat man, I was too late. He was gone."

"Yeah, me and Rafe, we settled that bastard's hash, pardon me, ma'am." Cookie winced.

She waved a hand as if shooing a fly. "But I need to know . . ." She looked at him again. He decided she had maybe the prettiest eyes he'd ever seen on a woman. Except maybe for Arlene's.

He thought of Arlene Tewksbury, cook and general boss of the ranch, who was not only a fetching lass, but she made the world's best biscuits. Ever. And since Cookie considered himself a learned man regarding all things biscuit, that was saying something.

"There was a woman," said the girl.

"Always is," said Cookie, a light grin on

his face.

"No, no, on the scaffolding with Jack and President Grant."

"Oh, you mean Mala. Yeah, she's okay, too."

"Mala? Hmm," said the girl, turning from Cookie. She lifted the bottle, then poured each of them a splash more of the fiery liquid.

"Oh, I see, you think Mala . . ." Cookie smiled again. "No, no, Mala, she's Jack's sister. Long lost and everything."

"Sister? Really?"

"Would Cookie McGee lie to you?"

"Who is this . . . Cookie McGee?"

"Who . . . ? Why," the feisty man puffed up his bony chest and said, "why, you're looking at him, ma'am."

"Oh, I see, I see."

She smiled fully for the first time and he knew she'd been funning him. But how had she known who he was?

She kept speaking. "No lies then. Okay, okay, so this Mala is Jack's sister." The girl smiled, then thrust out her hand. "And I am Marietta. The last name, it's not important."

"Okay, then, Marietta. That's fair enough."

There was a slight rustling at the far side

35

of the room and Ricardo parted the curtains in the doorway and stepped through.

"Doc," said Cookie. "How's he doing? He . . . going to . . ."

For all his limited English, Ricardo understood the look on Cookie's face. He smiled a weary look and nodded. "Sí, I believe he will live."

Cookie had never before felt like shedding tears of relief. Then the doctor spoke again. "But," he held up a finger. "He is not well. He has . . . how do you say," he turned to Marietta and spoke in Spanish.

She responded, then spoke to Cookie. "He says your friend may always be weakened because of this attack. He should not be moved as the wounds, though they don't appear to have hurt anything *importante* inside." She patted her rib cage. "He has lost much blood and has the strength of a weak child."

Cookie rasped a hand across his stubbled chin. "I see. How long before he can mosey? Longer we stay here, the bigger the trouble for you, girly."

"I am not concerned." Again, she shooed at him with her hand as if he had said something silly.

"I only have but a few dollars on me. I reckon it's the same with Rafe. But I can

pay you once we get back to the ranch."
Though with what, he wondered, would be
another story. He'd given Jack all his savings to gamble at the tournament. All gone
now. And any earnings from the gold vein
Doc had found in the cave at the ranch appeared to have pinched out.

This time it was Ricardo who spoke. He
stood straight, a mixture of boldness flexing
his nostrils and pride. In the pudgy face,
Cookie thought he could see the trim young
man Ricardo had once been. He looked at
Cookie but he spoke in Spanish. The girl
nodded. When Ricardo finished, she said,
"Mr. McGee, we will not take your money.
But we hope you will take our hospitality. It
is the least we can do."

"I don't understand. You act like you owe
me or something. That ain't right, ma'am."

The girl held up a hand to stop his chatter. "You may not remember this, but in
New Orleans during the war, you and Mr.
Barr stopped a wagonload of Mexican
women and children bound for a slave
market. You freed them all. Among them
were a woman and her child, a little girl.
That woman was Ricardo's sister, Rosa."

Cookie felt his jaw drop open. "Oh," was
all he could think to say.

Marietta spoke again. "Ricardo is my

37

uncle, Mr. McGee. My mother's brother."

"So . . ." Cookie pointed at the girl. "You're telling me you're . . ."

Marietta nodded. "Sí, Mr. McGee, we have met before. I am the little girl."

Cookie rubbed his chin again, then looked around the room, anywhere but at the two people smiling at him with gratitude. "Hearing that makes a man feel old," he said, his voice hoarse and low.

"You should feel proud."

"I . . . I reckon. Much obliged to you both. I . . ." he cleared his throat. "I should check on Rafe, see if he needs anything." He nodded at them both and ducked into the little lean-to room, relieved to be away from all that kindness.

He looked down at Rafe. In a whisper, he said, "It's nice to be remembered for some of the good things we done, eh, boy?"

CHAPTER THREE:
DOUBLE HEADER

Without looking at the barkeep of the Double-Nickel Drinking Emporium, Turk Mincher nodded at the empty glass before him.

The man behind the bar, one Alphonse Dalgato, caught the subtle movement of the customer's head as he adjusted an arm garter and glanced at his reflection in the backbar mirror. He was tempted to ignore the haughty gesture, but a tingle of warning in his gut told him no, hold off there, Alphonse. This man has a dangerous edge to him.

Choosing the wiser course, Alphonse knuckled up the left side of his waxed moustache, that side vexed him as it forever drooped lower than the right, and faced the man with a smile.

It was the brandy the fancy man in the red silk shirt was drinking. The stuff in the carved glass bottle that nobody had showed interest in before. Alphonse was also the owner of the emporium. And if this dandified stranger, with the fancy black clothes decorated with silver conchos and a red shirt making him look like a matador, wanted to sample the brandy, well then, Alphonse had no choice but to serve him.

Still, this was not ordinary liquor, but a bottle Dalgato had been talked into buying from a roving liquor drummer of two, no, more like three years back. He'd regretted it every damn time he had dusted the bottle since then. And that same bottle had survived two thrown chairs and a handful of whipped bullets, even as nearly all the other bottles around it had collapsed, at one time or another, in a spray of glass and booze.

Well, thought Alphonse, if this dangerous gent wants to spend the money to drink it, then by god, Alphonse was happy to oblige him in the doing of it. Even if he himself had always wondered what that juice would taste like. He had a thought it might be honeyed in flavor.

The plain label sported several simple curlicue lines in black, set off with red script in French that read, "D'Artagnan's, 1854," and the word "brandy" at the bottom. He'd never given over to indulging in it, though he'd seen it at the end of each night. Once he'd even picked up the bottle, all set to pry off the red wax, twist out the cork, when something had stayed his hand.

Isn't that like life? thought Alphonse as he walked over to the dandified man. Always something telling a body to wait, best not indulge in this or that. Not yet. It was only lately that Alphonse had begun to ask himself why? Why wait? Alone for years and then you have to wait? Wait for Mary Hanson to say yes, oh, yes, Alphonse, I'll marry you?

If she had said yes, then he had damned well intended to open the brandy. But she hadn't. Hadn't even let him ask. She'd left on the cursed train, never said goodbye, good riddance, not a word fired in his direction. And that had been that, and he'd gone back to waiting. And then the stranger walked in today, loose and lazy-like, smirking at everyone as if he, and not Alphonse, owned the place. And that was why this man annoyed Alphonse so.

With care the barkeep poured another two-finger measure into the man's waiting glass. Before he turned away, the man took the drink back in one gulp and licked his lips. "You may leave the bottle, bartender."

Alphonse wasn't certain he'd heard him correctly. That was why he stood still before the man, brandy bottle held before his aproned belly, head leaned to the right as if he were listening for the train.

"I . . . I own the place." Alphonse wondered why he'd said that.

"How very nice for you. Leave the bottle here, please."

The bartender set it down and turned. "It's expensive stuff, you know, that brandy . . ." He looked over his shoulder at the stranger, who nodded, a catlike smile on his mouth.

"And the cork."

Alphonse did as asked, then resumed tidying at the far end of the bar. The door clunked open and he looked up to see a pair of men — if they could be called that, mismatched and wrong-looking — walk in. They scanned the room, then made for the dandified stranger.

"So good of you two . . ." said the stranger, looking each of the duo up and down with theatrical precision before continuing, ". . . gentlemen . . . to meet me."

The taller of the two poked his head forward, smiling. He reminded Alphonse of a curious turtle. "Turk Mincher. Been a while."

The dandified stranger smirked. "Nice to see you two again." Mincher finished rolling a quirley, ran his tongue's tip along it to set the paper, then scratched alight a lucifer with a thumbnail. The entire process, from rolling to lighting, was a one-handed affair.

The taller of the two new arrivals flashed his eyes toward the groove-plank ceiling and smiled. "Mincher, you got to be kidding. You can't stand me and I feel the same about you. Plug here says much the same thing, though he ain't near so polite as me."

The tiny man, Plug, growled, parting an abnormally wide mouth to reveal blackened stumps painful to look upon. If they troubled the little brick of a man, he showed no sign.

Mincher continued as if the man hadn't spoken. "You are a curious looking pair, I'll grant you that. I see you still have that cutlery fetish."

He nodded toward Knifer, a tall, reed-necked man with an Adam's apple that bobbed like a bird's head working up and down when he spoke. A battered black beaver-fur top hat accentuated his abnormal height as much as his sticklike physique. He, too, offered a glimpse at the inner workings of his mouth, a vacuous pit wafting the stenches of dead things. Perhaps most curious of all, an array of bladed items protruded from sheaths all over the man's lean form.

The bartender walked up. "What would you like?"

"I'd like a fast horse and a slow woman." Knifer wheezed out a laugh. "But I'll take a beer. Both of us will."

"And you." Mincher shifted his gaze to the short man as if no one had spoken. "Still afflicted with that sawed-off gut shredder and, well, all the other obvious things about you that don't require pointing out."

"What you expecting, Mincher? The Queen of China?" Knifer giggled. Plug followed suit, though his offering resembled a ripple of piggy snorts that tailed off in a wheeze. Both men quaffed the foam-topped glasses of beer the bartender set before them and belched nearly in tandem. Knifer motioned for refills.

"You certain you would not like something other than beer to drink?" said Mincher, who did not so much lean on the bar as stand at it, one boot resting on the brass rail.

"You paying?" Knifer squinted at the dapper man, who nodded and beckoned the barkeep with a slight rise of the chin.

"So, what do you want with us, anyway?" asked Knifer once he and Plug each had a glass of whiskey standing beside a fresh glass of beer. He looked over at his little compadre, who nodded.

"What I want is to hire you two men. It's a job I would do myself, but I have other matters to attend to in places other than this town."

"Yeah, well, what makes you think we ain't busy, too?" Knifer pooched his bottom lip as if he might be on the verge of shedding a tear.

"Come now, Knifer, I know you two by reputation. I know that Mister Timmons doesn't hire people willy-nilly."

"Who? You think we was working for that fella who bosses you around? Ha!" Knifer slapped a long, bony hand on his trouser leg. The metal of hidden blades clanked. Dust, the stink of stale sweat, and the smell of long-ago fried meat wafted from him.

Mincher faced Knifer full on for the first time since the two men entered the bar. He was not a tall man, but he seemed so with his squared shoulders and flat-crown hat pulled low. Knifer's eyebrows rose.

"Nobody, and I will say that again, slower so you both understand me . . . no other person in all of the world tells Turk Mincher what to do. I offer my services for a time, but if the person paying for those services suggests I do something I am not wanting to do, why, you can sleep well at night knowing it ain't going to happen. Not that I give back their money, mind you. What sort of a world would we live in if a man gave away money handed him in good faith at the commencement of a business contract?"

"Mincher," Knifer spat a stream of brown spittle at a spittoon on the floor between him and Plug. He missed. "I got no idea of half of what you said, but why don't we cut to the thick of this here pie and see if the berries ooze, okay? I have a feeling being tied up with you in some dealing or other ain't a thing we are going to want."

Turk eyed the odd duo once more, then resumed his casual pose at the bar. He gestured to the barkeep and flicked a finger at the two.

Knifer leaned against the polished surface as if he were holding it from pitching forward onto him. Plug sat propped on a tall stool that Knifer had helped hoist him onto.

"Fair enough, fair enough," said Mincher while his two companions licked their lips and lapped up another round. "Why don't I, as they say, float the idea by you and you can see if it's something you would like to pursue?" He planted an elbow on the bar

46

and leaned toward Knifer, crooked a finger, and, distasteful as it was, beckoned the stinking man close to him. "One name: Rafe Barr."

The change that washed over Knifer's face was sudden and told Mincher plenty. It verified that the mess in Denver had been between them and Barr, and they likely wanted him dead. The trouble with that was Mincher didn't want them to get to Rafe before he did. So, he was going to have to do something about that. But first, he was going to get them good and drunk. It was not a task he was looking forward to. Crass as they were when sober he could not imagine what they'd end up like drunk. But that was how he needed them if he wanted to best the pair without harm to himself.

"I see by your expression you are familiar with the formidable man, eh?" Mincher forced a smile and poured himself a short drink of that godawful brandy. "Take your time. I assume you'll need your diminutive partner's approval to speak."

"Don't need it, but yes, he's game for most anything." Knifer exchanged nods with Plug, who, Mincher saw, had begun to weave on the bar stool.

"I think it's time we took our business conversation to a more private place. I never discuss money in a saloon."

At the mention of the word "money," Plug perked up. Mincher forced another smile. "If you care to meet me outside, I'll settle up here."

As they left, Mincher jerked his chin toward the barkeep. "Tally the rounds."

The barkeep did so, first by counting in the air with a bent index finger the glasses, and then, looking up at the ceiling, trying to recall how many drinks he'd poured for the three. "Four dollars. For them." He nodded at the empty glasses where Knifer and Plug had hovered.

"That," he nodded toward the brandy, "is a ten-dollar bottle that I was only planning on selling as a full bottle, not doling out drink by drink. It's imported, you know. All the way from the land of . . . Europe."

Mincher pulled a frown, then nudged his hat back off his forehead; the twin scars framing his face were difficult, he knew, for the barkeep to look away from. "The very land of Europe itself, you say? Well, let's hope they do other things than make brandy. That is godawful and the entire bottle isn't worth a silver dollar."

The barkeep's eyebrows rose and his thick cheeks colored.

"But I'll tell you what," said Mincher. "I'll

pay you ten dollars for the whole affair, their drinks and mine, and you can keep the rest of that brandy swill. Feed it to your hogs out back. Or maybe you'd like it for yourself." He smiled, clinked coins onto the bar, and took his time crossing the room to the door.

Alphonse Dalgato waited until the fancy dressed man had walked by the large window out front before he corked the bottle and set it down beneath the bar beside his balled-up coat. *Yep,* he thought. *You're damn right I'll keep it for myself. No more waiting.*

"Do you honestly think I would acquaint myself professionally with two fellows such as yourselves?" Mincher belched softly, tasting the brandy once more, his cheeks scrunching, nose wrinkling. He set his teeth tight together as if he might expel the rank drink. That was all he needed, to be stricken with an illness before he'd dealt with these two fools. He had to get them out of his way so he could deal with Barr on his own. He'd not let the man live in that alley so these two buffoons could take all the fun out of the situation he was creating.

"What . . . what's wrong with us, anyways?"

"Your tiny friend doesn't have much in the way of a stomach for drink." Mincher nodded at Plug, asleep, propped against the back wall of the horse stall. As soon as they stepped into the stable, where Mincher had assured them no one would be around to eavesdrop, Plug sat square in a fresh topple of dung.

Mincher doubted the sensation or the smell would rile the rank little beast. He was right. It hadn't alarmed Plug one whit.

"He always sleeps with that sawed-off gut shredder laid across his lap like that?"

"Why, yes," said Knifer, his horse-like gaze swinging toward Plug. And from his squinting, it appeared as if he was having difficulties focusing his gaze. "You see, Mincher, we been on a toot for a couple of days. We wanted to leave this here town right after we got our money from that fat fella from the Brotherhood of the Phoenix outfit, but we thought we'd treat ourselves to one beer each before we lit out."

Knifer smiled a snag-toothed, horsey grin. "Why, Mincher, you know how such things go, one beer led to two . . . days!" He brayed, doubling over in the middle. Plug grinned and his tongue slid out between his teeth. His eyes never opened and he merely shifted his head in his sleep.

Mincher was a little disappointed in himself, for he hadn't thought far enough ahead about this particular problem. These two were both armed, and he suspected no matter how drunk they were, they would still possess formidable skill with their weapons.

At close range, any of the blades bristling from Knifer's person — no doubt he had a few up his sleeves attached to trick gadgetry, others recessed in his boot tops and heels and toes — as well as the shotgun that foul little beast, Plug, cradled, would make quick work and require little aim to damage Mincher in such tight quarters.

The stable was empty. He'd seen to that. The liveryman wouldn't ever bother anyone again, as he was currently searching for his head in his adjoining quarters. It was now dark outside, not likely anyone would look for accommodation for his or her horse tonight. That would give Mincher hours to play. But he had to decide which of these two brutes would be first to give up their ghost.

Then it came to Mincher, and he acted on it as he always did in life when a shiny new idea popped into his head. "Say, Knifer, what if I was to do . . . this to your little pal!" The dandified stranger struck outward with his right boot, planting it hard and fast on the cradled shotgun, square in the middle of Plug's chest. The little man's eyes snapped open, bloodshot and unfocused. Mincher kept the boot jammed on the runt, pinning the thrashing beast and his deadly shredder in place. At the same time, he spun his torso and lashed up high with a blade of his own.

By the time he recognized he'd been sliced, Knifer was already snatching at his torso, but his hands flailed, swatting the hilts of his various knives — skinners, machetes, Bowies, needle daggers — without grasping any.

A squealing sound rose from his throat, but pinched out as a gout of steaming blood sprayed its redness outward. It came from the fresh gash Turk Mincher had sliced across the skinny man's reedy neck, midway between his shoulders and his chin. The slit opened as if forced by a cosmic hand higher up on the stubbly, grimy face. Knifer's eyes widened until they were round and bulging.

His mouth, the proper mouth, not the new, red maw, opened and closed like a beached fish gasps for water. His foul mouth clicked and gnashed as the blood spewed outward, slowing to a pumping drizzle. The smell of fresh blood wrinkled Mincher's nose. "Never can get used to that stink."

Knifer dropped to one, then both knees, his long arms whipping slower and slower to the sides, his agitation losing a last fight. The only sounds, a thin whistle from his throat, crawled up and out, helped along by a lowdown gurgling, gagging sound, as if heard through a wall.

Mincher turned his attention back to the tiny man he'd pinned to the floor with his boot. Plug's hands still gripped his immobilized shotgun, but his eyes were now as wide as Knifer's had been.

"That's right, little man. You never did expect to see such a sight, did you? I bet not." Mincher laughed a slow chuckle as if he'd been told a good ol' story on the front porch on a lazy afternoon back home. But now, it was time to deal with Plug, who'd begun to sober, squirming and growling. He was a boisterous little thing.

"I would normally grab onto you by the hair, yank your head backward, get a good look at that grimy neck of yours. But knobbed up as you are, there ain't much to grab. It looks as if your pate's been scorched clean by some blaze in the past. Besides, I might catch me something I can't shake so easy. You look diseased, little man. But that won't make no difference in about one, two . . . ."

Mincher's left arm, which had been swinging loose by his side, whipped from left to right, acting fast lest the little man wriggle free and turn that shotgun on him.

The gleaming implement in Mincher's hand, Plug saw, was a long straight razor. His eyes followed its arc upward. In the dim light from the kerosene lantern hanging from a nearby peg, Plug saw a long string of red-black blood slide from the blade. As it arched up, up, up, Mincher said, "That's right, little man, watch closely. I'm about to give you a shave!"

The razor swept downward, slicing a button of flesh off the tip of Plug's pocked nose. He screamed, but the boot on his chest jammed harder, cracking something beneath the shotgun that pressed into his burly little rib cage. His tiny, clawlike hands scrabbled at Mincher's boot, grasping, digging for purchase on anything. His nails sunk into Mincher's leg above the boot, raking grooves in the man's flesh.

"Ow! You little bastard, that hurt!" Back from right to left came the blade, gone was the jutting end of Plug's chin. He gurgled and growled and screamed all at once.

Mincher shoved harder with his boot, another cracking sound and Plug's tiny arms flew outward. Mincher jammed down once more with his scratched boot and Plug jerked his head fast from side to side as if tugged by warring strings.

"Take that, you foul little thing," Mincher said through near-gritted teeth, allowing himself a smile at the helpless look spreading over the little man's face and body. Now the entertaining part . . .

But Plug wasn't done in yet. His eyes focused upward on his dark-clad attacker, and a leering, wide smile split open and his black, jagged, diseased teeth came together hard, snapping and popping. He reminded Mincher of a black bear cub he'd seen bawling all over its dead mother after a trail companion had shot the she-bear in a case of misplaced defense.

Turned out the bear was only interested in a direct route to a huckleberry patch and was trying to maneuver herself and her boisterous cub around the two riders. But Mincher's trail pard at the time, ol' Feeney, he'd grinned and shot the mother, laid her low with nary a warning.

Mincher had been opposed to shooting the mother bear but he'd not reckoned on Feeney's speed. Then he had to reluctantly agree that the cub would likely die a foul death, alone and bawling and easy prey to every kill-crazy critter in that Montana wilderness, should it be left to fend for itself. So, he'd let Feeney shoot it, too. Mincher had nudged the little carcass up close to his mama and had not let Feeney skin either of them out.

But the episode had haunted him for months afterward. He would settle into his blankets of an evening, close his eyes, and in his mind, he'd see that little hairy bear cub, mouth bleeding and popping his jaws, snapping his teeth, blinking teary eyes and bawling out his last.

He'd never forgiven Feeney for it. So Mincher grabbed vengeance on down the road. It had taken a few years but Feeney's tongue went the way of the bear, wriggling . . . and then not. That had also been the turning point of their partnership. They'd parted and traveled their own paths for years.

Feeney had become Warden Talbot Timmons's right-hand man, keeping a lid on the oily man's doings at Yuma Territorial Prison. Then, not a month ago, Mincher had tracked down Feeney and had sliced the bald bastard's head off. Then he'd delivered it to Timmons, a bit ripe and fly-buzzy from the trail. Made for an interesting meeting with the double-crossing warden.

"Oh, little man, how the time does fly. But I'm getting a . . . head . . ." He sliced once, twice, ". . . of myself," and Plug's neck opened right up like Knifer's had. The runt gasped and wheezed, his neck juices flowed, and all too soon his eyes glazed.

Mincher found he was not a little disappointed in the entire affair. "Well, isn't that something?" He regarded the two bleeding men at his feet.

Maybe getting them further along the trail of inebriation had been a mistake. As foul as they were, the pair had inspired a sliver of disgusted wariness, and even a pinch of respect, in Mincher. They knew their weapons, and they were surprising in the number of years they'd kicked around the West, gutting and robbing and bumbling their way through one despicable debacle after another.

A new thought occurred to Mincher — he'd been mildly aware at times that Knifer and Plug had unwittingly drawn the law off his trail when he'd been but a few miles from them. But now they would not be his diversions in such cases.

He appraised each of the men, noting that while Plug seemed to have gasped his last,

Knifer, that beanpole, still showed signs of life; facedown though he was, his long, bony fingers slowly curled and uncurled in the dung-matted straw.

"Well now." Mincher bent low, squinting at the side of Knifer's head. It really was extraordinary; the way the man pitched forward he'd pried the new mouth in his neck open such that it appeared to be chomping on a mouthful of dirty straw.

"Ain't that about something?" Turk whistled and shook his head. "I have never seen the like, Mr. Knifer, if I may call you that. Now, look, I know, I know you can hear me, but seeing me is a whole other story. Being that you're chewing dirt and all, I do want to tell you that you and your little chum, Plug, was it? Yes, well, you two have disappointed me, to be perfectly honest. And I will tell you that honesty is one thing I always strive for in my dealings.

"My old Gamba, that was my childhood name for her, she always told me to be a good boy and don't tell no lies. So, I am telling you the square truth. You really should have put up more of a fight. I was ready, I tell you. But that little feeble show you offered me? If you was a circus, I'd demand my hard-earned coin back right now."

Mincher stared at the side of the man's flexing, vein-popped neck a few moments more, then stood. He looked down at the dripping razor in his hand and sighed before dragging the blade along Knifer's backside once, twice, and a third time to remove a stubborn clot of something more than blood.

"I expect I'll have to figure out what to do with you two rapscallions now that you are dead. Oh, excuse me, Mr. Knifer, I see you are still a-twitch. Nearly so, anyway. And I also see I have been too hasty in my cleaning of the blade. It appears I need to finish the job I began these long minutes ago."

With that Turk Mincher bent to his task, sawing in deep, clean, pushing strokes at the back of Knifer's upturned neck. The last of Turk's efforts resulted in Knifer twisting and bucking. Soon, that, too, subsided to an overall trembling, and then the long, thin man lay still.

"Now that," said Turk, pausing in his ministrations, "is nearly as good as a fine cigar. Only this blamed bone foils the fun every time. I vow I'll never get the hang of this, it's that vexing." He sighed once more. "Tired as I am, could be I'll need something with more cutting power. I bet this here livery comes equipped with a chopping block, and what does a chopping block need in order to be considered a chopping block?"

He leaned down, cupping a hand to an ear. "Knifer? Plug?" Mincher looked at each respectively. "No? Well then, I will endeavor to tell you. It needs little more than an axe. Well, and a man to wield it. I happen to be such a man."

A broad smile stretched his blood-spattered face. *That's more like it,* he thought. Felt good. He searched the barn for an axe and turned up empty-handed. Then a thought came to him and he grinned and snapped a finger. He toed Knifer at the waist and said, "Ah ha!" There, pinned beneath the man rested a tomahawk, tucked in the dead man's belt. "That's the winning ticket."

He fingered the blade, nodding approval as its keen edge threatened to slice into the meat of his testing thumb.

With renewed vigor, Turk Mincher resumed his grisly task of separating the men's heads from their bodies. A couple of whacks each with the tomahawk and the neck bones parted. He nudged the heads into separate canvas sacks, dumped in several cups of quicklime, then eased the sacks into larger sacks. He cinched the tops with the ends of the same rope and carried the dangling prizes to a stall at the other end of the barn.

There stood his prize, gleaming black stallion. "Hello, son. Two for the trail. What's that? Yes, yes, we'll take them to another town, somewhere we've had dealings in the past. Maybe with Marshal Vanderlink down Tucson way. He don't ask questions, and he always has cash for heads."

As if responding, the big black horse shook his head and whickered low.

"You and me both, mister. What say we saddle up and call it a night? First, I should deal with these bodies. Might be I can pin them on Barr and his chatty little sidekick. I'll think on it whilst I saddle up."

Turk hated to admit it, but he'd been a pinch gregarious in his cutting. That had resulted in more blood spray than he reckoned, certainly more than he usually worked up. Now he'd have to have his clothes laundered. Even if the blood from these two cretins wasn't visible on his black clothes and red shirt, he would know it was there. And if there was one thing he could not abide it was to go about begrimed when it had been a preventable situation.

No, he'd get cleaned up before he left town. That meant he had to find Barr and

61

his chatty compadre soon — if, that is, they were still in Santa Fe. Something told him they were. Turk bet himself a fancy cigar that he'd dealt Barr enough of a slip with his knife — two, in fact — that the man would not be trekking far from town yet.

The only unfortunate side of killing Knifer and Plug had been that he'd have to prevent them from stinking as long as he was in Santa Fe. And he would remain in Santa Fe as long as it took to find Barr once more. He still wasn't convinced he shouldn't have killed the man back in the alley. "Hell," Mincher said to his horse. "Maybe he died of his wounds. Might be I sliced him too deep. Thought I missed his vitals, maybe not."

He'd visited the alley a couple of days after and had seen no sign of the man. He had seen some scuffing, what looked to be drag marks poorly brushed out, as if someone had found the man, then had gone to hurried pains to disguise the fact they'd dragged Barr on out of there. Why cover it up? Had to have been that silly old man, McGee, that yipped around Barr like a little annoying dog.

"Now that there could be an interesting development," said Mincher as he brushed the horse's glossy black hide. "Another two wanted heads." And he grinned.

CHAPTER FOUR:
BACK FROM THE DEAD

"Cook," the big man on the rough-strung
rope cot, Rafe Barr, licked his chapped lips
slowly, fighting to keep his eyelids from flut-
tering. "Cookie . . . that you?"

The older man, his longtime trail pard,
Cookie McGee, spun as if he'd been goosed
on the backside. "Rafe!" He glanced around
the small, dark room before looking at the
man in the bed. "It's me, ol' Cookie's right
here."

He slid a rough-hewn mesquite-wood
chair over beside the bed, the spindles and
legs lined with cracks where the wood had
dried and twisted over the years. The seat
bore a dull sheen as smooth as river rock
from years of backsides sliding in and out
of it.

The man in the cot regarded his old
friend. Though Cookie was on the slight
side, he was all muscle and bone, not unlike
the chair. Both were tough, had endured

years of abuse, yet stood strong and steady when needed.

Cookie leaned forward, his arms resting on his knees, his bony fingers loosely laced. The men had been through years of tight scrapes and shenanigans together.

"Thought we'd lost you, Rafe," said Cookie. "Can I get you anything?"

The big man in the cot closed his eyes, wincing as he swallowed. "Dry . . . have any water?"

Cookie smacked his hands together and hopped to his feet. "Water? Do I have water? You bet I do." He looked around as if he'd misplaced it, then held up a finger. "Ah, be right back." He crossed the small room and opened the door wide enough to slip through. He peeked back in before he closed it. "Don't go nowhere!" His nervous chuckle hung in the air after he clunked the door closed.

He returned within a minute, opening the door as he spoke with someone. "Gracias, señorita. Yep, you bet." He nodded and slipped back into the room, closed the door behind him, and slid the wooden deadbolt. He held aloft a wooden pail and a gourd dipper. "Didn't figure you'd be awake so soon, else I'd have been prepared."

Rafe tried to smile, but only managed to

close his eyes and offer a small nod. Cookie ladled up a dipperful of water and held it to Rafe's chapped lips. The big man gulped at the cool liquid. He twitched his jaw and water drizzled down his chin and neck. He didn't care; it revived him and he sighed.

"Sorry, sorry," said Cookie. "Take 'er easy, don't go all greedy on me now. Slow and sure . . ."

They made it through two dippersful and Cookie set the gourd back in the bucket. "Best let that settle, else you'll bring it back up and rip open your wounds."

"My wounds?"

Cookie looked as if he'd been caught in a fib and was trying to figure out how to back out of it.

"Suppose you tell me . . . what happened."

Cookie rasped a callused, bony-knuckled hand across his stubbly beard. "Okay then, never let it be said Cookie McGee don't give in to his pal's whining. You recall the kerfuffle with President Grant? How we saved him and Jack and Mala from a mighty lynching?"

Rafe nodded with the slightest move of his head. "It's fuzzy, but, yes, I do."

"Okay then, that's something. After that, I got Jack and Mala and Doc on the road home — they're fine, by the way. Well, Jack's bum leg ain't lookin' none too good, but he's young. And when he's not on the bottle, that Doc knows a thing or two about doctoring." Cookie nodded as if he'd discovered a fine fact that needed sharing. "Course, he don't need to know I said that."

"Imagine that," said Rafe. "You paying Deathbed Jones a compliment."

"Hush up now, else I'll lose my thoughts. Where was I?"

"Doc . . . the president."

"Oh yeah. They all went back to the ranch. Not that blasted President Grant. No, sir, he went back to Washington, DC, where all those politician rascals go. Not that he didn't try to weasel out of me where The Outfit's headquartered before he left, mind you. I told him to whistle in the wind for all the good it would do to get me to yammer. Why, if a notion takes me I can be one of the tightest-lipped fellas you ever did see!"

Rafe lay in the cot. "I see you haven't changed, Cook."

"What makes you think I can?" Cookie thumbed his old fawn felt topper back on his bald forehead and smiled at Rafe. "What was we talking about?"

"How I got here."

"Ah, yes, well, you see, I stayed behind in town."

"Santa Fe," said Rafe.

"Yep, that's where we're still at. Ain't gotten far."

"Like this story," said Rafe, a grin tugging up one corner of his mouth.

"Why you whelp — here I be, tending you like a nurse, all hid away in here . . ."

"Where's here, Cook?"

The older man was about to answer when a soft knock sounded on the door. Cookie walked over and said, "Who's there?" in a whisper. A soft voice replied. Rafe couldn't make out the words, but it sounded like a woman.

"Oh, okay, okay. Thanks, señorita."

"You going to explain, Cookie?"

"Yeah, but we got to keep it down. Says she could hear us out there. Honestly, I wasn't talking all that loud, was I?"

"You do get riled . . ."

"Why . . . okay, okay." He sat down. "So, anyways, I roamed this here town for a couple of days, the whole while hopscotching ahead, around, behind, beneath those blamed soldiers from Fort Marcy! Hundreds all over town. Place was crawling with them, like lice on a log-camp blanket they were."

"Who were they looking for?" Rafe's eyes widened then, caught in a sudden thought.

68

"Was it Timmons?" He tried to prop himself on an elbow, groaning with the effort. "Did they catch him?"

Cookie rested a paw on his pard's shoulder. "Easy now, you'll do yourself harm. Lay back. And keep your voice quiet, will you? No, they didn't find Timmons. But then again they weren't after him."

"But what about the Brotherhood of the Phoenix?"

"Oh, they got the leader, that fat bastard, Turlington, thanks to you. He's likely in Yuma now, still run by that man, Warden Timmons."

"But Timmons is the mastermind behind the Brotherhood."

"I don't doubt that, Rafe, but according to Grant, Timmons has done no wrong. That warden's got them all hoodwinked."

The big man closed his eyes and shook his head slowly as Cookie continued.

"As I said, before Grant's fancy train pulled out of Santa Fe, me and him had a talk." Cookie squinted and nodded at Rafe. "Fat lot of good it did."

"How do you mean?"

"Seemed as if he was willing to play you out some slack, seeing as how you delivered Turlington to him. But somebody must have put a bug in his ear. One afternoon I was

69

all disguised up — looked more like a Mexican farmer than any Mexican farmer ever did — and I happened to overhear a gaggle of them soldiers in a cantina not far from here — best mezcal I ever did taste.

"Anyhow, they allowed as how their orders were to roust everyone who looked askew at them, but their real orders were to catch you. Seems Timmons reminded Grant that you are a wanted man, especially after that hubbub up Denver way. Lucky for you I come along when I did to bust you out of there. Elsewise you'd likely be swingin' on a hangin' tree like an overripe apple right about now."

"I seem to recall we had a little help from one of Doc Baggs's men."

"That fella in the cell with the key? Oh, pish posh! He was a drunk with a half-baked idea — a bad combination, in my experience."

"So, the soldiers were after me?"

"Both of us." Cookie nodded. "Still are."

"Then what are we doing here, holed up like mice?" Rafe's voice rose, still quiet but confused, anger creeping in.

"You ain't even healed up yet and already you're fixing to ride ramrod over the outfit hereabouts — and you don't even know where hereabouts is! Paying nobody no

70

never mind no how . . . ." Cookie McGee stomped in a tight circle, his arms rising and falling in counterpoint with his words. When he wound down to a standstill, he regarded the incapacitated recipient of his rage.

Another soft knock at the door. "Sorry, sorry," whispered Cookie at the edge of the doorframe.

Rafe got a good look at his friend in the dim lamplight. Cookie had aged what looked like five years since Rafe had last seen him. What had it been — a week? Two?

"I'm sorry, Cook. I expect you're doing all you can."

"You bet I am." He gestured to the door. "We are, that is. I ain't alone in this, you know. That girl," he jerked a thumb toward the door. "She's a hell of a man to have on your side, let me tell you." He nodded, arms folded across his chest.

"Cook," said Rafe. "You become more . . . inscrutable as the years roll by."

"Why, thank you," said the older, rooster-ish man, toeing the dirt floor with a worn boot. "Unless that don't mean what I hope it do."

"Case in point," said Rafe Barr from the bed.

"See? Now that's what I'm on about," said

71

Cookie, slipping into a renewed frenzy. "Let me finish my story, then you can quiz me all you like. Honestly, I never seem to get to the point around you. Squawkin' and carrying on, makes a man wonder if he'd be better off without friends at all!"

Another soft knocking at the door.

"Sorry, sorry . . ." Cookie shook his head as if he'd been whacked with a stick. "She's a touchy thing."

"Who is she?"

"Oh, the señorita? Marietta, she's sweet on Jack. But that's another whole story. Now, as I was saying, I rambled all over Santa Fe looking for you. Reason I knew you were still in town is because I found Horse. You remember your horse, don't you?"

Rafe nodded. "Is he okay?"

"Yeah, he's fine. But what a big lummox. Reminds me of somebody I know. Picky about his feed, don't like too much sunlight, don't listen worth a bean. Honestly, I never saw such a pampered beast before."

"Stinky okay, too?" said Rafe.

"Oh, you mean Stinky, my perfect little mustang mare?"

"With the excess of wind, yeah, that one. Reminds me of someone I know . . ." Rafe smiled, waiting for Cookie to bubble up

72

with a few choice words. He did. Rafe said nothing, but held a finger before his lips.

"I found you in an alley, wedged in so deep and dark, even at midday, you was barely more than a shadow on a shadow." Cookie fell silent for a moment. Then he rested a hand on Rafe's arm, and squeezed. "Thought you was dead, boy. I thought I'd lost you. Thought some back-alley bum did what all them graybacks and killers and thieves and bullets and bombs and rock-slides and snowslides and Lord knows what else we've survived over the years tried to do . . ."

He turned away and tugged out a be-grimed old cotton handkerchief, pinked with age. He blew his nose, another sharp sound, and they both paused, waiting for the girl to knock. She didn't.

Rafe was about to ask what had happened to him when sudden clear, dark memories tripped over each other, filling his mind. He recalled a shadowed figure leaning over him, outlined, no detail, remembered a voice, southern, cold, slicing like fine, honed steel. He remembered the lazy way the man spoke. He remembered silver smoke, the slow way the man pulled it in, the end of a cigarette glowing like a lone snake eye in the dark of the alley.

Rafe recalled the man's boot pressing harder and harder on his throat, remembered he'd been hit in the head, and couldn't seem to move his arms and legs. There had been a sharp pain . . . in his chest? His gut? Where? What had caused it?

"Yeah, yeah," said Cookie, watching his friend's face. "I see you are getting back your thoughts. Whoever did it stabbed you twice and left you for dead."

"But I didn't die," said Rafe, his voice colder and clearer than before. He worked his jaw, anger thudding upward from his feet to his brain, his fingers squeezing, clenching.

"I know. Might be he was toying with you. Like a barn cat on a field mouse."

"I have to get out of here, Cookie. I don't know who he was, but he did it."

"Did what?" said Cookie, trying to push Rafe's shoulder back down to the bed.

Rafe looked at Cookie, eyes wide, teeth gritted. "He killed Maria and the boy. He told me he did, told me how . . ." The big man's voice cracked, but he plowed on. "How he did it, what he did to them . . ." It was more than his body was ready for, and Rafe Barr collapsed once more with a groan into the narrow, sagging, rope-strung bed. Anger rippled through him, trembling his head even as his eyes closed.

"Okay now, Rafe. I understand, believe me I do. But you are fixing to ruin all our hard work if you keep up like this. You'll rip open your wounds and then where will we be? Heal up and let ol' Cookie worry about the rest, okay?"

"Cook," said Rafe, drops of cold sweat stippling his whiskered face. "I have to find him. Have to get out of here . . ." He lost consciousness.

Cookie sighed. "I know it, son. I feel as if the top of the sack's drawing tight around our necks."

Then he heard horses out front, sharp gringo voices, one of them barking orders, then boots on the wood plank floor of the little house's ramada.

CHAPTER FIVE:
RED CHEEKS ALL 'ROUND

"Excuse me, sir?" Ruby Stinson leaned her head into Warden Talbot Timmons's office doorway.

The occupant of the office was on his hands and knees behind the massive mahogany desk, mumbling and snarling at the locked, black steel safe squatting on the stone-flag floor.

He didn't hear his assistant's nervous inquiry. She stepped into the room, advanced several more feet, then stopped, a stack of documents clutched tight to her sunken bosom. Again, she spoke. "Sir? I have those papers you wanted, sir."

He still didn't hear her. Ruby narrowed her eyes. This was becoming annoying. She wasn't too sure if she even liked Warden Timmons, but nobody said boo to the warden of Yuma Territorial Prison. Especially not when he'd offered her the job after that wormy man, Winkler, up and quit, disappearing from town one night with no warning or sign.

It was Winkler who had replaced Timmons's longtime right-hand man, Feeney, who had turned up dead. Ruby had heard rumors that a frightening gunman — and at Yuma Prison, calling someone frightening was really saying something — turned up one day with Feeney's head in a bag. In this office. It was all very dramatic and, not that Ruby was about to admit it to anyone, a little bit exciting, too.

She had thought initially that perhaps the warden had taken a shine to her. They were roughly of the same age, after all. And she did live alone. As far as she could tell, so did he. A woman can dream, she told herself in the looking glass each night as she combed out her silvering hair. She braided and pinned it back atop her head, the same tight look she'd always worn, same as her mother had.

And now here was the warden, up to something odd once more. And since he'd returned that morning from Santa Fe, from meeting with President Grant, no less, he'd been in a mood more foul than usual. Ruby nibbled her bottom lip. She stepped forward, close enough now to see his backside shifting side to side as he wrestled with something — the safe?

She'd told him a dozen times at least to write down the combination, but he said she was foolish for even suggesting it. And now look at him, locked out of the prison's safe, growling and snarling and uttering words that no churchgoing man would know how to pronounce. He had well and truly changed. Perhaps it had been Grant? After all, he was a Union man.

Ruby stopped short of clearing her throat and speaking once more. For sitting on the floor beside the warden gaped the open top of a large, floral-print carpetbag. She recognized the bag, as the warden had been lugging it with much difficulty when he'd arrived back at the prison earlier that day.

It was what lay inside the bag that widened Ruby's eyes. Packing it tight were stacks of United States of America dollars — of all denominations. No wonder he'd refused to let one of the guards help him carry the bag up the stairs to his office. Who could trust another soul with that much money? Who would even have that much money?

The warden bellowed, "Dammitalltohell!" and rammed his palm hard against the safe door's spinning mechanism. Nothing happened to the safe, but Ruby gasped at the sudden outburst.

The warden spun on his knees, eyes wide, his teeth bared beneath his trimmed moustaches. "How long have you been there, Miss Stinson?"

Then his gaze followed hers as she looked, she couldn't help it, at the open-topped cash-laden bag.

"That bag is none of your business, woman! Do you hear me? Now get out of my office!"

She stood mesmerized for a moment longer, unsure of what was happening. Surely, she thought, the warden of Yuma Territorial Prison is allowed to have ample cash on hand to conduct such important affairs as he was responsible for. Surely . . . and yet, what if that's not what the cash was for?

Ruby snapped from her reverie, nodding. "Yes, yes, sir. I'm so sorry, sir." She backed out of the office, still clutching the papers. Once she made it into the corridor outside the office, the warden's voice boomed again, "And close my damn door, woman!"

She scurried back, tugged shut the door, and spilled the wad of documents on the floor outside his office. Heart thumping in her throat, Ruby hurried to gather them, and heard the warden pacing in his office and muttering. This time she made out a few of the words. And the warden was saying the oddest thing . . . something about a phoenix, a rising phoenix.

CHAPTER SIX:
BIG PLANS, I TELL YA . . .

"We have to get out of this town, boy. It ain't safe here no more. Marietta and her uncle, Ricardo, they've risked aplenty on us. I think you agree, now that you know why they have done so much for us, we can't let the law ride ramrod over them."

Cookie had been pacing the tiny room. Rafe watched him, moving only his eyes. It hurt too much to move anything else. But being bedridden was a maddening experience, especially when it came time for him to make water.

Every time, Cookie grew flustered and made it into an even more embarrassing situation by turning red-faced. And yet the girl, Marietta, didn't seem to care one way or another. She was stoic, kind when she needed to be, and quiet much of the rest of the time. Much like Maria had been. She reminded Rafe of her too often.

He agreed that while he and Cook owed

81

the girl and her uncle so very much, it was time to leave. But how? He was still muddle-headed and could not think of anything beyond vengeance on that bastard who did this to him and who did . . . the worst of the worst to his wife and son.

After all that, there was little room in his tired, wool-filled head for much else.

With that swirl of thoughts, Rafe Barr, a man unused to being taken care of by others, drifted into a deep doze and appeared at peace once more, at least from Cookie's perspective. Cookie didn't know that every time Rafe Barr slept, dreams bubbled through his head, not unusual for most folks. But most folks didn't discover the bodies of their wife and young son, abused, strangled, stabbed, and shot. And then Rafe had been blamed and jailed for the crime. Most people never experience that, but Rafe Barr had — nearly six years before, and every night since. Frequent visions of the moment he found their savaged bodies haunted him each day as well.

Cookie McGee had been his trail pard and best friend for so many years the old goat had lost count. He didn't waste time with numbers, anyway. He was accustomed to Rafe shouting in his sleep, swinging the occasional punch, and murmuring the names of his wife and son. But on this night when Cookie should have laid down in his own makeshift cot at the far end of the room, when he was still pacing, quieter now that Rafe had fallen asleep, Cookie heard Rafe murmur a name he'd given up on Rafe ever saying again.

Sweat-stippled and shaking on his bed, Rafe had said, "Sue . . . no, can't . . . Sue . . ."

And Cookie knew who Rafe was thinking of, dreaming of. He thought that while it opened a whole sack of snakes, it also might be an improvement on Rafe torturing himself over his family's murders.

Rafe repeated the girl's name and Cookie knelt by Rafe's bed. "Sue's fine," he said. He knew his sleeping friend was referring to Susie Pendleton, the bold, young, blond woman they had rescued from the vile grip of Deadwood's Al Swearengen. She was also the daughter — and only child — of California's Governor Pendleton.

It had been a shady sort of venture they'd been tasked with. Near as Cookie could figure, Rafe was supposed to be jailed for life, busting rocks in Yuma Territorial Prison under that vile weasel, Warden Talbot Timmons. But after five years of hard labor, Timmons had up and offered him freedom if he'd rescue the girl and bring her back to Yuma.

Cookie and Rafe did rescue the girl, but they realized early on the warden had nothing but evil intent where the girl was concerned. Timmons was going to use her to blackmail the governor, and land himself a juicy political position, no doubt. Such a notion did not sit well with either Cookie or Rafe.

When they rescued her — hauling hell-for-leather out of Deadwood — she'd been near death, addicted to Lord-knows-what sort of drug that bastard Swearengen gave her. But she'd bulled on through and proved herself a solid ranch hand. She'd gone off on her own a while back after a spat with Rafe. But Cookie knew it had been the right time; the girl needed to spread her wings. He hoped she'd get back together with her father.

Was my daughter, thought Cookie, *I'd want to know her, see the fine person she'd become.* Forgiving her would be easy. She was a good egg — even if she did tease him, along with Arlene Tewksbury, she of the wonderful meals and scratch biscuits Cookie could never get enough of.

Cookie paced in that little lean-to room, pondering hard and deep on who owed them favors over the years. The list was filled with a whole lot of folks, but few he'd dare approach. Then it came to him, no doubt thanks to Rafe's dozy murmurings — Governor Pendleton might take kindly to them. They did, after all, save his only daughter from a short life of misery. Cookie paused, tapping his chin and wondering.

Trouble was, he didn't know if the girl had contacted her father or not. He believed Rafe had sent the governor a telegram telling him his daughter was alive and well and would be in touch when and if she chose to do so. But if that was believed at the far end of the line was unclear. And what if the governor was in agreement with all the others who still thought Rafe and Cookie were killers and thieves?

"Has to be a way to figure it out, though," he said to the empty room.

In his cot, Rafe Barr twitched, wincing in his sleep as he raised a big hand to caress a face no longer there.

"And I'm telling you, Cookie McGee, that calling in favors from people we helped years ago is no way to live. Payment in kind isn't why we helped these people. Shouldn't be, anyway. At least it isn't for me."

Cookie stood a few feet away, arms folded

across his chest. "You 'bout done?"

"No," said Rafe. He wanted to swing his legs up and out of this cot, poke a thick finger in his old friend's chest, and shout in his face. But he was so weak he could barely move his arms and legs enough to stretch them before hot needles of pain lanced up his sides. "Look, Cookie. You do what's right in life because it's the right thing to do, not so you can accumulate favors to use whenever you feel like it."

"Oh, pish posh!" Cookie spun on a boot heel and stared at the wall. "Don't you think I don't know all that? Don't you think I don't live my life that-a-way? Course I do. You ain't the only one, mister high-n-mighty. But I got a bigger concern. I got a thick-skulled pard laid up in bed who can't raise a hand to help himself. I got a town crawling with soldiers tighter-packed than fleas on a scratchin' hound. And they're all looking for that thick-skulled goober and his fool friend — that's me, in case you're so daft you can't figure that out, neither!"

A sharp rapping rattled the door. "Señors, please, the soldiers . . ."

"Sorry, Marietta," said Cookie and Rafe at the same time.

They heard her sigh and walk away. Rafe sighed as well, then said, "What's the plan, then, Cook?"

The old rooster grinned and rubbed his hands together. "Well, it ain't much, yet. But as long as you're awake, I figure you could help me figure out how to get you from here to there."

"And where, exactly, is there?"

"California."

CHAPTER SEVEN:
FANCY MEETIN' YOU HERE

As he walked toward the cantina he'd visited a time or three since being cooped up with the increasingly surly Rafe, Cookie wondered what he looked like in the mouse-chewed serape, floppy trousers, and a godawful, too-big, drooping straw hat, all of which he'd borrowed from Ricardo the doctor.

He enjoyed gussying up — or down as the case might be — in disguises, something he and Rafe got up to a bit over the years. Last time was when he dandied as an attorney-at-law in order to spring Rafe from jail up in Denver. He and Rafe had both done a pile of spy-type work in the war, not so much of late. But things were looking up, even if he did resemble something a barn cat had played with and left for dead.

He'd argued with Marietta about the getup, though. Not over the holey serape and raggedy, loose peasant trousers, but she insisted he wear those silly rope sandals.

He didn't have any problem with other folks wearing them, but Cookie hadn't ever liked to see his feet naked. They were horrible looking things, all bumps and knobs and white as the flesh of a dead man. Made him shiver to think on it. But she'd insisted, said no man wearing a serape and these raggedy loose peasant trousers, would wear boots, even if they did look as puckered and worn as his did.

Cookie gave thought to taking offense to her comments about his boots, but he took a long look at them and reckoned she might be right about that.

"The truth stings," said Rafe, and then he'd smiled, actually smiled, for the first time since he'd awakened days before.

In the end, between the cloud of stink that perfumed up out of Cookie's boots and bloomed off his socks (more hole than sock), Cookie had won the argument. His feet matched and exceeded every description he had warned them with. Even Marietta agreed it would be kinder to everyone if his feet were stuffed back in their own boots.

"Aaah," Cookie had sighed as if in luxury as he donned his boots once more.

"Wouldn't you like me to make you a pair

of new socks?" said the girl. "They might not hurt your feet like those you wear now."

"You're being too kind, Marietta," said Rafe. "And you're wasting your breath. Last time someone gave Cookie McGee a new garment, it was a shirt, as I recall, he saved it for years, neatly rolled up in his bag, until the one he wore most regularly fell off in tatters. Then we ended up at that saloon in Gabo, Texas, you remember that, Cook?"

"Yeah, might be I do . . ." Cookie scowled at the wall and adjusted the serape.

Rafe looked at Marietta. "The barkeep, a woman who weighed more than the two of us combined and came to half our height, said, 'You get the hell out of here! I won't have a naked man sullying up the place!' That's when we knew it was time to break out the unused shirt."

Cookie turned blazing eyes on them both. "I washed before I donned that shirt. I washed!"

"For which we are all grateful, my friend." Rafe smiled and closed his eyes, tuckered out from the brief exchange.

Cookie pondered his chum's condition as he approached the cantina. He'd hold off on a drink until after he checked on Stinky and Horse. He made it a point to visit their two horses every day. Ricardo and one of his sons, Carlos, Marietta's cousin, helped him relocate the two beasts to a backstreet barn owned by Ricardo's other son, Juan. So far, the horses and their scant gear stored there had raised no curious stares or questions from snooping soldiers.

Cookie was about to pass the cantina, though he sorely wanted to stop in for a five-cent beer, when he heard a voice that rang a clanking bell in a dusty corner of his mind. He slowed, still keeping his shoulders hunched, the serape bunched up high, half-concealing his face. The rest of his bald gringo head wore the straw hat with the flapping brim.

Cookie backed up one, two paces, and peeked inside the open doors. He had to squint but he saw no one, though he heard the voice once more.

". . . no, no, I know they're here in Santa Fe, my good man. Or at least Cookie was when I last saw him. A friend of ours, the famed gambler, Jack Smith, sometimes known as Black Jack Smith, you see, because he's a black man, clever that, Jack told me Cookie told him he was going to look for his friend. Well, he's a friend of us all, one Rafe Barr."

When Cookie heard his name, Jack's name, and then Rafe's, he knew exactly who it was. He stepped into the dim innards of the barroom. And there at the bar sat Doc Jones, aka Deathbed Jones, a name unfairly earned years back when, alone and unsuccessful, he'd battled an outbreak of typhus.

In recent months, he'd been a carbuncle on Cookie's hind end. It seemed Doc, now a permanent member of The Outfit at the ranch, was also vying for the affections of Arlene Tewksbury, ramrod of the ranch kitchen. For her part, she'd not given either man a hint of encouragement about who she might or might not step out with. It was frustrating and gave Cookie a headache thinking on it.

But now, hearing the man's voice so close rattled him. It was a voice he'd not heard in weeks, not since Doc and the others had left Santa Fe driving that contraption, Ethel the War Wagon, as Doc had called it. He'd rigged up the ranch work wagon to be a rolling weapons depot that looked from the outside like a humble chuck rig.

Cookie sidled up to the man. He licked his lips and leaned over. "Doc?"

The effect was quicker than Cookie had expected. It also turned far too many eyes on him. The man on the stool turned to face him and Cookie saw the beginnings of the familiar wet-eyed look Doc got whenever he spent time in a bar.

"Why, is that you, Cookie McGee? I have been looking for you and Rafe!" Smiling, Doc craned his neck to look for the big man.

"Hush now, Doc. You got to stop tossing out those names." Cookie tried to make his voice sound low, but altering how he spoke was one of the biggest regrets of his work as a spy, which is how he liked to think of himself whenever he wore a disguise.

"But —"

Cookie's hand flashed upward, clamped over Doc's jowly face. Doc's eyes flew open. And Cookie looked past him to the two men nearby who'd tensed when they saw what was happening.

"No, ah, problemo here. See? Sí?" Cookie swallowed, then said, "Doc, we're in trouble in town. Wanted by the Army and who knows who else. You pretend you never met me before. Now stop saying our names and follow me outside."

Doc still stared at him with wide eyes.

"Doc, you got that? Nod if you understand."

Doc didn't understand. At least he didn't nod. Cookie sighed. The two men were still staring at him. "I'll lower my hand but don't yelp, okay?"

That time Doc nodded.

Cookie took a seat on the stool beside Doc and the two men backed down, still casting glances their way.

Doc sat rigid, staring straight ahead. "Do I know you, sir?" he said through his half-closed lips.

"Know me? Doc, it's . . . oh, I see, you're playing along. Okay, good."

"I, uh, I'm confused, sir. Something about you seems familiar, I'll grant you that, but . . ."

"You're good at this," whispered Cookie. "But enough's enough. Follow me on out of here when I leave."

Doc stood, knocking over his stool. He gripped the bar's edge, frozen in alarm.

Cookie slid off his stool and backed toward the door, keeping his head bent, his face concealed in brim shadow. "Ah, no, no, el mistako, see? Not me, don't know you."

Cookie reached the dusty street and angled toward the alley, and saw Doc following. The medical man caught sight of him as he was slipping between the buildings. Cookie catfooted down the alley, feet hugging the wall, and stopped only when he was well into shadow.

Doc poked his head in. "Cookie? For heaven's sake, man, I know it's you. What game are you playing at?"

"Come here, Doc. Hurry!"

Doc complied, a grin spreading wide on his florid face. "Now, that's better!"

Cookie leapt at him, encircled the medical man's neck with a bony arm, and hustled him deeper down the alley. Every time Doc tried to speak, Cookie gave his neck a harsh squeeze. After a couple of flexes, the harried man learned the routine and kept his mouth shut.

Before he ushered Doc out the end of the alley and left toward the horse barn, Cookie looked back up the alley, but no one from the cantina had followed. He released his hold on Doc's neck and pushed him against a wall.

"Cookie, what on earth —"

The rangy trail hound poked a long bony finger in Doc's face. "You shut your mouth right now, you hear me, Doc?"

"But —"

Cookie leaned closer, the tip of his finger pushing in on the bulb of Doc's nose. "Not another word."

Doc swallowed and nodded.

"Good." Cookie relaxed, lowering his pointing finger. "Now, I'm going to tell you what you need to know, but first you got to keep your mouth shut and follow me to that little stable yonder." He nodded toward a small ramshackle barn a hundred yards away. "You think you can do that without opening your yapper?"

Doc nodded again, eyes still wide.

"Then follow me." Cookie tugged his hat low, bunched the serape up around his shoulders once more, and slouched toward the barn. "And don't look suspicious," he said over his shoulder.

Two steps behind, Doc's eyes widened more. He looked left and right, then concentrated on his manner of walking. But everything he did suddenly seemed suspicious. "Oh dear," he whispered, then clapped a hand over his own mouth and kept walking behind the oddly sauntering Cookie Mc-Gee.

CHAPTER EIGHT:
LET THE SCHEMES BEGIN

An hour after bumping into each other in the bar, Cookie and Doc stood beside Ethel the War Wagon, as she was officially named, now safely tucked into the same barn where Horse and Stinky were holed up. The two horses Doc had used to pull the wagon to Santa Fe stood tugging hay from a shared rack.

"They give you any trouble?" said Cookie, eyeing the two work horses he knew better than he knew most folks.

"No, they did exactly as I asked," said Doc, smiling at the two bay geldings.

"Asked? Doc, you don't ask a horse to do nothing. You have to tell them what it is you're after."

Doc thought a moment. "Might not that be why your forays to town always end in jittery-eyed horses and you shouting, 'Whoa, you mangy critters!' on your returns to the ranch?"

To his surprise, Cookie didn't slip into a rant, but rubbed his chin. "No, no, I think it's because them horses have been molly-coddled by the likes of you. Horses respect a stern hand." He walked to Stinky's stall and reached a hand over the chest-height wall. "Ain't that right, Stinky?"

Quick as a blink the feisty little mustang nipped Cookie's fingertips, then returned to the hay rack. Cookie danced in a circle, cursing and doing his best to not shout any louder than he thought he could and not draw attention to the secret stable.

When the throbbing in his digits settled to a dull pulsing, Cookie turned his attention back to the wagon. He whistled, admiring the alterations Doc had made since he'd last seen it in action. "Doc, tell me again why you brought this duded-up wagon all the way back down here?"

"Jack said you were likely going to experience trouble of some sort. Since Ethel had been useful to you during the kerfuffle with President Grant and the lynchings, why wouldn't she be useful again?"

"Oh, don't go all blubbery on me, Doc. You know as well as I do the wagon's a fine concoction you put together. Trouble comes in attracting attention. Even with your changes, might be people here who recognize it, see? We'd not only have the law on me and Rafe, which we do already, but it'd land flat on you, too. No offense, Doc, but you don't strike me as the sort of fella who's been dogged by the law half his born days. Am I right?"

Doc shrugged and nudged his spectacles up higher on his nose. "Be that as it may, Cookie, and know that while I respect your judgment, realize I do have a brain of my own, sir. I anticipated all those woes you described and I believe you'll appreciate what I have done with Ethel."

"What's that mean, Doc? Should I be worried?"

"Not at all. Let me ask you a question, Cookie. I am a man of medicinals, am I not?"

Cookie squinted, not sure where this line of questioning might lead. "Yeah, so?"

Doc nodded. "Good, good. And such men often rove the countryside drumming up business and selling their wares."

Cookie nodded.

"That's why it has become a tincture wagon."

"Well, now, that's dandy, Doc. Good enough to get you back into the city unmolested."

"It's true, it's true. However, I will admit

I was accosted on the trail by a gaggle of drunken horsemen and one rather uncouth creature I believe was a female who out-cussed and out-drank the rowdiest of her companions."

Cookie smacked his hands on his trousers. "Hoo-wee! Sounds like my kind of woman!"

Doc sniffed. "I don't doubt it. Unfortunately, they tried to gain entrance to Ethel's innards."

"What?"

Doc nodded, a solemn look on his face. "It's true, apparently — and this is a sad effect I did not foresee when turning her into a roving tincture wagon — the cowboys sought tonic for themselves."

"What was wrong with them?" said Cookie.

"That's the thing!" said Doc. "Nothing at all — they merely wanted to prolong their drunkenness."

"Can't hardly blame a man for that."

"Yes, but at gunpoint?"

Cookie grinned. "How'd you weasel out of it?"

"I told them I was carrying a cure for a certain strain of pox that if mishandled could well lay low whoever samples it."

The old rooster's eyebrows rose.

"And furthermore," Doc raised a finger

skyward. "And I think you'll like this bit, I intimated the possibility that I had already been exposed to the pox and lived, but only because of my own tinctures. Others, I warned, might not be so lucky."

"What'd they do then?" asked Cookie, eyes wide.

"I didn't give them the opportunity to think about it. I laid right into them, asked them where they'd come from. 'Tularosa,' one of them said. I feigned shock and said that was the very nexus of the pox, and where I was soon bound — if I hadn't been detained by them."

"They believe you?"

"Too well, I'm afraid. I had to inoculate them against the pox. At their insistence, of course."

"Did you dig into their arms with needles and such?"

"Oh, heaven's no. I told them we'd made significant advances in the administration of remedies. While they watched, I whipped up a jug of a cure-all that I assured them if they all sampled it in equal shares would render them sufficiently free of harmful intruders. Though, if they experienced any ill effects, it was possible the pox already had them in its grip."

"What'd you give them, Doc?"

The little pudgy man peeled off his spectacles, squinted through them, and commenced buffing the lenses with his handkerchief. "I may have dosed them with a rather substantial wallop of my own special concoction."

Cookie's eyes widened. In a quiet voice he said, "What's it do?"

"It is a laxative."

"Oh, Doc, you are a devil. Remind me never to cross you."

"Too late," said Doc and stared at Cookie, who stared back in alarm.

"I'm joshing you, Mr. McGee."

Cookie sighed and smiled.

"Or am I?" said Doc, turning back to the wagon.

Cookie patted his belly tenderly and thought back on what he'd drunk and eaten in Doc's company over the long months he'd known the rascal.

The men spent the next half-hour inspecting the wagon, with Doc explaining attributes Cookie swore he'd heard all about before. But Doc, he was beginning to realize, might not be a man to be toyed with. Best let him ramble. Though, as the minutes wore on, Cookie reined in the medical man. "Doc, we have to get to California."

"California?"

"Oh, yes," said Cookie.

"Why on earth are we not taking Rafe home to the ranch to heal up?"

"That's the first place the scoundrels will look."

"Ah," said Doc, rubbing his chin. "Well, then, do you know where in California we are headed?"

"Yep, going to see the governor."

"Where might he be?"

"No idea, I figured somebody must know how to find the man. Maybe you?"

"I see. Well," Doc scratched the top of his wispy-haired head. "The state capital is in Sacramento, so it is a safe bet if we head there, we will find him."

"What's this 'we' business, Doc? You got a mouse in your pocket?"

"I . . . uh, no, not to my knowledge." Doc patted his tatty coat, then dipped his fingers into his vest pockets.

Cookie shook his head. "What I mean is, you ain't going nowhere but home to the ranch."

"And entrust Ethel to your care?" He shook his head.

"Gonna have to, Doc. Ain't no way around it."

"I beg to differ. You see, there is only one way to drive this wagon — and you don't

103

know it. I do, however, know all the nuances of Ethel's oft-persnickety behavior."

Cookie's face flamed red. "I tell you, Doc, you're gonna have to do as I say or . . ."

"You'll do what, my good man? I happen to know the route to Sacramento, been there a time or two myself, don't you know, and while it won't be an easy ride, it will be a pretty ride. But this all may be moot, as there seems little reason to take Ethel all the way to California."

Before Cookie could ask if he'd been offended, Doc ducked back inside the wagon. From outside, Cookie heard a rustling, clanking, and slamming. Several somethings fell and clattered on the floor. Doc emerged smiling and clutching a half-rolled map.

"We're not going to California? Doc, I think you best consider your next words careful-like."

"What I meant to say is you would be well served if you took the train."

"Doc, we can't go to the station here in Santa Fe. This town's buzzing with soldiers from Fort Marcy, all out for our blood, for some odd reason I don't want to speculate on right now."

Doc squinted his eyes shut tight as if he were dispelling a headache. "No, no, no. We take the Southwest Freight and Flyer from the railhead in Agave Junction. It might not be as mysterious and intriguing as Ethel and her varied charms, but it will get you there rather expeditiously."

"But how do we get out of Santa Fe? Didn't you hear what I said about the soldiers? Let alone all the way up to the railhead to catch the train to California."

"I am glad you asked," said Doc. "We'll be going . . ." he leaned forward, touching a pink finger aside his nose. "Incognito."

Cookie's wrinkled brow gave him away. "I thought the wagon's name was Ethel?"

"It is, my good man. I said, 'incognito.' "

"That's what I mean. You said in Cognito, blast it! Which one's it gonna be?" Cookie walked in a circle, windmilling his arms and shaking his head. "Surrounded by folks who ain't thinkin'."

"We can't take the train out of town as the military is checking every carload that goes in or out. But what's the one thing they might leave alone?"

Cookie shrugged. "A big bathtub?"

"No. A pox wagon."

"But we none of us has the pox, Doc."

"Doesn't matter. Think back on my encounter with the drunken cowboys from Tularosa. They only have to think we are pox-riddled. Oh!" Doc held up a finger, jutting skyward along with his eyebrows. "Hold on . . . we're transporting the body of a victim, the body of a dignitary, no less, back to California."

"So that's what you meant, going in disguise. Why didn't you say so? Use all them fancy words when a plain one would do the job."

"My apologies, friend."

Cookie rubbed his hands together as if he were cold. "What do you think? Trapper? Musician? Dandy? Not fond of that one, though I will say I was a fair-to-middling barrister not long ago in Denver. Good enough to spring Rafe from the hoosegow, I was." Cookie looked away lest Doc challenge him. Might be he'd heard they had help in the form of one of Doc Baggs's underlings.

"You didn't happen to lug along my trunk of disguises . . ." said Cookie.

"I'm afraid I did not think to bring it."

"But it's right there in the barn — that old steamer trunk! You would have had to trip right over it to get Ethel outfitted."

"Don't worry." Doc tapped his temple. "I have an idea. I believe it will be something far more effective than any of your old standby costumes. I'll need to gather the necessary materials and props, however."

"Doc . . . what do you have in mind?" Cookie spoke in a low voice.

Doc smiled. "Rafe will be in a coffin — I know it sounds gruesome, but it's brilliant, if I do say so myself. We can use our store of theatrical face paints to create the desired, albeit somber, effect. We'll tell anyone who inquires that we're traveling to California on behalf of the governor and his family, that way we won't really be lying. We'll be hauling the afflicted to be buried in the family plot. A top-name family!"

"What name?" said Cookie.

"Why, I don't know."

"That's right, you don't." He shook his head in disgust. "That's because you ain't experienced in such matters as disguises and whatnot. Where as I've been doing this for years. I could pull off most any getup, even big-name fancy folk." Cookie thumbed his lapels.

"That's good," said Doc. "Because I have a special one in mind for you. Now, do you know any women in this town? Particularly old ones, or widows."

Cookie's eyes widened. "Doc, I . . . I am shocked, I tell you! Never figured you for a rake and a rogue! We got work to do." He turned away, shaking his head. "Try to keep them urges of yours tamped down, will you?"

Not for the first time did Doc Jones wonder what Cookie McGee was rambling on about.

"Rafe?" Cookie poked his head into the dim room. "You awake?"

No answer.

"Rafe?"

This time Cookie heard a slight sound, as if someone were sliding a hand over rough whiskers.

"I am now," said a voice. The voice sounded weary, thin, old. And not at all like Rafe. Cookie had to get the big man out of here, even if it meant risking getting caught by the soldiers. Rafe was withering in this sunless little room.

He hadn't complained, wasn't his way, but he was a man of the outdoors, of the rough grass-covered hills of his Colorado ranch. He was a man of the cow trails and high country, too. Of the timbered slopes of the foothills of the Rockies. He was not a man of towns, let alone cities. And he was most definitely not a man to be trussed and cooped like a clip-wing chicken, in the dank little lean-to of a shelter at the back of Marietta's house.

It had been convenient for them, and Marietta and her family had been kind and gracious in tending to Rafe's slowly mending self and to their basic needs. But, Cookie realized as he hadn't before, it was now well-past time to go.

"Rafe, look at who I found wandering around old Santa Fe!" Cookie nudged the door open wider and ushered Doc Jones into the little room. Cookie followed him in and as he fumbled with the oil lamp, Rafe said, "Who is it, Cook?"

"Give me a minute, will you? My word, it's Cookie this and Cookie that. Ain't a man given a chance in life to do a thing before he's quizzed and rattled?"

Rafe sighed. Even after all the time they'd spent cooped up together of late, he still couldn't keep a straight face when his grumpy old trail pard slipped into one of his frequent rants.

"Doc?" said Rafe, forcing himself to lean on an elbow. "That you?"

"Indeed, it is, Rafe." Now that he could see inside the little room, the medical man stepped over to the bedside and began interrogating the wounded man, asking him the same questions he'd asked Cookie, who stood to the side with his arms folded.

"Told you that. Told you that, too. Yep,"

he nodded. "And that."

"Doc," interrupted Rafe. "Why are you here?"

"I should think that would be obvious, my friend," said Doc.

Before he could continue, Cookie cut in: "Gonna get you out of here. Got us a plan, Rafe." He winked.

For the second time since his rescue, Rafe smiled. "Well boys, that sounds good to me."

CHAPTER NINE:
EVERYONE PLAYS A PART

Doc motioned for Cookie to join him in Ethel the War Wagon's half-lit interior. He nodded toward a side cupboard. "Marietta helped me procure a suitable costume, or rather, a devious disguise, for you, Cookie. She brought it here earlier. It's in that cupboard. I have things to attend to, but you shout if you need help." Doc climbed out and gently closed the wagon's small side door, hiding a smile as he did so.

Cookie rubbed fingers across his stubbly chin. "About time, too. This escapade won't roll forward unless we have decent disguises, like I always say . . ." He looked to the doorway but Doc was gone.

Cookie tugged the handle of the cupboard, opened it, and pulled out a mass of black fabric.

"What on earth do you suppose this to be?" said Cookie to no one in particular as he hauled out the black costume. "Can't make sense of it."

Doc made it a good twenty feet from the wagon before he heard Cookie McGee's reedy howls of rage. Doc stepped up his walk, smiling.

In the wagon, Cookie sneered at the costume, then in the dim light of the wagon's interior, he held it up and turned it this way and that. "Ain't a bad idea at that," he said. "Even if I hate it."

Cookie gave a critical eye to the voluminous black dress with many layers to the skirt, an ample midsection, and a high collar with black lace overlaying much of the chest portion. Widow's weeds. He tugged out a small second bundle from the cupboard. It was a black hat with a mass of blue-black feathers jutting from one side, and several layers of veil to cover his face.

"Hmm," he said, tugging off the battered straw hat and plopping the lady's funeral hat on his head. He adjusted the veil and peeked at himself in the small looking glass Doc had installed on the wall across from the door. It was intended to assist in seeing who might be approaching the wagon should the door be open, but in this instance, it served to show Cookie what sort of a widow he might make.

"Nope, it ain't half bad," he said, adjusting the veil. "Doesn't mean ol' Doc ain't going to get a mighty comeuppance from Cookie McGee one of these days. No, sir, that fella's going to regret this mighty." He smiled and tugged on the dress to see how she fit.

"Something odd about this, Doc." Cookie jutted out his smooth chin and ran a bony finger around the high, tight collar of the black dress. Rafe had said he should at least appear freshly shaven should someone catch a glimpse of his face beneath the veil.

"Beneath this?" Cookie had said, fingering the three thick layers of patterned veil fabric. "Don't think that's possible, she's mighty thick."

"Humor me," said Rafe, wincing as he sat up so Marietta could help him tug on his mended and newly laundered shirt. "Though I don't think you can do much more to make me laugh, Cook."

"What's that supposed to mean?" Cookie scowled, smoothing the sleeves of the dress.

"Cook — don't ever change."

"What makes you think he can?" said Doc, winking at them both.

"My mother's mourning dress fits you well, Señor McGee." Marietta touched the old black dress, lifting the fabric and smoothing wrinkles as she walked slowly around Cookie.

"Ma'am, I don't feel right about you giving up your mama's dress and hat. It should be yours."

Marietta smiled. "It is mine, Cookie. And so it is mine to give away. Besides, I have no man, and since I have no man I will never be a widow, sí?"

"I reckon, ma'am. Odd way to look at it, though."

"Cook," said Rafe. "It's a gift."

The old rooster of a man smacked his hands together and smiled. "That's right it is. And I will wear it with pride. Course, it don't need saying that I don't want nobody to ever find out about this. Might confuse all those women out there who can't seem to get enough of ol' Cookie McGee."

Marietta smiled, even though she'd been opposed to the idea of Rafe leaving. "You are not well enough," she'd argued. "You need more time to heal."

Secretly Rafe agreed; he felt in body, at least, that he was not yet as mended as he needed to be. But in his mind, he was far worse off. He knew if he stayed one more day holed up in her back room, he was in danger of giving up the ghost, the ranch, the blue sky, mountain streams, of long rides thinking of nothing much at all.

Most of all, he was afraid of losing the hope of ever figuring out who did this to him, who did the same and worse to his wife and son. He could never again live a full life, his life, until he found out who that man was. Found out and did something about it.

And now here they were. Doc and Cookie had wheeled Ethel the tincture-wagon-turned-funerary wagon down the quiet rubble, ash, and junk-filled alley behind Marietta's humble home. Any of her neighbors who cared to notice were already aware of the presence of the wanted gringos in their midst and seemed happy to turn a blind eye to the proceedings, or else lend a hand themselves.

Rafe wasn't certain what sort of position of power the quiet, serious, and beautiful young Marietta held in the little neighborhood, but she — and her family — were respected by the others there, and Rafe counted himself fortunate. But that didn't mean he wasn't ready to leave. Even if it was in a coffin.

"Gives me the creepin' willies to see you laid out in that there box, Rafe, it surely does." Cookie lifted the matte of veils covering his bony face as he leaned over Rafe.

"Cook, if it's any consolation, seeing you dressed in widow's weeds isn't exactly reassuring."

"Hmm. I'll have to think on that one. You about ready?"

Rafe nodded. "Let's give it a go," he said. "If we fail, I won't have far to travel, anyway."

"Oh, now, don't talk like that, boy. I ain't about to let you ride off yet. And I sure as hell ain't going to meet my maker, nor appear before a judge, neither, wearing this big, gloomy frock!"

It took some doing, but they managed to make room in the wagon for the coffin by temporarily removing the chuck box in the back. Doc did most of the work himself, and supervised the rest. He made Cookie and a skinny Mexican boy, yet another of Marietta's cousins, swear silence about anything they may have seen regarding the true design of the wagon's inner workings.

Cookie had no idea what Doc was going on about. Doc suggested to Cookie that the boy might well be a mute, as he made no sounds the entire two hours the process took. Doc also allowed as how he'd never worked with anyone whose company he enjoyed so well. Cookie took that as a compliment until he realized Doc meant the silent boy.

Doc sighed. "No offense, Cookie, but you talk too much. Sometimes a man needs to think."

"Huh?"

"In peace."

Cookie turned a quizzical stare at him. "That don't make sense, Doc."

"In silence."

"Bah."

Their efforts resulted in them being able to load the coffin, in which Rafe lay atop several layers of old quilts, thanks to Marietta. The big man protested, but his growls fell on deaf ears.

"Enjoy it while you can, Rafe." Cookie scratched his rump. "Could be worse — you could be in a dress."

While Cookie and Doc tightened hinges, shuffled cargo, and stowed victuals, Marietta fussed with Rafe's pillow and kept trying to jam more padding into the coffin.

"Marietta," he said, taking gentle hold of her wrist. They looked at each other and he smiled. "I can never thank you enough for what you've done. I —"

"Señor Barr, it is I who —"

He shook his head. "No, Marietta. I owe you my life. You and your fine family risked your own lives for me . . ." Cookie uttered

117

another roosterish cackle as he sparred with Doc. Rafe smiled and shook his head. "For us. I don't have anything to offer you right now, but I want you to know you and your family are welcome at our ranch any time. For as long as you'd like to stay." He pressed a folded piece of paper into her hand. "Any time. And that's a promise." He closed a hand over hers. "This is a map and detailed instructions to our ranch in Colorado. You'd love it there. And I know someone there who would like to see you, so don't wait too long, okay?"

Marietta's normally silent, unreadable demeanor slipped. Her eyes moistened. "You . . . you speak of Jack, the gambler?"

"You bet. He mentioned you to me, to Cookie, to anyone who'd listen. But he was in a bad way. Doc and Mala had to haul him out of Santa Fe to heal up. He hated to leave without seeing you. So, Marietta," he waited until she looked him in the eye once more. "Don't let him down, okay?" He smiled.

"Oh, Mr. Barr, he would not want to see me."

"Never was a body more wrong, señorita!" Cookie walked over, carrying a small wooden box of tincture bottles. Doc stood behind him, nodding. Cookie continued,

"You're the only way to shut Jack up, so don't keep away too long, you hear?"

For a long moment no one said anything, then Marietta nodded and smiled. The effect was magical. Her beauty glowed anew and the three men cleared their throats, scratched their chins, and looked around, at anything but the pretty woman before them.

"Okay, now," said Marietta. "You noisy men must leave. You are a pain to me." But her words did not match the smile on her face. She tucked the map inside the top of her dress and took over the organizing of the wagon, her smile never leaving her face.

Once the coffin was in place and the top propped beside it, they hastily refitted the chuck box, now outfitted with all manner of tinctures, a scale, boxes, cartons, sacks of powders, and bundles of dried herbs swinging from strings and suspended throughout the wagon. A mortar and pestle sat secured in place by a leather strap — anything they could think of to make Ethel look like a traveling healer's tincture wagon and less like a war wagon.

"Wouldn't it have been easier to make Ethel look like a funeral wagon?" said Rafe on first seeing it.

Cookie and Doc exchanged raised-eyebrow glances. Cookie nibbled his bottom lip and looked away. Doc's veined cheeks bloomed bright pink and he looked in the opposite direction.

Cookie spun back on Rafe. "You couldn't have said something sooner, Mister Fella-With-All-The-Answers?"

Rafe sighed. "When you mentioned the coffin angle, I assumed the whole rig was going to be black and draped in death rags. You never told me it would be a snake-oil wagon. I didn't know until you dragged me out here in this box."

"What do we do, Rafe?" said Doc.

"Let's roll, boys. Time, the tides, and trains don't wait for most men. Definitely not for the likes of us."

CHAPTER TEN:
A POX UPON YE

"Odd looking train you have there, Doctor." The US Army lieutenant nodded at the animals hitched to the tincture wagon, two in front pulling, two being pulled behind, one lined to each rear corner.

Doc regarded the two beasts in the traces. "I cannot disagree with you there, sir. These two in the lead are solid pullers. The two trailing behind the wagon, the big bay and the little feisty mustang, they are the mounts of one of my passengers. They have been surprisingly forgiving. This is fortuitous, as speed, I am afraid, is of the utmost importance."

"Passengers, huh? Tell me about them. Wouldn't be two men by any chance, would they?" His gloved hand rested on his thigh, the flap on his holster unbuttoned.

"No, only one of them is a man. Or rather was a man."

"What does that mean?"

"It means I am ferrying a dead man, sir. And his widow."

"What?"

Doc nodded, a grimace tugging his puffy cheeks downward. "It's true, I'm afraid. You're welcome to look inside. You'll find a widow and her dead husband." He beckoned the soldier closer.

The man stared at him a moment, then urged his horse a few steps toward the front of the wagon. "You have something you wish to tell me?"

Doc looked to either side, regarding the four other soldiers who sat their own mounts off to the left. None of them looked inclined to do more than glare in a disconcerting way.

"Yes, you see . . . it has been, ah, how shall I put it, brought to my attention that the man in the coffin," Doc jerked his head toward the wagon behind him, "is not only possibly a victim of the pox . . ."

At this the soldier's eyebrows dipped and he tugged out a gold, silk handkerchief.

"But he is, in fact Mr. Wilfred Bartholomew the Second." Doc nodded, eyes wide.

"Is that important? I don't recognize the name," said the soldier, his voice muffled behind the kerchief.

"Don't recognize the name? Why, sir,

that's surprising, I tell you. Surprising, given the man's fame in the business world and social circles from East to West. Indeed, he was most celebrated in the court of Queen Victoria of England, as a titan of finance, of course."

"Why are you whispering?"

"Because, as I said, his widow is in there with him!" Once more Doc jerked his head back at the wagon.

"Is she dead, too?"

"What? No, no, not yet. But between you and me, she's not looking too well. The years haven't been kind to her and this sad time with her husband has only made life rougher on the poor old thing."

From inside a thumping sounded, following by a muffled voice. "I heard that!"

"Maybe she should be riding out here with you."

Doc nodded, "Don't think I didn't try to persuade her, despite her rather unpleasant ways, but she is nothing if not a doting creature; even unto death she will not leave her husband's side. You are most welcome to look in on them, sir. I would offer two words of caution: The old woman is distraught, positively beside herself and prone to lashing out like a cornered viper at anyone who dares disturb her time with her husband. The second warning is simply this: Though I dosed the body of Mr. Bartholomew with ample lashings of lime, every movement of the clock's hand when we are not moving forward toward our ultimate destination, we risk the pox emanating outward."

"Is that how it happens?" said the lieutenant.

Doc nodded, a grim, tight smile on his face. "I am afraid so, yes, sometimes it does." Doc winced, wondering if a lightning bolt was about to strike him low.

The officer clucked with his tongue and urged his horse backward two paces. "Nelson, Pilchik, go to the other side of the wagon, rap on the door, and verify there's a coffin and an old woman in there. I want you to get a look at the dead man, make certain he's . . . well, that he's dead."

"Is that really necessary, Lieutenant?" Doc tried to keep the alarm from his voice.

"Yes, Doctor. Purely a precaution. As you may know we've had a lockdown on the town since the lynching, or near-lynching, I should say, of President Grant. It is suspected that the two wanted killers are still in town, but so far we've not found them." He leaned forward, saddle leather creaking. "But, when we do, and we will, anyone who has helped them will be in a heaping world of hurt. Jail will be too good for them."

"Oh, dear, oh, dear," said Doc, fanning himself as if he'd become overheated. "Very well, then. But hurry it up. I can't be held responsible for what that old woman might do to your men."

The officer looked up and said, "Careful, men, the widow's distraught."

Those poor souls, thought Doc. *They have no idea what Cookie in a dress might do to them. Just as well,* he thought, tamping down a grin.

He heard one of the men knock on the door with what sounded like a gun butt or a quick rapping. "Open up, ma'am. US Army," said a voice. "Got to look inside. Ain't no cause for fear. Doing our jobs, is all."

The door creaked open. Cookie nudged it a little wider with the toe of one of his own boots. The ladies' boots had been far too pinched for him. He eyed the man peering in at him from atop his Army mount. "Why, you little ruffian! Can't you see I'm in the midst of mourning my dead husband! If I wasn't so worked up over that, I'd hop on out of here and take a round out of you and that other one, too. I see him hiding behind you!"

From within the gently lidded coffin Rafe said, "Tame it down, Cook — you sound like yourself, not an old weepy woman!"

"I understand, ma'am, but . . . I got my orders. I . . . uh . . . I need to see the body, ma'am."

"What? You whelp — that's my man in that box. And besides, he was sickly before he passed. Might be I am, too. You never can tell with these poxes. That's why they call them pox!"

From the front of the wagon, Doc groaned.

"Sir," said the lieutenant. "You aren't ill yourself, are you?"

"Why, no," said Doc. "I . . . I have become immune to this strain of the pox. As I have worked with such cases extensively in the past. I really do need to get this body out of here and on the road to the family plot in California."

"Won't you infect others along your travels?"

"No, no, not at all. The risk, at this stage, is low. Nonetheless, we intend to camp well away from others on the trail and I will alert anyone who ventures too close."

A voice from the other side of the wagon called out. "Sir, you want I should look at the body?"

The lieutenant sighed, rubbed his jaw with the kerchief, then said, "Yes, dammit. If we don't, word will get back to Colonel Maples and I'll be spinning in the wind."

Cookie kicked the wagon door wider and lifted the lid of the coffin slightly. Under his breath he said, "You ready, Mr. Wilfred Bartholomew?"

"Yes I am . . . Widow Bartholomew," said Rafe in a whisper.

Cookie slid the lid back enough to expose Rafe's chest and face. He'd been dressed in a decent shirt, a cravat that Marietta had dug up from somewhere. And Doc had produced theatrical makeup from one of Ethel's many hidden compartments. They'd whitened Rafe's face, oiled his hair, and applied garish red to his lips and cheeks. He lay still and did his best not to move.

"There," squawked Cookie in as high a pitched voice as he could muster and still sound righteously angry. "Yonder lies the body. You satisfied, young man?"

The soldier bent low in the saddle, leather creaking. His horse fidgeted and stepped closer to the wagon.

"Not too close, soldier," said the lieutenant. "Close enough to verify there's a body in that coffin and that it looks sufficiently . . . deceased."

"Did he say diseased?" said Cookie. "Pox ain't nothing to make fun of, you know!"

The soldier craned his head, squinting into the dim interior of the wagon. "Yes, sir, I reckon that's a dead man. All made up like they do at the fancy parlors where rich folks go to get tended when they've died off."

"Rich, ha!" said Cookie, sliding the lid back over Rafe's face. He heard the big man let out a long breath. "Used to be well off, but this lug couldn't never stick to home and make a go of things. Wandered all over tarnation and now I've had to hire a snake-oil man to drag his festering carcass back home to California!"

The soldier rode one step closer, reaching out with the toe of a boot. "Yes, ma'am. Sorry to have troubled you, ma'am." He shut the door on Cookie in mid-rant. From within, everyone heard Cookie's roosterish snarl and then a flurry of grumbled words.

The two soldiers cut around the front of the chomping horse team. The one who'd done the looking at the corpse said to Doc, "That woman is genuinely frightening. Don't half wonder if the dead man ain't better off . . ."

"That's enough, soldier," said his commanding officer. To Doc he said, "Best of luck to you, Doctor. And please, do your best to contain the spread of this pox."

"You can be certain I will do that, Lieutenant. Good day to you." He nodded and cracked the lines. The two wagon horses from the ranch churned forward in a lurching mass, followed by Horse and Stinky trudging in sullen silence behind.

Dust lifted as the horses pulled and the wagon rolled and creaked. For long minutes, Doc rode along, enjoying the steady grinding of the wagon, the clink and squeak of the traces, the stepping of the horses, feeling the slight movements of the lines, tug and slack, tug and slack, between his fingers. Then a small port slid open in the wall behind his back.

"Doc — it okay for us to talk now?"

Doc sighed. "I think you answered that question, Cookie."

"For an educated man, you don't make sense half the time, Doc."

"And the other half?" said Doc, smiling.

"Huh?"

"Never mind. How's Rafe?"

Doc heard Cookie ask Rafe how he felt. "He says for a man in a coffin, he's never felt better."

"Not many people who can say that," said Doc. "We'll make it nearly to Agave Junction tonight. I suggest we camp well outside of town, then figure out our next steps and proceed accordingly in the morning."

"Sounds good to us, Doc. I'm happy to spell you on the driving, but this blamed dress has got me all turned around. I can barely move in this thing."

As his head had been turned to the side, the better to speak toward the small sliding hatch, Doc spied movement on the road behind them. It was a lone rider trotting up on a black horse.

Doc put his hand to his mouth as if coughing. "Close the hatch, Cookie. Somebody's coming."

Doc turned an innocent, sidelong gaze toward the rider and snailed a pudgy hand up beneath his plaid frock coat. He patted the two-shot hideout gun he kept there, and took the lines in both hands once more.

The stranger was close now, and Doc saw the man wore a red shirt, over which sat a black vest sporting silver conchos. More of the same studded his black hat's low crown. He also wore black trousers, and black, square-toe boots, and sat in a black leather saddle that also bore silver conchos. At his waist, the man wore a pair of nickel-plate, pearl-handle revolvers. But it was the man's face that Doc found most arresting. He bore twin scars, thick welts pinked with healed age, that ran from above his jawline to his blunt chin.

The man was nearly abreast of him, intent, so it seemed, to squeeze in between the wagon and the stunty mesquites pocking the roadside.

Doc smiled. "Good day to you, sir." He touched his battered derby hat with a finger and saluted.

"And to you," said the man, returning Doc's smile.

To Doc's dismay, the man did not continue on his way, edging past them, but maintained his spot beside the wagon, keeping pace. Here was a man comfortable in the saddle. Rafe was one of the few men Doc had seen who rode as though born to it. This man was another.

"That is a mighty fine wagon you have there, sir." The stranger gestured toward the bulk of the wagon behind Doc. "Yes, sir, a mighty fine ride. Though, if you don't mind me saying so, she rides heavy. Almost as if she were weighted down with a hefty load."

"Is that right?" said Doc, wondering what this man's motive was. The stranger exuded something false, and unsettled the pudgy medical man. The horses, too, had become agitated, as though the stranger's gleaming mount had the same effect on them.

As if reading his mind, the stranger said, "And that team up front and trailing those two behind, hoo boy, you have yourself quite a setup."

"See here," said Doc, doing his best to sound offended, hoping it might mask the odd tension and the creepings of fear he was feeling. "I do not know you, but you ride up here bold as the noonday sun and proceed to criticize my wagon and my horses."

Doc looked straight ahead. Instead of hearing the man fall over himself with an apology as most folks would do in such a conversation, this man chuckled. It was a dry, hollow sound.

"I did nothing of the sort, mister. I merely related a couple of observations, that's all."

"Well, it was implied in the relating." Doc silently willed himself to shut up. This might well be a man who would not take trifling. Doc tried a smile on the man again. The man was still staring back at him, his own smile stretched on his face, as if painted there.

"I will ask you this — are you bound for the train station at Agave Junction, by any chance?"

"I . . . I am not sure. No, I mean, no,

that's not something we, that is to say I have no reason to go to a train station. My livelihood . . ." Doc waved at the wagon. "I travel, you see. In this . . ."

The stranger sucked his teeth, then with his reins in one hand pulled the makings for a cigarette from his vest pocket and rolled a quirley, one-handed. Then he lit it, also one-handed, with a single flare of a match dragged briskly along his thigh. He pulled in a deep, long draught of smoke, plumed it out slowly, and said, "Now then, that's better. Reason I asked about the train station at Agave Junction is because I am headed there myself. Bound for California and I don't see any reason to tucker myself or my horse out on the dusty road from here to there. Take the train, I told myself. And since I am my own best counsel, why, I listened to myself. And here I am."

He puffed again on the cigarette, blew out the plume of smoke, and fixed Doc once more with an eye. "Thought perhaps you would like to share the road, campfire later."

"Ah, well, you see, I was planning on turning well before that town. People to see, commitments to keep."

"Doc, may I call you Doc? Judging from your wagon that's a name you go by. I reckon you're not familiar with these parts.

There's no turns betwixt here," the man smiled and pointed at the ground beneath his horse, the cigarette scissored between his fingers, "and the town of Agave Junction. So, you might as well either turn around right now, head yourself back to Santa Fe, or roll on ahead to Agave and figure out a better story once you get there."

The man offered a wide smile. "Besides, that town is bound to be full of folks needing tonics and tincture for their aches and pains. I know I do. Who knows, Doc? You might make a sale later, over the campfire." He winked.

For two hours the man rode alongside, chatting enough to instigate clipped comments from Doc, whose heart throbbed far too fast beneath his sweat-soaked shirt. The man set his teeth together tight. The longer the man rode too close beside them, the more agitated the four horses became as well.

In a lull of strained chatter — strained in part by Doc, the stranger, for his part, appeared as relaxed and chatty and happy as anybody could riding a horse on a hot-as-hell day — a sudden thought came to Doc. "Um, yes, ahem, and what did you say your name, was, mister?"

The stranger turned toward Doc. There

were those twin scars again like worms on the man's face. "I never did say, as a matter of fact. No, I did not . . . mister." He winked at Doc and slowed his horse, dropping back.

Doc snapped the lines, rolling his team forward, urging them with a few quiet clucks of his tongue. Maybe he'd be shed of the odd man after all.

Doc gave it a few long moments, during which he'd begun to breathe easier, his heart, bumping and thumping in his chest, began to calm itself, and even the horses seemed less annoyed. Then he risked a look behind. There was that red-shirted stranger, smiling and nodding at him, off Ethel's rear corner.

Doc swallowed and, though his heart had clawed its way back up his throat, he leaned with the lines, slowing the team. "Whoa, whoa now." The horses danced to a stop, the squeaking and squawking of the wagon abated, and the damnable man reined up, too, staying just off the back corner of Ethel.

Doc set the brake and knotted the leather lines around it. A quick knuckle rap came to Doc's ears from inside the wagon. He licked his lips and risked a low, rapped response on the little sliding door. Cookie pushed it to one side, talking before it opened. "Doc, it's hot as hell in here! What in the blue —"

"Hush!" whispered Doc. "We're not alone. Close it and be quiet." He grunted and huffed and made a show out of straightening his trouser cuffs and tugging on the backs of his brogans in case the man sidled up again in that infuriating silent way he had.

Doc popped up, looking along the top of the wagon. The man was still there, still smiling, sitting his horse as though he had nothing else to do.

"What is it you want, mister?" said Doc, doing his level best to quell the quaver in his voice.

"Want? Me? Why, I don't want a thing, save for a spot of companionship along this here dusty road. I couldn't help but notice you have not turned back, so you must be taking my advice and heading on into Agave proper. Wise choice, as I said earlier, there will no doubt be folks in dire need of your tonics."

"Yes, well, I . . . I . . . we shall see." Doc climbed down on the opposite side of the wagon and, leaning close, said in a loud voice, "I am about to make water in the dust of the road, should you wish to inspect that, too."

He heard the stranger say, "Ah, you do

have a hell of a sense of humor, Doctor."

In truth, Doc didn't know what to do. He suspected Cookie and Rafe would have — at least when they weren't holed up in a wagon — dealt with this man in some bold fashion, run him off somehow. Alas, thought Doc. I might as well be alone out here for all the good they will be able to do me. One is a crotchety old goat in a dress, the other is laid out in a coffin, unable to do more than sit up, take sustenance, and fall back again, tuckered from the effort.

Doc sighed and, waiting for help from within that was apparently not going to bloom, he hoisted himself back into the seat and untied the lines. Before he released the brake, he looked back over his right shoulder. "You seem to be under the illusion I am in need of company, sir. Let me relieve you of that faulty line of thought. I am not."

The man, still smiling, nudged his horse forward until he and his horse stood once more alongside Doc. "So with that logic, that must mean you are carrying passengers."

"Uh, no, no, I . . . nobody here but me. And the horses, of course. They keep me company."

The stranger regarded Doc, close and cool, with two dead eyes, though his mouth still wore its perpetual smile. They sat that way for long moments, Doc feeling as if he were being hypnotized by a serpent from an old fireside tale.

The stranger slid a lone finger along his hat brim and nodded. "In that case, Doctor. I bid you good day." He heeled his horse into a walk. He'd traveled twenty feet when he looked over his left shoulder and said, "But I don't believe you. Until next time, please pass my well wishes to your companions."

Doc watched him as he heeled the horse into a lope. He sat there with the lines in his hands, shaking between his knees, one foot resting on the brake. He sat still long after the stranger's dust clouds drifted apart and all trace of him had vanished far ahead up the road.

He did not breathe again until a soft rapping sounded behind him. Doc let out his breath in a stutter and rapped back.

"Doc?" whispered Cookie. "Okay now?"

"Yes, yes, I think so. For the time being, anyway. We are alone. Open the door and let some fresh air in there."

Doc set the brake once more, looped the lines, and climbed back down.

Cookie poked his head like a cautious rabbit out of the cracked door. "Who was that, anyway? Another soldier?"

Doc looked up the long, empty road ahead. "No, not a soldier."

"Well, who then?"

"A curious fellow."

"Hmm," said Cookie, peeling off another layer of feminine garments. "Well, that makes two of you!"

The three men decided it would be best to camp that night right where the stranger had left them. At Rafe's suggestion, Doc steered the team northward, rolling Ethel well off the track, where they would be partially hidden from any travelers who might be out.

Rafe wasn't able to do much more than clench his fists and offer encouragement, but soon Cookie and Doc had the horses picketed, fed, and watered. Then they set about building a small cookfire and warming food Marietta had prepared for them. The smells of the bubbling, spicy frijoles and tortillas twitched all their noses.

Cookie insisted on sticking to his plan, convinced soldiers, a posse, or a lone lawman was headed this way from Santa Fe for them. Though he shucked the voluminous black bulk of the widow's weeds, he stomped around camp in bloomers, sagging underthings, and the veiled feathered hat. He claimed the veils helped keep the campfire smoke from reddening his eyes.

"I reckon that means you'll wear such a hat from now on." Rafe chuckled inside the wagon. They'd propped him up and he looked robust, considering the long hours he'd spent in a sweltering wagon with Cookie cursing and mumbling in his ear.

From the campfire, but six feet from the wagon's door, Cookie pointed a long, bony finger at Rafe. "You keep that up, mister, and I might not bring you these biscuits and beans. What do you say to that?"

"You try to starve me, McGee, and you'll find I'm not as feeble as you think."

Despite the somber mood draped over him by the stranger, Doc smiled. "It's good to hear you two are back in top bantering form."

It went on like that through supper, and soon twilight gave way to a dark purple sky.

"How about a cigar, Doc? It's been too long and I am on the mend."

"I think not, Rafe," said the medical man. "That's the last thing your body needs right now."

Even as he said it, from somewhere secreted beneath the mysterious underthings, Cookie pulled a fresh, long, fancy cigar from his dynamite holster. He stared right at Doc, eyes narrowed.

Doc shook his head and said nothing, the barest beginning of a grin working at his mouth.

Cookie paired the cigar with a wooden match and, leaning in the wagon doorway, handed them to Rafe. "One of them special-occasion cigars President Grant give me for you. But I reckon you know all about those, eh?"

Rafe chuckled and said nothing. Soon a blue cloud billowed out the door. "Ahh," came the sound of Rafe's satisfied voice. "You know what always makes a fine cigar even better?"

Doc smacked his hands together. "Since we are dispensing with all good sense, I have just the thing." He tugged out a jangling wad of skeleton keys from his trouser pocket, disappeared around the back of the wagon, and returned from rummaging in one of Ethel's secret locked drawers with a pint bottle of bourbon. "For medicinal purposes only," he said, proffering the bottle across the fire to Cookie.

"Of course," said Rafe, puffing away.

Cookie licked his lips and arranged their three tin coffee cups. "I like your kinda medicine, Doc. I like it fine."

Soon all three men were toasting everything they could think of to toast, from good riddance to good fortune to good luck. It had been a long time since any of them had enjoyed themselves, even in such a modest fashion.

If only they had known a scar-faced stranger in black had been watching them from atop a wash to their northwest, a stranger who was now hunkered down in that wash, smiling and slowly smoking a cigarette . . . If they had known, the three men might have had a very different night.

"I do wish you would reconsider. I can take you to California in perhaps two weeks' time, traveling safely within Ethel and her many hidden charms."

"Doc," said Cookie. "We've been over this —"

"You'll risk opening those wounds, Rafe. Why, you'll reach Sacramento soon, within a few days, and then you'll have to ride your horse. I don't see how you are going to do it." Doc shook his head, letting his hands flop at his sides. He looked as if he'd received bad news in the post.

Rafe sighed. "Doc, we appreciate your efforts more than you know, but we have things to do. As for my ailments, well, I'll

142

have to deal with the aches and pains as they come." Rafe stuck his hand out and Doc shook it, still wearing a frown.

"Take Ethel back to the ranch. We'll be along as soon as we find the bastard who turned my life inside out. No reason others should suffer any longer because of me and my troubles."

"Oh, pish posh," said Doc and Cookie together. They looked at each other and grinned.

"You're okay, Doc," said Cookie. "Always thought so." The two men shook hands and Cookie straightened his veiled, feathered hat. "How do I look?"

"Frightening," said Doc. "But convincing."

"One out of two ain't bad." Cookie lifted the veil, spit a thin brown stream of chaw juice, and said, "I'm going to make sure they don't separate Stinky and Horse in the stock car. They've taken a right shine to each other."

Doc looked down at Rafe. "Perhaps it's for the best. If this is the sort of shenanigan you two get up to, I am not certain I am cut out for it. I'll mosey back to the ranch with the two horses and Ethel, and set my shoulder to whatever task the formidable Mrs. Tewksbury may have in mind for me.

Best of luck, Rafe. I wish I could be of further assistance."

"We're not out of the woods yet, Doc. Your time may come again. Besides, you've already saved the day twice now with that amazing wagon of yours."

"How about a third time, eh, Mr. Barr?"

Rafe smiled. "Let's hope it's not necessary, Doc. I'd prefer to keep that in the bank for a rainy day."

"That sounds like a fine idea to me."

Cookie reappeared, stomped up, and stood before them, arms crossed. Doc and Rafe exchanged raised eyebrows.

"What's that look mean?"

"It means," said Rafe, "you do not have the most delicate style of walking."

"I don't have time for all that. We're about to roll on out of here. Besides, if I was a woman, I'd still be me, right? Stands to reason this is how I'd walk!"

Rafe looked at Doc again. "What were you saying about luck?"

Doc chuckled and made for the open end door of the baggage car. "Safe travels to you both."

They'll need all the good thoughts I can muster, thought Doc. He stepped down from the car as the train commenced its slow, slipping grind forward.

He knew he wouldn't be able to see Cookie and Rafe, who were safely stowed in the baggage car, Rafe still laid out as a dead man in the coffin, and Cookie as his grieving widow who refused to leave his side. The arrangement had taken much conniving and convincing to pull off, but a wad of cash, nearly all of Doc's savings — he'd brought it suspecting Rafe or Cookie may have need of it — made the critical difference in their being allowed to travel in such an unorthodox manner.

"Ain't the first time such as this has occurred on our train," said a slop-bellied but affable junior porter. "Don't you worry none. I got keys to the whole of everything on this here train." He leaned close to Doc. "I'll see they ain't molested nor interrupted. I know how old widows can be. My mama, she was inconsolable for pretty near nine years following Uncle Eli's death. He weren't my daddy, but you'd never have knowed it. Him and Mama were that close."

And now, Doc stood on the platform eyeing the passing cars as they sped up and past. *Funny,* he thought. *There was a time I would have fought for a place on this mad expedition. But now I have little desire to travel, unless it's back to the ranch. Which is where I am going to go, as soon as I purchase*

145

a few supplies.

He was jostled by an immense woman in a pink-and-white dress. She was crying and waving at someone in the passing car, and didn't seem to notice him.

Compelled by her simmering histrionics, Doc, too, looked toward the moving passenger car before them. He saw a sad-eyed young man in a stiff collar and oiled hair offering small waves back to the woman. Doc felt obliged to wave to the boy, too. He raised his hand, but it froze halfway up.

Facing out of the window beside the weepy boy was the stranger on the trail from the day before. Still smiling. Still scar-faced. Still wearing that black hat with the silver conchos, the red shirt's collar poking above the black vest. Still staring straight at Doc with those glittering, snaky, dead eyes.

Before he rolled out of sight, the stranger raised his finger and slid it along his hat brim in a salute, as he did when he rode up the day before.

Doc stared for a long time as the rest of the train rolled by, faster and faster. Near the end were the two baggage cars, then the stock car, then the caboose. *Oh,* he thought. *What do I do now?*

The fat woman's open, shuddering sobs pulled Doc from his reverie.

"I've lost my last boy to the world," she said, addressing Doc as she snuffled into a soiled handkerchief. "They're all gone from home now and I fear I will never again look upon their shining faces."

"I feel much the same way, ma'am." He offered a weak smile he hoped conveyed reassurance. He nodded to her. "Pardon me." Then he made for the telegraph office.

Two minutes later, he found himself next in line at the window.

"You, hey you!" The man in the booth jerked his chin toward Doc. "Get on with it or move on. We're busy today."

Doc shook his head and stepped forward. "So sorry." He recited a quick cryptic message, hoped it would be decipherable at the other end, and paid the man. Then he walked back toward the wagon.

Slowly, as if in a daze, Doc inspected the wagon, double-checked the traces and lines, and climbed aboard his seat. The only thing to do was head back to the ranch. Perhaps a better solution would occur to him as he rolled northeastward toward the hidden spot, tucked in the rolling foothills of Colorado's Rockies. For once, Doc doubted that even a drink would help improve his outlook on the situation.

CHAPTER ELEVEN:
CLICKETY-CLACK,
CLICKETY-CLACK . . .

"I can't see how women put up with wearing such foofaraw, do you?"

Rafe shrugged. "Seems to me a dress could be a mighty comfortable thing to wear."

Cookie recoiled as if he'd been slapped. "You got to be joshing me, Rafe. You any idea what I'm wearing? I got more layers on than an onion. Why, I'm trussed up like a holiday bird!"

Cookie stretched and tried to reach behind himself to scratch his back, all the while he kept talking. "I got on this here dress, which you will note is as heavy as a lifetime of sinnin', and it has near as I can count three layers of fabric going on. Not to mention the buttons and lacings and whatnot." Cookie looked toward the car ceiling, lost for a moment. He shook his head and continued. "Then there's the stockings, the strapping to hold 'em up, some sort of sock-type of things, then my own socks, and then the blasted lady undergarments! You top it all with this here crazy hat and gloves and fan and this little drawstring satchel and I have the makings of a mighty brutal ride coming on." Cookie hung his head in misery.

Then he looked up, winked, and leaned closer to Rafe. "I got my longhandles on underneath — can't risk letting them lady things touch me. Maria said it belonged to her poor old dead mother, but you never really know who wore this getup before me. I don't trust that Doc didn't pull this thing off a dead woman himself. I know he has it in for me. Could be she was riddled with the pox!" His eyes widened. "Oh lord, I hope I have taken enough precautions."

Rafe didn't reply.

Cookie squinted at him in the dark of the baggage car. "You okay?"

Then he heard a whimper and saw tears sliding from the corners of Rafe's eyes.

"Oh lordy, here I been yammering on about my woes and you're likely enduring agonies of your own. What can I get you, Rafe? More of Doc's tincture for the pain?"

Rafe shook his head, said, "No more, can't take any more."

"I know, but you got to. You got to work

through the pain, Rafe. That's all there is to it. Thought you was tougher than that."

Rafe continued to emit thin sounds and the tears flowed freely.

Cookie leaned closer. "You . . . you're laughing? You son of a gun! I'll give you something to laugh about . . ."

The handle on the north door of the car rattled and squawked as it slid back along its tight track, inch by inch, tight from the heat. Cookie looked up.

"Pardon me, ma'am." It was the junior porter. He took off his blue railroad cap and held it against his chest. "Didn't mean to intrude on a private moment. I know how devoted you are to your man. The whole crew has commented on it. Some of the passengers, too. We all think it's . . . something . . . different. Special, I mean, something special. Yep, that's it."

"Well," said Cookie, adjusting his veils and tugging down his dress. "What do you want . . . sonny?" He wondered if maybe his voice wasn't ladylike enough. He'd have to work on that.

"You don't mind me asking, but that body you got in that coffin . . ."

"My husband, yes."

"Yes, ma'am, well, he . . . he don't stink all that much. Only reason I ask is I have always considered the noble art of undertaking as a noble . . . undertaking, if you know what I mean."

"Not really, no," Cookie's voice slumped a little. He cleared his throat and fanned himself with the black lace fan.

"I mean . . ."

"We limed him up in good shape."

"Pardon me, ma'am?"

"You got dung in your ears, boy? We limed him, the body, limed him up in good shape. So he wouldn't smell up the place. But I tell you what, you best get back to the engine and tell that train jockey to lay a heavy hand on the throttle, as I think the effects of that lime will wear off soon in this heat."

"Oh, oh, yes, ma'am."

"Now, sonny. Get to it. Every minute we lose is another minute we all won't know what might happen to poor Wilfred here. Why, he could take to falling apart right before our eyes. You don't want that on your mind, do you?"

"No, no, ma'am."

"Okay then, get to it. I have a few more things to tell Wilfred before we bury his old smelly, cheatin' self."

CHAPTER TWELVE:
CAUGHT IN THE ACT

"You are a hard man to track."

The junior porter, name of Randolph, swung around his ruddy, pudgy face. He'd been rummaging in a woman's burlap sack that he knew contained some sort of baked tasty. Had to. The day before he'd seen her wispy little granddaughter rise from their seat and scurry down the aisle and into a luggage alcove, then return a minute later with what looked like a ragged hunk of brown sweetbread with some sort of glazing, possibly sugar icing, atop.

That was in one hand. The girl's other clawed tight around a crumbly mess that surely had been cookies, perhaps with nuts and raisins. Oh, the thought of those toothsome treats gnawed at Randolph the junior porter most of the hours since he first saw this happen. He knew he had to do something about it. The trouble was, he was no thief; he'd hardly ever filched anything before.

But he was hungry; he was a working man now, for the railroad line, and he could never seem to get enough food to fill his belly. It felt sometimes as if he could not carry on throughout the day and perform the work expected of him.

He blamed his boss, that pinch-faced head porter, lording it over him and the other fellas on the train that they were no better than trail bums lucky to have the work, lucky to be under him. All that did was gnaw away at Randolph, nearly as much as not having enough food to get through his days.

And that's what brought him to the little luggage alcove, elbow deep in the old woman's burlap sack. He figured if he could find something tasty in there, they might not miss a handful or so of crumbs. But the stranger's voice behind him caught him off-guard and knocked his knees together hard and fast.

"What? What?" That was all Randolph could think to say. In truth, that was a reflex word for him, popping out of his mouth like a spooked rabbit whenever he felt cornered. It was the one word he could count on when he didn't know what else to say, or when he was scared. Same thing most of the time.

"I said you are a hard man to track."

"Oh," Randolph slid his arms out of the bag, not daring to let go of what felt like a biscuit — not a sweetie but something he could sample, nonetheless. "You need something, mister . . . ?" That's when Randolph the junior porter turned around and faced the stranger seeking him.

The man was an odd-looking duck, no doubt. Had a set of freakish scars running down his face, one for each side. Looked to Randolph as if he'd been chiseled out of pasty rock; his face was all angles and shades and glinty specks in each of his black eyes.

At least he was smiling. Randolph withdrew his arms from the sacking and did his best to slide whatever he'd managed to snag his hands on into his trouser pockets. Some of it he felt sure was dribbling down to the floor. He heard something hit — a crust, maybe, or a dried fruit bit. Oh, how he hated this stranger.

"What do you need, then? I am the junior porter of this train." Randolph stood taller, crammed his rescued crumbs deeper into his pockets, then clasped his hands below his sagged belly.

"What I need and what I want are two

different things." The man smiled as if this was some sort of joke he and Randolph could share. Randolph did not understand it, and it must have showed on his face because the man leaned closer.

"Isn't that the question of all time, then, huh?"

"What?"

"What is it we need? Or maybe I should have said what is it we want?" The man's smile slipped and he turned his head to the right, but kept those dark eyes on Randolph. The porter swallowed.

"I want the key to the baggage car. You know, where the widow and the dead man are holed up."

Randolph swallowed again. "Uh, that's not . . ."

The stranger held up a hand; the palm facing the young porter looked as if it had been scrubbed with lye, pink and perfect. Like a painting of a hand. The man's fingers were oddly square at the tips. That would be the thing Randolph the junior porter for the Southwest Freight and Flyer line would remember as he died a few minutes from then. That and the sweetbread he never got a chance to sample.

CHAPTER THIRTEEN:
RESPECT MY AUTHORITY

"Who are you?"

Cookie jerked awake, whapping his head against the stack of rope-lashed wooden crates he'd made into an uncomfortable but functional reclined seat. His feathered hat jostled but didn't fall from his head.

"Huh?" he said, voice lower than he'd allowed it to be for days since he'd donned the dress. In the brief moment from waking to regaining coherence, he realized he'd been sleeping sounder than he intended. Out of recent habit, he lashed a hand out for the coffin, then felt his fingers slip inside the rim — the lid was askew. Rafe would have to play dead and be seen doing it.

The man who'd intruded stood in the doorway, lit from the back by daylight filtered through something. Trees, thought Cookie, blinking his eyes hard and trying to wake the hell up. "Who are you?" he said to the skylined man.

"No, no, no. That's what I asked you . . . lady?"

"Oh, oh, yes," said Cookie trying to raise his voice to the odd squeak he'd been using. He didn't know if it sounded ladylike or birdlike, but it wasn't his voice and it was the best he could manage.

"Where's Randolph?"

"Who?" said Cookie.

"Randolph! The junior porter — you must have seen him. He said he was going to tend to the animals in the stock car, and check the baggage car, too. That's why I haven't made my way back here yet this run."

The man stepped closer, halted, then walked one more step with caution. He bent forward, jaw set as if he were about to answer a question he was unsure of. "That a coffin?"

Cook stood, swaying with the click-clackety-click of the train as it rolled toward California. "Yes, why yes, it is." He cleared his throat. Being a lady was a whole lot more work than he thought it was going to be. He'd never forgive Doc for saddling him with this disguise. Of all the getups Cookie had stored in that old trunk in the barn — old miner's clothes, dandy suit, doctor's getup, even Reb and bluebelly uniforms.

And Doc had to saddle him with widow's weeds.

"It's my husband, Wilfred. We made arrangements with the railroad and with your junior porter to transport Wilf here back to his family's bosom in . . . Sacramento. Yes, that's it. Him and the two horses. They were his pride and joy, you know. Going to bury him with them. Or them with him, I mean."

The man stiffened, then stood tall. "You mean to tell me you have two dead horses in here, too?"

"Dead horses?" Cookie's voice cracked, dipping low for a second. "Why, no, not at all, sir. They best not be dead. We entrusted the young porter with their care and we aim to see he keeps with his promises. I paid a pretty damn penny to have them horses looked after in the stock car. And even more for me to ride here in the baggage car with my dear Wilfred." With that Cookie let out a practiced sob and flung himself from the waist up into the coffin. He landed on Rafe's chest, forgetting for the moment the man was still recovering from stab wounds.

Rafe wheezed.

"Sorry," mumbled Cookie. "Snoopin' bastard won't leave."

"I don't like it," said the man. "Not one little bit of it, you hear me, ma'am?"

Cookie pushed himself upright and faced the man. "You think I like that my husband's dead as a fox-kilt hen and I have to drag his carcass back to California? Hmm?"

That set the man back on his heels for a few seconds. "Be that as it may, ma'am. You . . . we can't have you riding like this. How long have you been back here?"

"Been since we started, what do you think?"

"No, ma'am, this won't do. You must return to your seat, after you nail shut that coffin lid. There is no way I can allow a dead man to remain exposed any longer." He took one step closer, then stopped. "Jesus — what is that smell? Is that the body?" With frantic, clawing fingers the man tugged his shirt collar up, untucking it from his waistband, and knocking his tie askew as he pulled the collar of the rumpled white shirt over his nose.

Cookie nearly lifted the veil from his face, but lifted enough from the bottom to draw in a good, long sniff. "I don't smell a thing off. You sure you're okay, young man?"

"It's . . . it smells of death . . . or perhaps sweat in here."

Cookie cocked his head, sniffing at his armpit. "Oh, that's me. Ain't had a bath in ages. It's this godawful dress I have to wear." He advanced on the mortified man, and shook a lace-covered bony finger at him. "You better hope you never end up a widow, mister. It's one hell of a task, I tell you."

"Yes, well . . . I'll be back to check on you later. To . . . to make certain you've done as I've ordered. You will seal that coffin tightly and you will find a place in the first passenger car; there are seats at the rear. Away from other folks. So you may mourn in peace."

The man pinched his nose harder and coughed. He paused in the doorway, trying not to look back over his shoulder. "If you see Randolph, the junior porter, tell him to report to me at once. Oh, God, the stink!" He gagged. "I have to leave now." He hustled from the car and crabbed with one hand at the door handle, sliding it shut with a loud bang.

"Well, hell, don't that beat all. Now he's onto us." Cookie turned to Rafe. "Say, Rafe, you don't smell all that bad. Don't take it personal."

"Cook," said Rafe. "I don't think he meant me."

"What? Why, that little . . ."

"Forget it, Cookie. We have decisions to make." Rafe sat up with a grunt.

160

Cookie smacked his hands together. "Yep, got to think of something, Rafe. Might be I could gouge some air holes in this box for you."

Rafe slid the coffin's lid back. "No way, Cook. This has gone on long enough."

"Well, what do you suggest I do about it, mister smart man?" Cookie folded his arms and waited for an answer.

"We're going to do something about it. Together."

"Oh, and what's that?"

"The only thing we can do — we're going to leave."

In the dim light, Cookie thought he saw Rafe smiling.

"You remember the Horkins Gang?" said the big man.

Cookie was about to shake his head no, but then he did remember . . . Lemuel Horkins and his three brothers. Really, it was two brothers and a sister. But the girl had been homelier than a mud stump, so he preferred to think of her as a boy.

And then he knew what Rafe meant to do. "Oh, no. No, no . . ."

CHAPTER FOURTEEN:
TIME TO MOVE, BOYS

"You don't mean it," said Cookie in a low whisper. He flipped back the veil from his face and repeated himself.

"Cook, we need to get on out of here and do it quick. We don't know exactly when that nosy head porter is going to return, but I'd wager it won't be long. He looks to be the persistent sort."

"But the Horkins escapade? You ain't up for that. Look at you. Why it's barely been what, a couple of weeks since I found you, all but wearing out your knuckles knocking on death's door! You try to pull a Horkins off this train and you're liable to drive yourself headfirst right on through that door, splintering the whole damned thing in the process. I ain't such a saintly man that I care to see ol' St. Peter any time soon. And certainly not when you've riled him like that."

"That's why," Rafe grunted as he pushed

himself up out of the coffin, leaning on Cookie's shoulder and gently stomping his boots on the floor to work up his circulation. "When the time comes, you'll need to prairie dog up out of the roof of the stock car to pick the best time for us to pull a Horkins. I'm thinking a slow bend."

"Oh," said Cookie, rubbing his hands together. "Even better with an incline."

"And level surrounding terrain, otherwise, as you say, we'll be sunk before we float."

"Ain't that the truth."

A short time later found them in the stock car that, for all its room, on this particular journey, looked to Rafe to house no other beasts than Cookie's fiery mustang, Stinky, as well as Rafe's bay, Horse.

Cookie mumbled that as insulting as trailing Ethel had been for the two mounts, the rattling, echoing din of the dark stock car must have been worse punishment.

Despite the sharp, pulsing pains in his rib cage and overall sense of fatigue from weakened muscles, Rafe smiled at his friend's whispered comments directed at their horses. The man was far more interesting and complex than most people who met him would suspect. It had taken Rafe nearly a year of friendship with the coot, challenging at times though it had been, to fully realize what a unique fellow was Cookie Mc-Gee.

Cookie moved about the car with the sureness of someone who'd been there before. And he had, a couple of times each of the days they'd been on the train journey to California, visiting with the horses. Rafe, however, hadn't yet been to the stock car. Ever since he'd climbed out of the coffin, Rafe had been the recipient of Cookie's eagle eye. "You feel okay? Not going to pop your stitches, are you?"

"Cook, I appreciate your concern, but ease off. I'm fine. Now, where's my bag? I want to change into my trail gear."

"Over there," said Cookie, undecided if he was going to sulk or forget it. A nicker interrupted his thoughts.

"Cook, there's another horse in here."

"Oh, yeah, forgot to tell you, big black beast back there, stallion, I think. I ain't got close enough. He looks surly."

It was dark in the car, but enough light sliced in through the slat-board walls to allow Rafe to get a look at the horse. "He's saddled," said Rafe.

"What? He is?" Cookie joined him by the far-end stall. The big demon-eye horse stared at them. He wore a black leather saddle, studded with silver conchos, bridle, saddlebags, the works. "Looks as though someone's got the same idea we do."

Rafe shrugged. "Likely whoever rides him has made accommodation to disembark from the train at the next water stop."

Cookie hefted Rafe's saddle. "Don't much care. As long as they go their own way, and as long as it's not our way." He nodded, as if agreeing with himself.

Rafe began stripping off the smelly shirt he'd been wearing in the coffin. He decided against checking his wounds beneath the thick layered wraps Marietta had swaddled around his trunk.

Each man went about his tasks, Cookie taking it on himself to saddle the two horses before Rafe tried to, something Cookie didn't doubt the big lug would attempt. Rafe used his soiled shirt to wipe off the funereal face paint he'd worn in the coffin, then donned his clothes, secured their bags, and checked their weapons. Soon, all was loaded, strapped on, and ready.

"Cookie," said Rafe.

"Yeah?"

The big man nodded at his compadre. "The dress."

"What about it?"

"We'll make faster time without it. Don't you think it's time to shed it?"

"Here? But . . . but it's Marietta's. She might want it back someday."

"Cook. Are you trying to tell me you like wearing that thing?"

"What?"

That did it, thought Rafe. Now the rooster's dander was up.

"You whelp. I'll show you!" With that, Cookie began unfastening the buttons and clasps that held the dress bound about him, one at a time. He turned his back on Rafe. "Help me with these buttons."

Rafe sighed and set to work on the line of buttons running up the back of the voluminous black dress. "My word, Cook. How'd you do them all up?"

"Doc helped."

"You mean to tell me you haven't once taken this thing off since we camped with Doc?"

"Nope. Like I've said in the past, when I'm in disguise, I give it my all."

Rafe squinted in the dark car, struggling with the few remaining buttons. "From the smell of this thing, I'd say you did that. And then some . . ."

"What are you mumbling back there?"

"Nothing." Rafe smiled. "There, now get rid of that thing and pull on your regular clothes."

166

"Ain't much more to tug on," said Cookie, smiling as he peeled off the layers of stained, smelly, sodden undergarments to reveal his own clothes beneath. He smiled at Rafe. "There now, what do you think of that?"

Rafe's eyebrows rose. "I think maybe you should ride downwind of me while you dry out."

"You ungrateful cur!" Cookie would have continued but Rafe had tightened Horse's cinch and was in the middle of trying to mount up. "Want a hand?"

"No, I'm okay." But Cookie shook his head and jammed a shoulder under Rafe's backside and stood, helping the big man into his saddle.

"My word, Rafe. Been feeding you too much!" He cackled and scampered up the side of a stall, then reached up and scrabbled in the dark overhead until Rafe heard a dull clunk — the latch on the roof hatch. Cookie climbed higher, and swung the hatch skyward. Daylight angled in, illuminating the dusty air of the stock car.

Rafe gave him a moment, then shouted, "What do you see?"

Cookie didn't respond for a few seconds, then ducked down. "Lots of smoke from that blasted engine, but we're coming on a pretty good setup. She curves northwestward, then rises. That should slow the beast. North side of the track is best — perfect for the door of the car, elsewise we'd be in a world of hurt." Cookie slipped down, leaving the hatch open as smoky light shined in. "She's not what I'd call level, but beats the hell out of the slope on the south side. You still game?"

Rafe ran a palm over his throbbing sides, the fresh puckers of his newest wounds, and hoped his flesh had grown together well enough to sustain the wrenching ride to come. "You bet, Cookie McGee. You're the eyes of this outfit. On your word, we'll get to it."

"Whoopee!" shouted Cookie as he scrambled to the door and unbuckled the bars and slid back the deadbolt on the wide side door of the car. He cackled as he wrestled the door, sliding it open wide enough for them to exit.

Rafe felt much the same mix of eagerness and giddiness at finally doing something, anything, other than playing at being a dead man. It had been about to do him in. Now he felt as though he'd guzzled a bottle of cure-all tonic, and for once, the promises of the huckster's patter were true.

Cookie gave his cinch one last tug, then climbed aboard Stinky, who was champing and stomping, same with Horse. At the far end of the stock car the black horse nickered, then with a head toss, offered up a full-throated chortle.

"Ha! He wants out, too!"

They sat their horses, holding them back from the open door as they fidgeted in place. The train began to slow; the steady chug-chug-chugging slackened as the train dealt with the twin challenges of a long curve and an incline. As the long train slowed and struggled, the two men gauged the best moment to "pull a Horkins."

And then, each man seemed to know the time had come. They looked at each other, nodded, smiled, and heeled their mounts.

It felt to the two men as if the moment were caught by a slow-moving clock. Time ground down as they sailed out that wide-open door, hooves poised, cuffing at open air, two men, vests rising high, hats tugged low, stampede straps cinched tight beneath chins, one arm raised high, as if riding a bronc, teeth gritted tight, ready for the inevitable slam to earth that awaited them . . .

From within the car, beyond the big black stallion, a shadow peeled away from the far back corner, behind a ragged stack of musty hay. The shadow cleared its throat, stroked the black horse's neck, and said, "Well done, boys. I say . . . well done."

He angled over to the gaping door, leaned against the frame, and squinted into the sooty breeze. He caught sight of his quarry and touched his hat brim in salute. Then he pushed from the doorway, returning to the black. "I expect it's time we follow suit."

He opened the horse's narrow stall door, eased the horse out of the small space, and walked him over before the door. He tightened the cinch, mounted up, and in the same motion sunk heel into the big, gleaming horse's barrel, and out the door they jumped.

They landed hard, but solidly. The man reined to a halt and surveyed the vista to the east. Between the scattering of ponderosa pines, he spied twin dust clouds receding northward.

As his own dust cloud rose, then drifted up and away, Turk Mincher rested one hand, reins held loose, atop the saddle horn. With the other he built a cigarette. He finished, licked it smooth, thumbnailed a match, and set fire to the smoke. He pulled a cloud down deep into his lungs, then expelled it.

"Let's move." And horse and rider loped slow and steady, northward, into the trees.

CHAPTER FIFTEEN:
A SOCIAL CALL

"I thought you said this ranch was supposed to be some sort of secret?" Mala set the cooled pie on the kitchen table, then glanced out the window.

"Not much of one anymore, I'm afraid." Arlene Tewksbury pushed a stray strand of graying hair away from her eyes. "Which one of The Outfit's swinging back this way? Must be Doc."

Mala shook her head and continued to stare out the window. "Not that I can tell."

Jack hop-walked across the kitchen, parting the calico-pattern curtains of an east-facing window. "Coming down from town way. One, that I can make out." He sighed. "I'm surprised it took them this long."

"Who?" said Arlene, sticky biscuit dough clinging to her hands as she held them up before her and craned her neck to see out the window.

"Cavalry," said Jack. "You all know Grant.

171

The man makes hollow promises he has no intention of keeping."

"Bit harsh, don't you think, Jack?" Mala looked at her brother.

He shrugged. "Might be. But that's not one of the boys, nor Sue, either, even though she rode west when she left."

"Then who?"

"Looks like . . ." Jack squinted. "Ferd, from town."

It didn't take long before the rider thundered into the ranch yard proper, the big dun on which he rode breathing hard, and as he slid from the saddle, Ferd's red cheeks puffed as if he'd run alongside the great beast.

Arlene met him in the yard, still wiping her hands on a towel, Mala following close behind. Jack leaned against an upright on the covered porch.

"What on earth is wrong, Ferd?" Arlene laid a hand on the chunky man's shoulder. He tried to speak, gasped, and held up a finger.

"For heaven's sake, man," she said. "Take your time."

He shook is head. "Gimme a minute," he said. He saw Mala, looked from her to Arlene, then continued. "Got a telegram for you . . . plus, there's men . . . from the government. I can't be sure, but they had that look."

"Is something wrong, Ferd? An emergency?"

He shook his head. "Nah, least I don't think so."

"Okay then, go on in and sit down," said Arlene. "I made a pie and you can have a cup of coffee, tell us all about it. Jack will want to hear this."

Arlene grabbed the horse's reins. "I'll cool him off, then tie him at the trough. You two head on in."

As Mala and Ferd walked to the house, he said, "Who are you?"

"That's a mighty bold question, mister."

From the top of the porch steps, Jack laughed and they looked up at him. "Don't mind Ferd, Mala. He's naturally nosy. Can't help himself, he's a bartender."

They reached the steps and Jack said, "Ferd, allow me to introduce you to my sister, Mala. Mala, I believe you've met Ferd."

She looked him up and down, and unsmiling, said, "Yep." Then she walked into the house, the door closing behind her. Jack's eyebrows rose.

"She's a corker," said Ferd.

"Yep." Jack held the door open for him.

Arlene entered the kitchen and helped Mala with the pie and coffee. "For heaven's sake," said the older woman. "Ferd, are you going to tell us what's going on or are we going to have to beat it out of you? And who's the telegram from?"

"Is it something bad, Ferd?" said Jack, his smile gone.

"Oh no, I don't think it's bad. Odd, more like it. It's from Doc." Ferd patted his dusty coat, then reached into an inner pocket and pulled out a folded piece of yellow paper. With his other hand, he slapped at other pockets as if he were being stung by bees. "Can't find my specs."

"Oh, Ferd," said Arlene, snatching the paper from him. "Stop fidgeting and eat your pie."

"What's it say?" said Jack.

Arlene cleared her throat and pulled out her own spectacles from her apron pocket, her already red cheeks reddening. No one dared say a thing, but Jack and Mala hid their grins.

Arlene read it out loud: "FOUND THE STRAY BEEVES STOP SENT THEM TO CALI STOP AM COMING HOME STOP DOC."

"What do you think . . ." said Jack, then caught himself, meeting Arlene's gaze. "Oh, yeah, good. All set with the strays, then."

"Yes, yes," said Arlene, flashing raised eyebrows at Mala. "Looks like Doc was the man to deal with the strays."

Ferd looked up from his pie and spoke around a mouthful. "You sent Doc out to round up stray critters?"

"Oh, yes," said Mala, refilling Ferd's coffee cup. "Doc's a man of many talents." Jack and Arlene nodded.

"You said something about men from the government?" said Arlene.

The barkeep looked at them all as he forked in another mouthful of pie. "Oh, no . . . I didn't mean there was nothing like that coming."

"Then what did you mean?"

"I was fixing to ride on out, bring you the telegram. It come in this morning, by the way, when a fella blew in from . . . oh, I forget. Said something about the government or soldiers or some such, sent by the president hisself, are headed to Dibley."

"And?" said Mala.

Ferd shrugged. "Well, that's it. Except for that blamed horse."

Jack glanced at the window. "I didn't know you owned a horse."

"Don't," said the man, chewing more pie. "He's borrowed. I don't ride much, never did, in fact. Got a mile or so out of town and the fool beast went crazy on me, ran like he was being chased by wolves! It was all I could do to steer him in this direction." He mopped his forehead with his napkin. "I tell you, I don't believe I breathed but twice before we barreled up over that hill yonder. I ain't never been so happy to see a sight as this house. Wasn't sure I could recall how to get out here."

Arlene, Mala, and Jack stared at the man, their eyebrows pulled together.

"Say, where's Rafe and Cookie at?" He swiveled his head around, looking down the hallway leading away from the kitchen, as if the men he named might suddenly appear.

"Not here," said Jack. "Now why don't you tell us more about these soldiers sent by Grant."

"I told you what I know."

Jack smacked a palm down on the table. "Look, Ferd, you don't ride in here like you did, then tell us nearly nothing. Something about whatever you heard made you ride on out here."

The man gulped back a mouthful of pie, looked longingly at the rest of the pie, and folded his hands on the table before him. "It's that, the man who told me this. He had a look about him, kept an eagle eye on

176

me while he told me. Like he was watching me or my reaction to what he was saying. If you know what I mean."

Arlene groaned. "Yeah, Ferd. And odds are he was waiting for you to pay us a visit so he could follow you out here."

"No, no," Ferd said, smiling and tapping his temple with a stubby finger. "I outfoxed him, see? I pretended I didn't know what he was talking about, then I waited for him to leave."

"And then?" said Jack.

"Then I went to Haskell's and got that fool horse. Set me back a whole dollar." He nodded at each of them in turn.

"Oh, for heaven's sake," said Arlene as she rummaged in her apron, pulled out a coin, and handed it to Ferd.

"And did you see where this mystery man went after he left the bar?"

"I think he took a room at Miss Dulcie's."

"You think?" said Arlene.

Ferd shrugged.

"Then I'd say you were followed," said Jack.

"Naw, I tell you I took precautions."

"Not enough," said Mala, looking out the kitchen window toward the east. Arlene joined her, closed the curtain, and looked at Jack. "There's a rider at the top of the hill."

177

It was Ferd's turn to groan.

When Arlene turned back to the window and peeked through the curtain, the hilltop was empty once more.

"Don't make me ride that hell beast back to town. Oh god, that thing is a killer waiting to happen." The fear pulling at Ferd's face was real, but it didn't sway Arlene Tewksbury.

"Ferd, you get back on that horse and ride to town."

"But what about that man you saw?"

"What about him? You led him out this way. You lead him back. If he stops you, you tell him poor old Granny Tewksbury needed her medicine and you were bringing it out from town."

"But . . ."

"You best mount up, Ferd," said Jack. "And for pete's sake, ride tighter, keep your boots in the stirrups, and don't give him his head."

The man looked at Jack as if he'd spoken to him in Chinese.

Jack sighed. "You have to keep the reins held back, like this." He pulled his hands toward his chest, holding imaginary reins. "Mount up and I'll show you."

Ferd looked once more at them, saw no

178

sympathy, and managed to struggle into the saddle.

He surprised them by keeping the beast in control as he rode away, headed back toward town. At the crest of the hill, Ferd tried to raise his hat and wave once but the horse lunged and carried the pudgy barkeep, arms flapping and legs swinging, over the rise, and then they were gone from sight.

Jack shook his head. "His heart's in the right place, anyway."

"Even if his brain isn't," said Arlene, looking at the brother and sister. "If they do come, one or ten or fifty, we have to convince them this is your ranch, not connected with Rafe or Cookie."

"You mean me and Jack?" Mala shook her head. "They'd never believe me and Jack own a place like this."

"Why not?" said Arlene. "Maybe, maybe we can convince them you two are a couple and I am your aunt."

"Arlene," said Jack, smirking. "You peeked in your looking glass lately?"

The older woman tried to hide a smile of her own behind her hand. "Oh, your housemaid, then. I don't know or care. This is our ranch, our home. Rafe and Cookie said so, and they own it legally."

Jack nodded.

"That gives us the right to do and say what we please," continued Arlene.

"And invite who we want and boot out who we don't want," said Jack.

"I don't know about you," said Arlene, looking from one to the other. "But I for one have never heard of anybody named Cookie McGee or Rafe Barr. Now, we best figure out what that telegram means and then cobble together a war plan. But first, I'm going to make fresh coffee."

A short time later, over cups of hot, steaming coffee and thick slices of pie at the table, they agreed to go about their daily business as if Ferd's visit hadn't been anything but a normal chat session by a friend from town.

Jack reread the telegram for the twentieth time, then tossed it on the table. "I'd say it means Rafe and Cookie are headed for California, though why I have no idea."

"Maybe it's best we don't know," said Mala.

"What do you mean?" Arlene looked offended.

Mala shrugged. "If we don't know where they are or what they're up to, those government men can't beat it out of us."

Jack and Arlene grew silent. It was apparent once more that they knew very little of Mala's life before they found her in Santa

180

Fe. From the scant hints she'd given, it hadn't been an easy time.

Arlene cleared her throat. "That's true. Out of sight, out of mind, as the saying goes. Now, back to the question of who we are and what we're doing here should we be invaded."

Jack nodded. "I think it would be more believable if we were freed slaves working as ranch hands for you, Arlene." She reluctantly agreed. Arlene would play a formerly wealthy widow struggling to keep her family's home and business solvent. The war ravaged her family to the point she could only hire seasonal help with her meager herd.

She took cold comfort in the fact that none of this was wholly untruthful. She was a widow, Jack and Mala had been born into slavery, they all worked to serve the needs of the ranch, and the war had been hell on the people she now considered her family — Rafe, Cookie, and the gang.

During the few hours left before dark, the three each caught each other peeking out windows as they gathered firearms, shells, and a couple of cases of Cookie's stockpile of his favorite "boom-boom sticks." They cached them in various spots throughout the ranch house, the barn, and the little bunkhouse.

Jack wasn't able to rove the grounds as much as he wanted to, but whenever he tried to help, he got himself barked at more than once by both women. Finally, on the porch, as the sun tapered down on its long slide to sleep, he turned his broad shoulders on them at a tense moment in which they both talked at once, their voices increasing in worry and anger, their words tripping over each other's.

When he didn't speak, didn't turn around, and made obvious his pent anger with them, their chatter of concern dwindled. He stayed put a few moments more, then, without turning, said, "I may not be much of a man anymore —"

Arlene spoke, "Oh honey, that's not —"

He held up a hand.

"As I say, I may not be much of a man now, what with my gimpy leg and . . . and everything else, but I can, by God, take care of myself at this point. Don't mean I don't appreciate everything you've both done. Arlene, you have been through this leg business with me twice, but you have to leave off this, this . . . this harping on me!" He turned and his lean face was a rigid mask of wide-eyed, barely tamped rage. "Or I swear I am going to ride on out of here and not look back. I am Black Jack Smith and I had one hell of a life before I ended up here, and I'll be damned in the fires of whatever hell I got waiting for me before I yes-ma'am and no-ma'am my way through another day here with you two."

Neither woman said a thing, but stared wide-eyed at him.

He continued: "I know you mean well. I know it as sure as I know what to do with the cards in a deck, but I cannot, I will not, live like this anymore. Do you both understand me? It's the way it has to be. That's it."

None of the three spoke for long moments. Then Mala tossed a damp dish rag at her brother. "Make yourself useful and clean up that mess you left. I am not your slave."

Slow grins rose all around.

"Yes, ma'am," said Jack, and he turned to straighten the mess of old newspapers, a penny dreadful, crumbs, a coffee cup, spoon, and soup bowl he had indeed left beside the chair where he'd spent much of the day. He was a long way from healed, and he would require many hours a day with his bum leg outstretched, but for the first time in a long time he felt something like a man once more.

CHAPTER SIXTEEN:
HELLO THE HOUSE!

"We supposed to ride on up to the governor's mansion on Stinky and Horse here and say, 'Howdy-do, Governor Pendleton! We ain't met yet but you know us. And what's more, you owe us!' " Cookie shook his head and made a clucking sound.

Rafe plucked the stub of a cigar from his breast pocket and inspected it, then clamped it between his lips and set fire to it with a match. After he worked up a solid cloud of smoke he said, "So tell me, Cook, when did you sour on your own plan?"

"My plan? Mine?"

"Yep, that's what I said. I reckon this proves your memory's shot, but is your hearing going, too?"

"Okay, okay, I suppose I earned that. But Rafe, you better sleep with both eyes open, 'cause I'm going to take a round or two out of you and I ain't going to tell you when it's about to happen. You hear me?"

"Yep."

"Yep, what?"

"Yep, that is about what we're going to do once we get to the governor's place. Maybe use nicer language, though. We wouldn't want to offend him."

"Fine," said Cookie. "Then you can do all the talking. How's that?"

"Works for me." Rafe plumed blue smoke skyward and reined up beside a granite cornerpost holding up a tall, black, steel-rod fence topped with decorative — but sharp-looking — lances with spearpoints jutting skyward.

"What are we stopping for?" said Cookie.

"No better time than the present." Rafe nodded toward a tall, white mansion with black storm shutters and a broad open span between it and the fence at which they'd stopped.

"You mean to tell me that's the governor's mansion?"

"You seem disappointed," said Rafe.

"No, well," Cookie shifted in his saddle. "I thought it'd be . . . I don't know, bigger."

"He's not a king you know."

"I know that, don't you think I don't know that?"

Before Rafe could reply, a wide-shouldered man wearing a black suit and a bowler hat on his head stepped out to the middle of the sidewalk. "Hey," he said, from beside a gate directly lined up with the front door of the mansion, two hundred yards away. The man widened his stance, then thumbed back his black coat to reveal three things: an ample paunch that looked to Cookie like a filled black-cloth feed sack, and the other two things were revolvers riding low, nickel-plate with bone handles, tucked into gleaming black leather holsters. "What are you two men up to?"

Cookie squirmed in his saddle and rasped a bony hand across his stubbled jaw. Rafe knew that was a sign that his pard was about to spice up the situation. Time to act.

"Well," said Rafe, holding out a hand of warning toward Cookie as he nudged Horse into a slow walk toward the man, parallel with the formidable fence. Every ten yards or so another shaped granite pier stood resolute and supportive of the thick steel fence. They came to within thirty feet of the man when he said, "That's far enough."

Rafe nodded and reined up. "What we need, friend, is to talk with Governor Pendleton."

The man's cow eyes narrowed. "Ain't nobody by that name here."

"Technically," said Rafe, lighting a fresh

186

cigar slowly, taking pains to ensure each move he made was measured enough that the man followed them with his eyes. "The first part of that is a title, not a name."

"What?"

"You should have said, 'Ain't nobody here by that title nor that name.' "

"Huh?" said the man, looking as if he saw a man cheat at cards but didn't know what to do about it.

"Don't worry," said Rafe, blowing out his match. "I won't tell him."

"Tell who? Tell who what?"

"Why, the governor that you didn't make proper reference to him and also that you denied his existence. Here, at least. Which is a lie. And lying, as we all know, can be grounds for treason." He blew out thick smoke. "Usually that's punishable with a jail term."

"Oh, lord, mister. I can't afford to lose this job. They're hard enough to come by."

"And even harder to hold, eh, pal?" said Cookie.

Then the man seemed to remember his position and nodded at them. "Right, then," he said, smacking his meaty hands together. "Let's see about all this."

"Only if you take off those guns."

"Now, I don't hardly think so. That is not

about to happen, mister. You step on down off those two horses and hold those hands up, level with your damn jug ears."

"Jug ears!" Cookie gritted his teeth. "I will box your ears, you overgrown whelp!"

There was something about the gate guard's demeanor that Cookie saw Rafe smiling about. "What's so funny?" said Cookie under his breath. "This brute's about to draw down on us."

"Nah," said Rafe, low, out of the side of his mouth. "He's an oaf, no doubt. But he's afraid, Cook."

"Afraid?" Cookie looked at the big man fidgeting before them. Then he grinned. "Yeah, he's made of paper, he is."

"You two . . . what are you talking about?" said the man. "I'm telling you how it's going to be. You step on down!"

"You heard the man, Cookie, let's step on down." Rafe nudged his horse forward until he was twenty feet or so before the man. He swung down from the saddle, but slowly as if he might break in two if he moved quicker.

"What's wrong with you?" said the man, eyes narrowed.

"Oh, I'm a little stiff from the trail is all."

"You still move better than that old man," said the gatekeeper, nodding at Cookie.

"Keep talking, sonny," said Cookie, remarkably still grinning. They tied off their reins to the fence, then advanced until they were within ten feet of the oaf.

The man rested his thick hands on the butts of his guns. "Don't you come closer. I'm authorized to kill on sight anybody I deem, ah, is a threat to the gov— to my employer."

"I'd say you failed in your first task," said Rafe.

"How's that?"

"Confirmed who lives here. Now why don't you tell your employer that he has two visitors. We'll wait here."

"Nope," said the man, shaking his head. "Can't do that. Strict orders."

Rafe advanced on the man, angling so his own back was to the nearly empty street, Cookie by his side. With finger-snap speed Rafe shucked a Colt and trained it on the man, who hadn't moved his own palms from resting atop his two gun butts.

"Now," said Rafe. "My friend here is not so old that he can't relieve you of your guns. So lift your hands slowly and rest them on your ears."

"My ears?"

"Yeah," said Cookie. "They still work, don't they?"

The oaf nodded.

"Then do what the man said."

As soon as the oaf raised his hands, Cookie stepped close and slid out the two six-guns. "Don't worry," said Rafe. "You'll get them back. But not until we've talked with your employer. We don't mean him any harm."

"Yeah," said Cookie. "We go way back with the governor."

"Sorry about this, friend," said Rafe. "But I'm going to have to ask you to take that wooden chair you were sitting in when we rode up and scoot around the corner of the fence. That way you won't be seen from the road or the house. That's it."

Rafe followed the man around the bend in the shrubbery and said to Cookie, "Could I trouble you to fetch the horses and a rope? Don't want to leave them out on the street in front of the governor's house. Might be unseemly."

"Right you are," said Cookie. Each man knew not to use the other's name in front of strangers. "And I believe we should stopper his mouth, too. It's a big one. No telling what sort of ruckus it could make."

The oaf's eyes widened. "You're sure you're not gonna kill me?"

"Only if you want us to," said Rafe, no hint of a smile on his face.

From the other side of the fence, Cookie giggled as he retrieved the horses. "Only if you want us to. Ha!"

The trussing completed, the two men approached the broad front steps, a shade-giving portico providing relief from the late-day sun. Rafe grasped one of the two brass lion-head knockers and rapped on the door. A muffled echo died away, replaced with crisp, clicking footsteps. One half of the big double door swung inward; a slight low squeak rose from its hinges.

"Yes? May I help you?" The man who said it was no taller than Cookie, but a touch on the paunchy side. He was dressed smartly in black trousers, polished shoes, and a black vest over a white shirt and a black bowtie riding at the neck, the shaved pink flesh of which jowled over the shirt's collar. A thin line of gray-black moustache, clipped and trim, bristled beneath a bulb nose. The top of his head sported hair darker than the moustache, oiled and parted in the middle and smoothed flat against his round head. His eyes, half-lidded, seemed to take in everything but the two men on the step below him.

"Yes, sir," said Rafe. "We're here to see the governor."

"Do you have an appointment?"

"No, but he will want to see us. We're old acquaintances."

The man lowered his head, then eyed each of them in turn, his nostrils flexing as he looked at Cookie, as if sniffing him from a distance. "I assume the gate guard had reason enough to let you pass. The governor is a busy man. I will tell him you are here. I doubt he will see you today. Your names."

A moment passed in which no one spoke, but all three looked at each other.

"Ahem. Gentlemen, the day, as the uncouth say, is a-wasting and I am a busy man. Your names, please, so that I may inform the governor."

"Now see here," said Cookie, one finger rising like a flagpole.

"Pard," said Rafe, forcing Cookie's hand down.

"We prefer to make this a surprise," said Rafe. "We are old acquaintances in town for a short time."

"That is a thin excuse for not wanting to proffer your names, but I will convey the message. My task is not to judge, merely to serve."

"Then get to it," said Cookie, his front teeth showing behind tight-pulled lips. Rafe sighed.

The butler's left eyebrow rose as if tugged

by a string. He stared at Cookie as the door closed with a heavy clunk. They heard his footsteps tapping, receding. The distant sound of another door reached them, clunking shut.

"Let's back down a step or so, Cook. Don't want to crowd the man."

They waited a full two minutes.

Cookie fidgeted and began sniffing, knuckling his nostrils, running a finger in his ears and nose.

Rafe eyed him once out of the corner of his eye.

Cookie saw him. "What? I got dust in my nose from the trail, is all."

The sound of footsteps, deeper, longer strides, drew closer. Both men cleared their throats and squared their shoulders. The door swung inward.

The man at the top of the steps before them was a tall, thin man dressed in a swallowtail jacket, gray-striped trousers, black brogans, and a sapphire-colored silk ascot. His full head of hair, as with his trimmed full beard, was silver peppered with black. Despite the lack of a smile, his crossed arms, and the bruise-colored hollows beneath two weary, wary eyes, Rafe saw the resemblance to his daughter, Sue. He also sensed the man was kind. Would have to be, he told himself, to have a daughter like Sue.

Still, the man wore the look of a fellow who was plain worn out, beaten down by whatever grinding life he found himself in. Rafe had seen it every day on every face during his five years in the hellhole Yuma Territorial Prison. He hadn't had a mirror, nor had he ever felt the need for one in his life — that's what mountain streams and ponds and lakes were for — but he was certain he, too, had worn that look in Yuma. And often since.

"Governor Pendleton?"

"Yes? How did you get through my gate? I gave that lummox strict orders not to let anyone through."

Rafe shook his head. "Please don't hold it against your gate lummox, Governor. We overpowered him. He'll be okay."

"What?" The man stepped backward, then held his hands palms up, shaking his head. "No, I don't want this. I am the governor, dammit."

"We know who you are, sir," said Rafe. He too held his hands up, and smiled. "We're friends."

The governor stopped backing up, but he remained tense, wary. "What have you done with my gate guard?"

Rafe ignored the question. "We're friends,

sir. The ones who helped Sue."

The tall gentrified man's face clouded as his eyes narrowed. He canted his head forward as if he could recognize these two men he'd never before met in person. "Barr? McGee? Is that truly you?"

Rafe and Cookie both nodded. "I'm afraid we don't have any proof with us. We're traveling light these days."

"I can well imagine — if you are who you say you are."

"Oh, we are, sir," said Cookie. He nodded, then took off his hat with a flourish and held it before his belly, worrying the brim with his thick-knuckled fingers.

"The name of the man who . . . who held my daughter hostage."

Rafe nodded, speaking softly. "That would be Al Swearengen, sir. And I regret that I was unable to incapacitate him permanently. One day, perhaps."

The governor's eyes softened. He nodded, as if coming to an agreement with himself. "Very well. Please come in."

"Thank you, sir." Rafe then said, "Oh, your gate guard. I'm afraid we tied him, I didn't want to do that but he wouldn't let us pass and we really need to see you, sir."

"He's a good sort," said Cookie. "Big mouth on him, but he shouldn't lose his work on our account."

The governor nodded. "I'll see to him. You have my word he'll be treated fairly. Though I will give him a talking to."

"Our horses are tied not far from him, inside the fence."

"I'll send Henry for the stable boy. We have ample room in the stables out back."

Their host kept several yards from them, nodding toward the butler who beckoned them to follow him. The governor said, "Please follow Henry. I'll be with you momentarily." He opened a door to their right and disappeared into a room.

They held their hats and meandered behind Henry, the butler, into a sunlit room with a white marble fireplace and a black, cold firebox. The windows wore heavy green-velvet curtains held open with gold ropes with tasseled ends. The room was cozier than the cavernous, echoing front hall.

The butler backed out the double doors, bowed his head once at them, then shut them in. Both men stared at the doors, but they heard no locks click. Nonetheless Rafe strode quietly, keeping to the thick Persian carpet, and gently tried the doorknob. It turned and he opened it slightly. He closed it again and walked back to Cookie.

Both men stood before the fireplace, looking and feeling out of place in the plush surrounds. The doors opened wide again and the governor walked in. He still wasn't smiling, but he strode to them, apparently no longer afraid.

He walked by them to a sideboard laid out with a cluster of cut-crystal decanters containing various colored liquids. "Whiskey?" he said, holding up a tumbler.

Rafe and Cookie nodded, and said, "Thanks," at the same time.

When each of the three men held a glass with an ample offering of whiskey and had each sipped, the governor cleared his throat. "Susan. How is she? Where is she?"

He looked Rafe straight in the eye. They were of the same height.

It was Rafe's turn to clear his throat. "I'm sorry, sir. I . . . I don't understand."

"My daughter, dammit!" The man's cheek muscles bunched and flexed. "I am sorry."

"You mean you haven't heard from her?"

The governor shook his head. "Not since that initial flurry of letters from you and her assuring me she was safe and being well cared for at your secret location."

"Our ranch." Rafe nodded toward Cookie, his business partner. "When I last saw her, oh, a few weeks back, she was well. Going to ride out. She had said she was ready to see you again." Rafe turned to Cookie for confirmation.

"That's right, Governor, sir. I seen her nigh on a month ago myself, and that's what she said. Heading here to see you. I told her it was about damn time, pardon me, sir . . ."

"We've all been encouraging her to do that, sir."

"Then what happened?" The governor set down his glass.

Rafe let out a long breath. "She's either in trouble, or she lied to us and has something else up her sleeve."

The governor surprised them by smiling. "I hope to God she's safe, but I'd bet my last dollar she told you what she knew you wanted to hear. You may have noticed by now that the quickest way to get Sue to do exactly what you don't want her to do —"

"Is to tell her what you want her to do," said Rafe, a smile tugging up one corner of his mouth.

"Here now, she's a good girl. I don't think it's right us talking about her like this." Cookie's eyebrows rose as the governor and Rafe both looked at him. "Oh, sorry, Governor, sir."

"That's all right, Mr. McGee. I'd agree with you, except that as her father I feel I've earned a certain number of words, per week, to spend on griping about my dear, frustrating, perplexing daughter."

Rafe grew serious again. "Cook, did Sue say anything to you about where she was headed, what she had in mind?"

"No, just that she was coming to see her pa. Sorry, Governor, sir."

"You don't have to keep saying that, Mr. McGee. My name's Cuthbert."

"Okay then, if you call me Cookie."

"Fair enough. Now, what are you driving at, Mr. Barr?"

"It's Rafe, please. I'm only now recalling something Sue told me. That it was time for her to go off into the world and make her own mark."

The governor sighed and rubbed his temple. "That sounds like Sue."

The rock that burst the large, multipane window in the front wall of the governor's mansion was sizable. "Big as a man's head," said Cookie later, while toeing the hefty missile.

He and Rafe and Governor Pendleton had been in the middle of a fine meal of roast pork, potatoes, thick gravy, and all manner of vegetables with fancy names Cookie had never heard of. He doubled up on the spuds and tripled the pork and gravy to make up for leaving the mystery vegetables off his plate.

Rafe and the governor had been swapping memories of the war when the rock interrupted the meal and the conversation. The serving boy screamed like a pin-stuck hog, though he was on the skinny side, and the cook, a burly woman with bright red hands and cheeks to match, barreled into the room, knocking wide a set of swinging doors that separated the dining room from the hallway leading to the kitchen. The butler flinched but otherwise stood quietly behind the governor's chair, as if carved from stone.

Truth be told, even Cookie yelped a little. Rafe reacted as he always did — he went into action, dropping low and rolling out of his chair. By the time his knees hit the blue-and-red Oriental carpet, the big man had dragged a Colt from a holster and thumbed back the hammer. Cookie followed suit, and even managed to snag a thick slab of pork on his way down. Only the governor sat still, eyes wide and a hand across his mouth as if suppressing a scream.

Rafe hissed, "Governor!" and tugged the man out of his chair and down to the floor.

"What do ya reckon, Rafe?" Cookie scanned through the gap between the bottom of the tablecloth and the floor. "I see something over there." Before anybody could stop him, Cookie crawled on hands and knees under the table, straight to the object he'd seen.

He whistled and stood to one side of the shattered window, grunting as he hefted whatever it was. "Hoo-wee, whoever lobbed this has a mighty good arm."

"Cook," said Rafe. "See to the governor. I'm going to try to track them."

"Without me?"

"Stay here!" Rafe low-walked to the door at the back of the dining room and followed hallways until he found a side door. He slid the deadbolt open and swung the door inward, Colt poised. No sound came from the dark without.

He slipped out the door, closing it as quickly and as quietly as he was able, so the bare trace of light from inside would not leach out.

He felt his sides protesting with each low step he took, and ignored them. The hot stitches in his side, he knew, were from his wounds, but they were healing, so he chose to ignore them as best he could. He'd be damned if he was going to treat himself tenderly any longer.

It took Rafe two minutes to figure out that

whoever had tossed the rock through the window was no longer in the yard. Who would be? The guard at the gate had gone home an hour before, his services only required during daylight hours. Rafe would suggest hiring a night guard as well. He spent another fifteen minutes searching the front walkway and gardens in widening circles in hopes of finding a clue. As to the why, he'd pin down the governor on that point soon enough.

He bent to his task, keeping an eye, as much as he was able, on the shadowed edges outside the light cast from inside.

"Anything, Rafe?" said Cookie, peering down at him from inside the dining room. He was chewing on something.

"I see this little event hasn't interfered with your appetite," said Rafe, not taking his eyes from scanning the earth of the flower bed at his feet.

"No, thank God," said Cookie.

"Governor okay?"

"Yep, went upstairs, didn't say why. Said he'd be back in a bit." Cookie leaned outward, careful not to snag himself on ragged glass. "Betwixt you and me, Rafe, I think the poor man's nerves are as frayed as my socks."

"I agree with you . . ." Rafe looked up.

"For once."

"Ha — that must mean you're comfortable being wrong most all the time, then!" Cookie cackled and wrestled with a particularly toothsome hunk of pork.

"That cook ain't much to look on, but she's a fair hand in the kitchen. Course, she can't hold a candle to Arlene's, I mean Miss Tewksbury's, cooking."

"Again, I can't disagree with you, Cook."

"Twice in one night? Wait, let me get a hold of the local newspapers, they're gonna want to take this down."

"Cook?"

"Yeah, Rafe."

"Any clues on that rock?"

Cookie wiped his greasy lips with his cuff. "That's what I come over to the window for, risking myself being in the light whilst you hide in the shadows. Then you got me answering questions instead of telling you what I meant to, why you're a regular troublemaker, Rafe Barr."

"Louder, Cook, I don't think all of Sacramento heard you shouting my name. Which also happens to be the name of a wanted man, in case you hadn't forgotten."

"Okay, okay. Don't get your bonnet in a twist."

"Cook?"

"Yeah, Rafe."

"The rock?"

Cookie rubbed his hands together, disappeared from the window, and reappeared hefting the big, gray lump. "Somebody scratched something on the rock. Look here — it says, '2 DAYS.' "

"Two days?" said Rafe. "Hmm. What might that mean?"

"I asked the governor and you know what he did?"

Rafe shook his head.

"Well, at first he didn't say a thing. Turned whiter than he was, sort of like the color of old milk. Then he said, 'I'm going upstairs. I'll be back soon.' "

Cookie turned from the window. "Hey, hey, don't take them plates up! You got to clean, you clean the glass off the floor. It ain't harmed the platters none. I was about to tuck in again." Cookie looked at Rafe and shook his head. "Can't get decent help no more."

Rafe smiled and rubbed his side. "Nothing to learn out here. Too dark. I'm coming in. And Cook?"

"Yeah, Rafe."

"Don't ever change."

"Ain't about to." Cookie winked and circled the table. "Now, where was I?"

Cookie was amazed that, with little more than nods, arched eyebrows, and flared nostrils, the butler, Henry, was able to direct the meager house staff in cleaning the room of glass and righting the situation as if he'd been born to the task.

He sent an errand boy to fetch a glazier, and within the hour a harried man and an assistant arrived lugging wooden crates with panes of glass, and an assortment of odd tools, and managed to replace the six sizable squares of glass that had been smashed.

Rafe and Cookie weren't certain what to do with themselves now that the governor had disappeared up the grand, winding staircase. They went out back and visited the stable to check on their mounts. They saw the horses had been well tended, and their gear was secure.

"You reckon we should mosey?"

"No, Cook. The governor is hiding something. He's in trouble and we have to find a way to help him."

"Oh, we can sure try," said Cookie, rubbing his chin. "Good thing we was here, huh? Two days, that rock said."

Rafe sighed. "Doesn't seem likely, but maybe the governor is being targeted because of us. Hell, I don't know. But I do know we have to talk with him before we leave."

By then the two men had reached the back door to the house. "Think we should go on in?" said Cookie.

"I'll knock," said Rafe. His big knuckles were poised to rap on the door when it swung inward.

There stood Henry, the butler. "Gentlemen, I have been asked by the governor to show you to the drawing room."

They followed the servant down the long hall.

"Rafe," whispered Cookie. "Don't tell me they got a special room for making pictures?"

"What?" said Rafe, then he smiled, hiding it behind a hand. "Oh, I think he meant the room we were in before. You know, with the fireplace."

"And the whiskey," said Cookie.

"That, too."

Once again, they found themselves drumming their fingertips on their elbows, staring at the walls, now painted with shadows from flickering oil lamps. And once more the governor opened the doors wide, and though he looked, if possible, more haggard and with deeper sunken eyes, he managed a smile. Rafe couldn't be certain but he swore he saw a flash of relief cross the politician's face when he saw them.

"Gentlemen," said the governor. "I am so very sorry to have subjected you to that madness at the dinner table. Random action. I suspect local ruffians. Simply appalling."

"No need to apologize to us, Governor," said Rafe, "but I don't for one moment believe it was a random occurrence. Nor do I believe local ruffians are to blame."

The man of the house paused in splashing glasses with whiskey. He looked at Rafe. "I beg your pardon?"

"Governor, I've spent too many years of my life listening to people make nice and cover up the truth. Let's cut to it."

The governor regarded the big man through narrowed eyes. Then something inside him seemed to collapse and his shoulders sagged. He passed the whiskey tumblers around and nodded. "Okay, Barr. You're right. Something is going on, but . . ." he stared at the drawn curtains as if looking out the window.

"Governor?" said Rafe, turning a cigar in his big fingers as if admiring it. Cookie was admiring the fact that his tumbler of whiskey was still half full and the cut-crystal decanter on the sideboard was, too.

The governor sighed and turned to face them. "I am being blackmailed, to be blunt."

Rafe nodded, sending blue smoke toward the plaster-filigree ceiling. He was not surprised. "Who do you think is responsible?"

Another sigh, then: "That's the big question, isn't it? I know who, and I know why, but I am caught like a fly in a spiderweb. And I don't know how to extricate myself."

"Maybe we can help," said Cookie. "You'd be surprised what sort of shenanigans we get up to."

The governor smiled, then nodded. "I don't doubt your abilities in the least, gentlemen, but I do doubt there's an acceptable solution to this . . . . this mess." He sipped deeply from his glass.

"Let us worry about that part, sir. Why don't you tell us about it, from the beginning?"

"Yeah," said Cookie. "And what does 'two days' mean? That's what was on the rock that come through that big window."

The governor's face went ashen once more. "The message."

"Usually is one," said Rafe, glowering at Cookie for derailing his efforts at persuading the governor to talk.

"Governor," said Rafe. "You mentioned

you know who it is, and why."

The governor nodded. "I suspect the name will not come as a surprise to you. That's what makes your arrival so . . . fortuitous."

"What's that mean?" said Cookie, eyes narrowed.

The governor was about to answer when Rafe cut in. "The name, Governor."

Again, the man sighed, nodding. "Talbot Timmons, warden of Yuma Territorial Prison."

"That rascal!" shouted Cookie, smacking his free hand against his leg. "I knew we'd not heard the last of him!"

Rafe's face maintained its hard set. He nodded.

"Then you're not surprised," said the governor. "I didn't think you would be, given your history with the man."

"What does he have on you, Governor?"

"I beg your pardon?"

"That's the second time you've said that tonight, sir. No need to beg a thing from us. But if you want to tilt the odds in your favor, you might want to pour us all another whiskey, then let's sit on these fancy couches and get down to it. We'll need to know everything, from the beginning to now. And don't be tempted to skip any parts you may be embarrassed about. We may be rough around the edges," he glanced at Cookie and smiled. "But we are discreet."

"You speak as though you men have been down this lane before."

"Oh," said Cookie. "You'd be surprised how many folks we've helped who've found themselves over a barrel."

The politician nodded, offered a weak smile, and sank back into a corner of the couch. He seemed to have grown older, sagged inside.

"It's not the blackmail. It's these past few years. The demands of a life serving the people — which I do not regret. Yet I never expected so many people with so many problems to demand so much. It's as if they abdicate all personal responsibility and entrust that I, or rather the government, that is, will take care of them. Like a mother mopping the brow of a fevered bairn."

Rafe kept silent, maintaining eye contact with the man. The governor needed to talk, that much was plain. And maybe in a roundabout way he would get to what was truly troubling him, what had been causing this mess he now found himself in.

The governor paused, sipping his drink. "That's not true, though. No, this is a job, a task that I am capable of. I always rise to the situation required of me. No, it's not the governorship, it . . . it began with Sue leaving. No, with Sue running away. There is a difference. She's a grown woman now, it's true, but when she left she was still a child, filled with fanciful thoughts and impractical notions. Then she left and heaped all manner of trouble on herself."

He gripped his mouth with a white hand as if he might say something more he'd regret.

Cookie cleared his throat, then spoke in a low, even tone. "I think you'll find, sir, that she's come through her troubles in fine shape. You got no reason to worry about her now. She's a strong one, is Sue."

"I appreciate that, Cookie. But I'm her father, of course I can't stop worrying about her." He smiled and leaned back in his seat. "I'm afraid it's a lifelong affliction, men." Before he could stop himself, he asked, "Do either of you have child —" Then he caught Rafe's eye and saw the distant, lost look nested deep there. Another lifelong affliction. "I'm so sorry, Rafe. I . . . it was callous of me to have forgotten."

For a moment Rafe was still lost in memory, of his smiling wife holding their baby boy, then those pictures dripped away, replaced with his last visions of them, as he

211

wrapped the sodden blanket about them, the mother still holding the son. He'd buried them in the rain, together, deep in a muddying hole. And they were still there, at the ranch, waiting for him to return.

He cleared his throat. "There's something else, isn't there, Governor? Something more. The blackmail and . . . ?"

"Yes, blackmail, death threats, someone claiming to have some sort of power over me."

"What could Timmons have on you, sir?"

The governor shifted in his seat, staring at the wall. His fingertips drummed about the rim of his empty tumbler.

"All respect due, sir, we're not leaving until you fess up."

"How dare you . . ."

But Rafe held up a big hand. "Save the fake indignation, sir."

"Oh, all right. Very well, then. When I first ran for this office I . . . unwittingly earned a favor with an organization."

"What sort?" said Cookie, leaning forward.

"I found myself beholden to an entity I was unaware of, operated by men I was unfamiliar with. I made certain promises I really had no business uttering, but I was caught up in the hubris of the moment. My

victory seemed a certainty, you see. I felt . . .
I felt all powerful. I was foolish, I see that
now. But in all honesty, at the time it
seemed as if nothing could possibly happen
to me."

"But it did," said Cookie.

"What was the name of the organization,
do you recall?"

"Yes, of course. They won't let me forget.
They call themselves P.I. Limited."

"Does the P.I. stand for something?" said
Rafe.

"Phoenix International, I believe."

Cookie's mouth made a sound as if air
was leaking from a puncture. "How big are
they, Rafe?"

"What? You know of them?" The governor
sat up in his seat.

Rafe ignored him. "Bigger than we
thought, Cook. When did you say this was,
Governor?"

"Ah, three years ago, the spring of the
year, when I was campaigning. I didn't
know at the time they were bent on mis-
deeds."

Cookie snorted. "That's the least of what
they do, Governor, sir."

"I'm confused. Who are they? I demand
to know what you know of them."

"As you're aware, Governor, in the war

213

Cookie and I were agents, double agents. We operated on both sides of the fence. We had a few run-ins with a Phoenix Shipping, down in Savannah, turns out it was a front for a group of Confederate sympathizers, mostly old-money, plantation owners and the like, who were hell-bent on doing anything it took to make certain the South did not lose the war."

The governor snorted. "Hardly sounds like the men who approached me. They were an international shipping firm. With a fleet of schooners up and down the coast."

"I don't doubt it, sir. They have, or had, a whole lot of money at their disposal."

"What was the favor you, ah, didn't know you were accepting from them? And what did they end up wanting from you in return?"

The governor shook his head. "The long and short of it, gentlemen, is if anything unsavory leaks out, I'm done. Not merely with politics, but as a trusted financier and businessman. And the thing about it is, while I like my fine life and my large home and all the wonderful things it brings, I would prefer to be a pauper and have my wife back here with me. I sent her away abroad when this unpleasantness began. I would also very much like my daughter back on speaking terms with me. I thought we were making inroads in that direction, but she appears to want to continue shunning me."

"Governor," said Rafe, rubbing his chin.

"Oh no," Cookie rolled his eyes and paced the room. "I've seen that look before, Governor. It means we're all about to be in a world of hurt."

"What's that supposed to mean," said Rafe. "I was only about to say —"

"I know what you was about to say — that you have an idea. Am I wrong or am I right?"

"You're right." Rafe offered a tired grin.

"I'm all ears, gentlemen," said Governor Pendleton. "World of hurt or no . . ."

Cookie knocked back his last swallow. "Don't say Cookie McGee didn't warn you!"

"What I think we can do," said Rafe, ignoring his crusty companion, "is set a trap for your blackmailer."

The governor nodded, his eyes sparking for the first time since they'd met him. "Go on, I'm listening."

"How about we lure him here?"

"That should be simple enough," said the governor. "After all, I apparently have something he wants."

Cookie nodded. "And two days to deliver it."

As Rafe and the governor exchanged nods of agreement, Cookie, who'd angled on over to the sideboard, and appeared to be inspecting the drawn brocade-and-satin curtains, said, "What if your blackmailer had something you wanted?"

"But I . . ."

"No, hold on a minute, Governor," said Rafe, holding up a hand toward their host.

Judging from his drawn brows, the politician was not a man accustomed to being told to do anything.

"What do you have in mind, Cook?"

Rafe was not surprised to see his pard shrug and say, "I can't think of everything! You suggested a way to lure him here, trap him, you said you have something he needs or wants, and so my next thought was what if the tables were turned?" He raised his lanky arms, then dropped them to his sides. "After that . . . well, a mind needs fuel, you see?" He shifted his gaze to the decanter before him.

The governor, it appeared, didn't become so powerful a man by not reading people well. He glided over to the sideboard and said, "Gentlemen, we're on to something here. Not certain what yet, but I believe this calls for a top up to our drinks." He lifted the glass top of the decanter with a clink. "Unless, of course, Mr. McGee, you've had enough of these festivities for the evening? Perhaps Helga could fix you a glass full of warmed milk and a platter of her ginger snaps?"

Cookie's wiry eyebrows rose like birds taking flight. A look of genuine terror settled on his face. "Ginger what? Warmed-over milk?" He dragged a cuff across his whiskered lips. "No sir, all the same with you, I'd as soon have a splash or three of that fine stuff you got right there in your hand. Sir." He nodded, his tongue running along his lips.

"Very well, then Mr. McGee," said the governor while he poured them all another generous round. "We've sorted my woes down to two basic ones: The whereabouts of my daughter and the issue of blackmail." He sipped his own whiskey. "As to Sue, if I know her as well as I fancy I still do — she was a spitfire as a girl and from what I hear that's only become a more prominent trait as she's matured."

"That's true," said Rafe, the whiskey helping loosen his still-sore body, and random thoughts of Sue flitting through his mind. When he'd first rescued her, even as frail and as dark-eyed and physically downtrodden as she was, there was still something there. She still had spunk enough on the trail in the days following to tell Rafe and Cookie what she thought, even as the withdrawal from the drugs bedeviled her, even if she was incorrect as to their motives.

"She's a wonder," he said, then in one of the few moments Cookie could ever recall, Rafe blushed and fixed his attention on his whiskey glass. Moments of silence passed, but Cookie saw the governor's squint of assessment creep into a light smile before disappearing.

The politician cleared his throat. "As you say, I suspect there is a way to lure that wretched man here."

"What's the thing he most wants from you?" said Rafe.

"That's easy to answer — he wants my job."

"What?" said Cookie, nearly but not fully committing to spraying his whiskey across the room. "Who'd want that? No offense, sir."

"None taken. I've asked myself that same question many times, believe me. But this is only a suspicion, I should make that plain. He's never asked for anything specifically, save for money."

"What if we promise him that money, but only on the condition that you meet him face to face, and here at your own home."

"Here? Why would I do that?"

"Does it matter? Your loved ones aren't here, and you know the place, he doesn't. We could get a leg up on him."

Cookie rubbed his hands together as if he were kindling a flame. "Yep, I like it. Glad I nudged you fellas into this line of thought. Now Rafe, what's the plan?"

"That, my friend, is what we're about to discuss."

Helga stood close by Cookie's chair, her thick, pink hands locked atop her bosom. Cookie didn't dare look up, nor chew the mouthful of ham and biscuit he'd already forked in. Finally, Henry the butler cleared his throat. Cookie heard Helga's low growl as she bustled back to the kitchen.

"That woman's sweet on you, Mr. McGee." Rafe winked and popped another bite of biscuit into his mouth.

Cookie reddened. "Yeah," he said in a low voice, looking to either side. "But she can't make a proper biscuit to save her backside."

"And that would take a mighty mess of biscuits."

"Why, Rafe Barr, I do believe you poked

fun at that poor woman's . . ."

Rafe's eyebrows rose. "Ample backside?"

It was some minutes before Cookie could stop coughing. And then it became worse when Helga bustled in, red-faced and waving a great, two-pronged metal fork. "Vat ees da matter here? You poor little man, are you all r-r-right?"

Cookie nodded, gulping down more water. "Went down the wrong pipe, is all."

"Oh," she said, scowling at him. "I don't like a man who smokes on the pipe. That is a smell that never leaves a house!" With that she slipped back through the side door to the kitchen.

"Well, what do you make of that?" said Cookie wiping his eye corners.

Rafe forked in more egg. "Pretty clear to me. You're going to have to ask her to step out some time."

"What?"

"Or take up smoking the pipe."

CHAPTER SEVENTEEN:
FOXY IN THE HEN HOUSE

The sun felt good on Jack Smith's face. He'd been back at the Barr-McGee Ranch for weeks now and had spent the early days of it buttoned up tight in that stuffy little downstairs bedchamber in the still-unfinished ranch house. It was convenient for Arlene and his sister, Mala, to tend to him. But being tended by others was not what Jack wanted — even if he needed it.

He was up to hobbling about on a crutch or two, depending on how ambitious he felt, but the process of healing was taking its own sweet time, forcing him to lay low for hours a day. He wouldn't admit it to the ladies, but being doted on had its advantages, despite his scolding them about treating him like an invalid.

He sat back in his chair out in the sunlight of the dooryard, resting his hands on the blanket they'd stretched over his legs. They'd even rigged up a couple of planks on chairs to accommodate him. He closed his eyes and tried to ignore the pain in his game leg, throbbing like a cannon blast every time he shifted. He avoided that as much as possible, but a man gets fidgety, wounded pin or no. Verdict was still out on whether he'd be able to use the fool leg in the future as much more than a post to prop himself up with.

Doc Jones had said if he took care and didn't push his luck he might not lose the leg to a blood disease. The thought of Doc holding him down and laying into him with a bone saw made a sweat pop out on Jack's forehead. No way could he let that happen.

Bad enough that the same leg had taken forever to heal months ago after he'd been savaged by El Jefe and his Hell Hounds right here at the ranch. Thankfully Rafe and Cookie had let him stay on until he healed. Then when he had, he'd taken the fool notion into his head that he needed to slip back into his old life, gamble more, visit a town that had more going on than the ranch did. That plan had not worked out well. The poker tournament had been a false affair from the start. He'd been attacked, and his leg busted up again, maybe worse than the first time. Then he'd nearly been lynched, and he'd lost all of Cookie's money, to top off the entire headache of a visit.

The only good thing to come out of the horrible episode had been finding his long-lost sister, Mala. That she'd been a southern man's plaything was something he would never come to terms with, but at least they found each other. Ain't nothing going to pull them apart ever again. He would not let that happen. He had family once more, real blood family. You put that with the family of his friends here at the ranch, you had the makings of something good. Rafe and Arlene and Cookie and Doc — and Sue Pendleton, the lovely daughter of the California governor. Wonder what she was up to?

Pretty as Sue was, Jack's dozing mind called up memories of another beautiful face, a young Mexican woman who'd saved his hide outside that bar in Santa Fe the night before the tournament opened. They'd not talked for long, but the look they had exchanged struck him like nothing Jack had ever felt before. Trouble was, he didn't even know her name. Didn't know how to find her, nothing. If only he could get back to Santa Fe — but that didn't seem likely to happen anytime soon.

With that thought on his mind, Jack dozed in the sun like a well-fed cat. And he didn't wake until something blocked the sun before him, shadowing his face. He roused slowly, still thinking of Sue, wondering if he'd ever see her again.

"I leave for a month and everybody lays around in the sun, no regard for getting ranch work done."

Jack woke and squinted up, but saw only a dark shape skylined before him. Someone on a horse looking down. "Who's that?" His right hand visored his eyes, his left crawled backward, fumbling to slip beneath the blanket for his . . . that's right, he'd not carried his revolver since he got back from Santa Fe. Been no need, all busted up and infirm as he was.

"Relax, Jack."

The person slipped down from the saddle with a soft thud of boots on gravel. Jack struggled to clear the sleepiness clouding his mind. He saw it was a slender person, and whoever it was leaned closer. He tensed, cursing his leg even as he winced from the pain his sudden movement caused.

"Jack, relax . . ." The figure walked closer, reins held in one hand, and bent to his level. The sun cleared away and he saw then who it was.

"Sue?"

"Hey, Jack, it's me." She bent close, her

face inches from his. "See?"

She smiled.

"That really you?" he said in a hoarse voice.

"It is . . . hey, I'm sorry I startled you, Jack. You must have really been snoozing." She playfully rapped the back of her hand on his arm. "How about a hug for your old trail pal, huh?" She stood, spreading her arms toward him.

"Sue . . ." He tried to sit up taller in the wooden chair. "I . . . I can't get up easy yet, Sue." He flicked a finger at the blanket. "My leg, got it hurt again."

"Oh, Jack, I'm so sorry, I didn't know." She bent to him, kissing him on the cheek. "What happened?"

He pulled away. "You really have been out of touch, huh?" He hadn't meant that to sound as caustic as it came out, but there it was, like his mama used to say, running across the floor before you can catch it.

Footsteps sounded on the porch. "Can I help you . . . miss?"

Sue swiveled her head toward the house. "I . . ." The words caught in her mouth. A tall, pretty woman stood on the porch, drying her hands on an apron. She reminded Sue of someone misplaced, as if she should be twirling slowly across a ballroom floor.

225

Elegant, that was the word she'd use to describe her. Even if the woman was looking at Sue as if she'd belched in church.

"Oh, no, I'm . . ." Sue looked down at Jack.

The woman walked down the broad porch steps and approached Sue and Jack. "Jack, everything okay?"

"Yes, Mala," said Jack, rolling his eyes at Sue. "Sue," he said, "I'd like to introduce you to Mala." He gestured from one to the other. "Mala, Sue."

They shook hands lightly, eyeing each other. Jack watched the exchange with interest.

Mala kept her eyes locked on Sue, but said, "Jack, can I get you anything?"

"No, no, Mala. I'm fine."

"Okay, then. We'll be eating in twenty minutes or so."

"That sounds good," said Jack. "You'll stay for supper, Sue?"

Sue held the reins in both hands. "I don't want to impose."

"No problem, is it, Mala?"

Mala didn't respond right away.

Jack said, "Mala?"

"Oh no, of course not. I'll tell Arlene." She turned back to the house, then looked to Sue once more. "A pleasure to meet you,

Miss . . . ?"

"Sue. Just Sue."

Mala nodded, a wooden smile on her face, and went back to the house.

Sue watched her leave, and didn't notice Jack had covered his eyes with a hand. His shoulders worked up and down in silent laughter; his head moved slowly side to side.

Sue looked toward the barn. "That Mala, she's . . . she's very beautiful."

"Yep," said Jack, squinting up at her. "Yes, she is."

They exchanged a glance.

"Jack, what is it?"

"She's also my sister."

"Your . . . sister?"

"Yep," he said, grinning.

"But . . . but I thought . . ."

Jack nodded, still grinning. "I know. That was fun."

"Oh, you! You could have told me. That was awful."

"Awful as leaving while I was gone to Santa Fe? I kinda thought you'd be here when I got back."

"You knew I had to go, do some things on my own. I'm only passing through, Jack."

"I see." He was going to say more but she was looking around the place again, her eyes roving from the barn to the house, beyond to the paddock and bunkhouse.

Jack watched her a moment, then nodded as if he'd come to understand something that had been unclear. "He's not here, Sue."

She looked at him. "Who? Cookie? Where's that old badger at?"

"They're both gone. Have been since before Santa Fe." Jack found it odd that Sue didn't ask him about Santa Fe. It was as if she knew what had happened there, the attempted lynching, President Grant, all of it. But how could she have found out?

Any question he might have been about to ask was cut short by Arlene's shout from the porch. "Sue! You're back!" The solid woman bounded down the steps, her arms out, and collided with Sue, wrapping the young woman in a big hug.

"Oh, it's so good to see you," Arlene backed away, blew her nose, and dabbed her eyes. "Look at you, wherever you've been, they could use a lesson in how to feed a growing girl." She put a red, chapped hand on Sue's shoulder and turned her, inspecting her. "Land sakes, you're skin and bones."

"I'm fine, Arlene, I swear it." It was all Sue could do to keep from laughing at the woman's distress.

"You put that horse in the barn and get

228

cleaned up. I'll help Jack."

"I can help him, Arlene."

"I know, but we have a system worked out. Don't we Jack?"

Jack nodded. "Yep, that's a fact. She scares me and I run straight back to the house."

Sue looked at them both, Arlene offering Jack a fake scowl, and Jack covering his head with his hands, as if Arlene were about to pummel him. Sue'd missed them, missed this place.

She turned toward the barn, leading her horse. Cookie was gone looking for Rafe. Rafe, who knows where he was. And Doc, where was he? She had forgotten to ask. This wasn't the homecoming she'd planned in her head, over and over on the trail.

After she settled the horse in its old stall for the night, then scrubbed the trail dust as best she could from herself, Sue walked back across the yard. Jack's chair and makeshift leg extension sat empty. She regarded it, then made for the house.

When she reached the door she paused. Inside she heard two distinct voices, Jack and Arlene, and here and there, Mala. Each seemed to surmount the others in a desperate plan to one-up the others. Soon she picked out familiar words, her name, plates and cutlery being set on the table.

Sue made more noise than necessary, clunking her boots and smacking the front of her split skirt, trail dust still rising in a fine cloud. The voices inside quieted and she opened the door.

Mala, looking even prettier than she had earlier, now smiled at her in what seemed a genuine way and held out her hand. "Sue, please excuse my manner from before. I'm . . ."

"She's protective of her big brother, that's all." Jack winked and dodged Arlene's swatting hand as he reached for a biscuit off a heaped platter.

Mala nodded. "I didn't know who you were. And Jack's been through so much."

"We all have," he said, his stern expression full of meaning Sue could only guess at.

"Yes, well," said Arlene. "You're safe now, that's what matters. Everybody sit, sit, sit! Before it goes cold."

Steam rose off the platter of sliced roasted beef surrounded with potatoes and carrots.

"No chance of that," said Jack.

"I swear," said Arlene. "It's almost like having Cookie underfoot. I'll be glad when you heal up. You're a regular scamp."

"No Doc?" said Sue, looking around the barely populated table.

Mala was about to speak, then caught Jack's eye and busied herself with filling his plate.

Sue didn't notice as she sipped a cup of cold water. "Where did that old sawbones get to? Let me guess, off to Ferd's for a drink or three."

Arlene laughed. "I bet he wishes that was the case, but no, he went to Santa Fe with Ethel."

"Ethel?" said Sue, a forkful of meat halfway to her mouth. "Who's Ethel?"

Jack laughed with tears forming at his eye corners. Arlene and Mala had no idea what he was laughing about but they were so pleased to see him happy, they began laughing, too. Even Sue had to join in.

"Ethel is not so much a who as a what," said Jack. As best as he was able, he explained the war wagon Doc created.

"Wow," said Sue. "Go away for a month, everything changes."

"So," said Arlene, finally sitting down herself. "What have you been up to, Sue?"

For a moment the question caught her off-guard. Jack, Mala, and Arlene stared at her. "I, ah, I've been . . . in . . ." She couldn't very well tell them she was now a Pink, an operative for the Pinkerton Detective Agency. What's more, on her first assignment she'd been tasked with infiltrating the notorious new gang, The Outfit.

She'd been told by Allan Pinkerton himself that the gang was headed by escaped convicted killer, Rafe Barr, and his ruthless sidekick, Cookie McGee, the same men who had saved her from certain death at the hands of Al Swearengen in Deadwood. It had been all she could do to keep a straight face as her new employer revealed this.

"I've been visiting my aunt. In Iowa. I thought I'd stop by for a visit here before I head to California. It's about time I get reacquainted with my father."

"In California?" said Jack before he could shut himself up.

Sue regarded him with raised eyebrows. "He's the only one I have. Why?"

For a long moment no one said anything. Then there was an awkward shuffling of plates and reaching for food.

Arlene cleared her throat. "Now that's the best idea I've heard in a long time, Sue. I bet you're looking forward to seeing him again."

"I am." She nodded, then looked at her plate. What had been succulent food moments before now tasted like straw. "I am at that."

Jack changed the subject, talking about

anything other than the awkwardness that had bubbled up among them. It didn't do much good.

After the meal, Arlene persuaded Mala and Jack to leave the clearing up to her and Sue.

The older woman scrubbed her stewpot with more gusto than it required, her mouth set in a thin line.

"What's wrong, Arlene?" said Sue, her gut muscles clenching. Arlene's tight-set mood was beginning to worry her.

Arlene sighed and turned to face Sue. "You aren't here for an old-home reunion, are you?"

"I don't know what you mean, Arlene. I came here to . . ."

"I know why you said you came here, Sue. Doesn't mean I believe you."

"Arlene, I've never lied to you."

The older woman shrugged. "Makes no never mind to me, Sue. You know how everyone here feels about you. In case you don't, that means we all think the world of you, but if you came here hoping to find Rafe and Cookie, maybe convince them they'd be better off explaining their side of things to a judge instead of trying to put things right on their own, in their own way . . . then we have nothing to say to each other."

For long moments neither woman spoke. "And if I didn't?"

"Hmm?" said Arlene, acting as if she didn't understand.

"If I didn't come here for the reason you said?"

"Then," said Arlene, sorting through glass jars of spices, "I'd say you had given up on your dream of working for the Pinkerton Detective Agency."

Sue felt her face heat from her neck to the crown of her head. "I . . ."

"Yes," Arlene nodded. "You told me a few things in confidence, things I will never say to another soul, save for you. But in sharing, it is my belief you allowed me a right to offer my opinions from time to time. And that I will continue to do. Otherwise, I'll keep my mouth shut."

Sue was about to speak when the cook said, "But!" Arlene held a thick finger upright before her face. "If you are planning on tracking them down and bringing them to justice, such as it is nowadays, to further your career as a Pinkerton detective . . ." Arlene turned away and went back to tending to her scrubbing. "Well, I don't have to tell you that any future visits you plan on making to this ranch will be frosty affairs. And not just from me."

Sue's shoulders slumped and she closed her eyes. She hadn't felt this small and childish and alone since her mother's funeral. When she opened her eyes, Arlene was holding out a piece of paper. It looked like a much-folded telegram. She looked at Arlene, who nodded and wagged the paper. "This is why we were so cagey about Doc at the table earlier. Go ahead, read it."

Sue took it and read it, then read it again. "Does this mean they're . . ." Her words trailed off as she reread the cryptic message from Doc.

Arlene rubbed the girl's shoulders with her work-reddened hands. "Sue, honey, visit your father. It's long overdue. And if you happen to bump into Rafe and Cookie . . . well, tell them the stew's on and the biscuits are hot. I'm not sure about Rafe, but I know that will get Cookie's attention. I've never seen a man who could polish off a platter of biscuits like Cookie McGee."

Later, Arlene walked out onto the porch, her hands rubbing her lower back. She sighed and looked into the purpling night sky, then glanced to her left. "Oh, I'm sorry, Sue. I didn't see you there. Can I get you anything?"

"No, Arlene. I'm fine. That was a lovely meal. And that pie — oh, if I ate that way every day . . ."

"You'd be better off. That aunt of yours needs to hire a cook." She let her gaze linger on Sue's face.

The young woman shifted in her seat, looking away. "Oh, Arlene. I . . ."

"Rafe's a tough man, Sue. You know that as well as I do. More so — you've known him longer than I have. But I do know a smidge or two about living. Sometimes a thing can happen in your life to scar you. It dulls your edges and makes you wonder if life is ever going to be the same again."

Arlene sighed and looked out at the dark night. "My Ronald died right over there in that bunkhouse. We were squatters here, didn't know the ranch belonged to Rafe, or anybody. I had to bury my husband alone, up there, near Rafe's wife and son. It seemed fitting, as if they'd all have company. Then Rafe came along. And after he simmered down," she smiled, "he offered to let me stay if I wanted. And that's when I got to know you all. Why, it was as if the clouds parted and sunlight such as I hadn't seen in a long, long time lit up my whole world once more."

She turned to face Sue. "I still miss my Ronald. But now I wake up each day and smile again. I believe that's how Rafe will be one day. But his pain is a deep one and not only because of his family's killings. But because of the way he was treated, turned on by his own government, what he gave his all for. I expect the worst thing that could happen to him now is if his friends turned on him, too."

Sue didn't reply. They both stared into the darkening night.

Arlene touched the girl's shoulder. "I've set you up in your old room. If you need anything . . . fetch it yourself. You know this house as well as any of us. It's your home, after all, Sue."

"Thank you, Arlene. I'll be in soon."

The older woman went back inside. Sue didn't move in the rocking chair. To the south, a coyote yipped. Another answered. Within moments a chorus filled the night air, ringing the ranch with their odd, pretty song.

Sue wanted to be happy that she was back at the ranch, but she knew she wasn't there for the right reason, and she hated herself for it. She knew that in the morning, she'd ride out for the station at Gunnison Fork, to climb aboard a train that would take her to California.

CHAPTER EIGHTEEN:
DÉJÀ VU . . . AGAIN

Sue squinted from the glare of the midday sun and tugged her hat lower on her forehead. The horse she'd hired from the livery in Moleno was a solid beast, if plodding. But she'd wanted to make the last day of her journey home on her own terms, in her own way, not reliant on a hired buggy to take her to her father's mansion. And now that she was so close, she found herself wanting to turn, to race eastward, back to . . . where? To Chicago and the Pinkerton Agency? To the ranch? She sighed and wiped the salty sweat from her lips with her sleeve's cuff.

Very little about the trip from Pinkerton headquarters in Chicago had gone as she had expected. She had thoughts of a grand homecoming on her return to the ranch, and while it had been nice to see Arlene and Jack, and to meet Mala, the visit had felt odd, the way a mouthful of off-food made you question everything on the plate.

She hadn't thought going back to her father's house would cause her to feel so worn down, so dismal. Sue wasn't even sure she really wanted to go back home. But that was part of the problem, wasn't it? Her father's house wasn't any more her home than the Pinkerton Agency had been. Her thoughts drifted to the ranch. Despite the visit's odd moments, that place felt right and comfortable, what a home should be. Why couldn't she have that same feeling of anticipation and happiness now that she was coming closer with each hour to her father's place?

It could be her stepmother. They'd never really gotten along, not that each woman had minded. It had bothered Sue's father more than them. To his credit, he'd never given up on trying to get them to tolerate, if not like, each other.

Sue sighed and guided her slow-stepping horse around a hip-high jag of shale jutting close to the edge of the narrowed roadway. Later she would curse herself for not paying more attention to the trail, to the rocky overhangs and shadows that might conceal a man in wait. Until it was too late.

And when it was too late, all Sue Pendleton could do was push out a quick scream as something dragged her from the saddle.

But she struggled, thrashing like a roped mountain cat. She lashed out high with a boot, then drove the heel down at her attacker. It had little effect, so she tried again. The second blow connected with what felt like a leg, maybe a knee.

"Daah! Why, you little vixen!"

Sue shouted and kicked, drowning him out, only allowing the one sudden thought to intrude — it was a man, not a thing that surprised her anymore. Then a gloved hand slid over her face, bent her nose as she struggled, shouting, "No! No!" before it clamped tight about her mouth, mashing her lips into her teeth. Still she kicked and elbowed and squirmed.

She managed a handful of cloth, a shirt, perhaps, and tugged at it but the man wrenched himself away while tightening his arms like steel barrel bands about her flailing midsection.

He dragged her backward and shoved her against the rough bark of a Ponderosa pine, pinning her right arm. Sue bucked and thrashed harder, but he managed to snag her wrist with his left arm. She was aware that her attacker was fumbling for something with his free right arm. Sue didn't care what, but she would in a few short moments.

She thrashed more than ever as she heard a dull "pop" sound, then a clink, a slight gurgle. It was a musty, pungent smell, like naphtha or lye; she couldn't place it. Even in her frenzy of fear and anger she wondered was the man drinking whiskey? And then a moistened rag was clamped sloppily over her face.

That smell, it was . . . was . . . No, don't breathe! She cursed herself, felt her arms begin to droop, as if weighted at the tips; her head bent forward, she fought this last wave of the attack, but . . . no use . . . drugged. She'd been drugged . . .

It was Deadwood all over again . . .

"There now, you see? I am not such a bad person as all that. Eat your food, now, girl, before it grows cold. Nothing as distasteful as whistleberries sitting in a dollop of cold fat."

Words, words, all those words tumbling like rocks, clacking and colliding down a steep gravel slope, rolling, hitting others bigger and bigger until the slamming, colliding sounds became words, a man's voice.

She opened her eyes, not of her own choice; they popped open and all was fuzzy.

There was a fire, bright orange, pushing heat at her, its smoke clouding her face. But it was inside, in her mind, that felt most strange. It felt to Sue as if someone were pulling cotton ticking soaked in ether one strand at a time, out of her head, from her nose, her ears, her mouth, stranding out of her eyes, and it hurt like hell . . . "N-n-naah." She snuffled, trying to get the words out. "Nooo!"

"Ah, I see I misjudged you."

The man leaned forward. Sue saw his shape, something about him sounded familiar, looked frightening. He was a snake man, leering, fire shadows flicking his face.

It felt like a year of days passed before shreds of this strange series of moments, this experience she was in the midst of, began to become familiar. The man's staring face settled back into a normal shape, then his nose, his chin, a hat — she hoped it was a hat and not an odd-shaped head. She waited, not daring to try to talk again. She fought with sleep or whatever it was that had snatched at her earlier, pulled her down and blackened her mind. More time passed.

Sue glared at the man, one hundred and more thoughts rushing through her mind like a mountain freshet gorged with water.

She moved her tongue in her mouth, ran the tip along her teeth, inside and out, pulled her lips apart, and forced her eyes wide.

She focused her eyes on the man across the fire. Had he molested her? She didn't think so, but . . . she remembered her time at the Gem in Deadwood, when Al Swearengen would keep her in a stupor and she'd wake to find him atop her grunting, his whiskey breath and food stink clouding her face.

She didn't think this man had done that. Yet. "What . . . do you want?" She'd managed what sounded like real words, though they leaked out as barely a whisper.

The man rose, his knees popping as he did so. He wagged a finger and paced the far side of the fire. "Now see, that there, little girl, is the question. You have whacked that nail on the head, no doubt. What is it I want? In general, in life? Or, say, from you in particular?"

Sue tried to relax her clenched jaw muscles. "What gives you the right . . . to bother me? Do you understand what I'm saying, damn you? I was on my way to . . . that's my business. You dare to ambush me?"

Her captor laughed, a bold sound. "This is where you're supposed to say, 'Don't you know who I am?' Hmm?"

Sue fell silent. Why would he ask that? And then she knew. He'd gone through her things. Papers in her satchel bore her name. Letters she'd received from her father while at the ranch.

"Yes, yes, I can tell by the little lost look on your face that you feel I unfairly violated your belongings. Well, to that I plead guilty. But I wanted to know what you were doing out here all alone, by yourself, traveling on this dangerous road. All alone."

"You said that already."

"Smart girl, too," he snorted. "By the way, you best commence to treating ol' Turk right nice or he's liable to resettle on that notion he'd all but abandoned once he found out who you are . . . Miss Fancy Pants who's going to make me a whole lot of money."

That stilled her tongue and her heart. What did he mean? And was he Turk? Should she know that name?

"Yes, ma'am, I can see you are the sensible sort, too. Course, you better be, considering what I know of you and your, shall we say, past, that you wouldn't mind if ol' Turk was to . . . well, I expect you know what I'm on about." He sat down again across the fire from her and hooked a finger through the loop handle of his tin cup. She saw steam rising from the coffee.

If she expected to get the better of this savage, she had to keep her strength up. Had to eat. Even if he prepared it. What if he sprinkled something foul on the food?

"You are a bastard and a fool if you think I'm going to put up with anything you try to inflict on me." She shook her head, drawing her lips back in defiance.

Turk Mincher sighed and leaned against the rock. This promised to be a long evening with his captive. "Look here, little miss, you are not in a position to question me." He shook his head in time with his words. "You are in a position to thank me, however. And if you wanted to add a little helping of something else on top, why, so be it."

He stretched his legs out and wiggled his toes in his boots. They cracked and popped. It had been a long day in the saddle, a series of them, in fact. Since departing from the train, he'd been trailing at a distance, his quarry, Rafe Barr and Cookie McGee, the heads of whom would keep him in whiskey and women for a long ol' time. He had a decent idea of where they were bound, so he gave them their lead, knowing that putting more distance between them and him would lessen the chance they'd get wind of him. That Barr was a tricky man, but so far Turk was confident he had managed to remain undetected.

Mincher rode a few miles northward, looking for a trail he'd learned of two years before. It was rougher, not well-traveled, but it would allow him to parallel the route of the two men from a safer distance. And wonder of wonders, he came upon this loveliest of ladies on this bare stretch of road leading to California. And what do you know? It was the woman Barr had saved from that runty pig up in Deadwood, Al Swearengen. The woman Talbot Timmons was willing to pay handsomely for. This was proving to be a most fruitful trip.

While Turk admitted the Gem's owner was a businessman of the first order, he also knew the man was foul beyond all hope, not redeemable in any sense. Mincher didn't doubt the man would rut with a dead hog if the situation arose. No matter, now here he was with this fine creature. Why, anything at all might happen.

"You know, girly, I was you I'd give special thought to pleasing ol' Uncle Turk with candied words and perfumed ways. You was lucky I come along when I did, after all. No telling what sort of trouble you'd find yourself in by now. Mmm-hmm, that's right." He nodded and smiled at her.

Sue licked her lips. "Turk. Is that short for turkey?"

He could have frowned, could have reached across the fire and snatched her shirt by the throat and dragged her clean across the flames, watched her take flame and light up the night sky. But no, tamp that thought down Turk, he told himself. Keep in mind she is the daughter of the governor of the United State of California, and the likely love of one Rafe Barr, criminal to the highest degree — at least in the eyes of the law.

Turk was beginning to see value in not having gutted the big man completely in that back alley in Santa Fe. And he was seeing even more value in using this girl, making her pay his way, maybe even for the rest of his days. Why, this girl could be your savior, Turk, he told himself. Keep your knife sheathed, your pecker trousered, and your strangling urges reined in.

Mincher worked his jaw muscles tight and hard, bunching like little apples beneath the scarred skin of his cheeks. His eyes, dark shards, glinted dull light from the dwindling fire. When he spoke his voice was slow, drawn out dead from a dry hole in a burned-out forest floor.

"Like I said, that food will not keep all night. It was prepared by me for the purpose of providing you sustenance, and you will eat it." He leaned forward. His leather gun-belt creaked like an old chair, his voice croaked to match it. "You will eat it."

"And if I don't?" said the girl.

Mincher sighed once more. Then he set to a most-pleasurable task. He plucked the makings from his left breast pocket, rolled a quirley, licked it, struck a lucifer alight on his trouser leg, and set fire to the cigarette. He pulled in gray-blue smoke down deep, then pushed it out. "If you don't eat the food I prepared for you, then I will force it down your throat with my own hand. Every last bean."

Turk Mincher smiled.

CHAPTER NINETEEN:
A TALE OF TWO PRIVIES

Mincher exhaled, pushing out a boil of gray smoke. He cleared his throat. "Let me tell you a story."

"I'd rather you didn't," said Sue, looking anywhere in the dark but at the half-lit face across the fire, flickered by dancing flame.

His low chuckle unspooled like a snake stretching full out for a night's hunt. "And I'd rather you were kinder to me, but if there is one thing in this life I have learned it's that we aren't likely to get the thing we most desire. Some can, but not all of us. With effort, we can learn to like other things, things we didn't think we'd like at first. That making sense to you?"

Sue couldn't help herself. "No. Nothing you have done makes sense. But as I'm your prisoner, I don't have much of a choice, do I?"

"There now, you see? Admitting to your

failings is the first step toward saving your-self."

"Saving myself?" she said. "From what?"

Mincher leaned back. "Why from me, of course. Now, where was I? Oh," he snapped a finger, stabbing the air and pointing at her. "That's right. Once upon a time not long ago there were two men, not a forget-table pair, or so I hear. One was a tall drink, gappy in the tooth department, greasy hair and all-around a hard-looking rig. His partner was a physical opposite of the former." Mincher leaned forward. "He was a tiny thing, likely a dwarf."

He nodded to his captive as if that would help confirm the claim. "The littler man was no less ferocious, however. Some might say he was the worse of the two. But as with all frightening folks, these two men met their match one fine day. Or was it a night? You see, these two individuals were not good men. They were bad, bad, bad, killing and robbing and leaving sad people behind them as often as they could."

Sue shifted, grunting as a sharp pain pulsed in her leg. If she didn't stand soon, she felt as though her body might seize forever in this painful, lashed position.

"Stop fidgeting, my dear, and I will tell you the rest of the story. You understand?"

The man's words and the cold, dead tone on which they rode chilled Sue. Almost without thinking she nodded.

"Good. Now about those two men. You see, the hero of our story, he decided they had to be stopped. One way or another they had to be stopped." Mincher leaned forward as if waiting for Sue to speak.

"What . . . what did the hero do?" She tried to sound interested, because something about the man had changed since he began this story; something starker and more serious had settled on the meager, cheerless campsite, like a veil of cobwebs, blunting and dulling all beneath it.

He nodded, no smile this time, as if pleased with her response. "The hero, for that's what he is, the hero . . . well, I am getting ahead of myself . . ." A burst of laughter rippled from his grim mouth. The sound was even more unsettling to Sue than his cold voice had been.

"A head. Ah, but you don't know what that means yet, do you, dear? You will." He touched a finger to the side of his nose. "You see not long ago, in Santa Fe . . . Oh, you are familiar with Santa Fe, New Mexico, I assume?"

She nodded.

"Good. Yes, not long ago in that fine town,

252

two headless bodies — now you understand my burst of humor — were discovered. But not together! Oh no, no. One was in a latrine, yes as foul as that sounds, it was found in a latrine behind the house of a noted local busybody. If I am told correctly, she goes by the name of Miss Tinkler, of all the names. Can you believe that?"

Again, he stared dead-eyed, mirthless-mouthed, at Sue. She was unsure how to answer. She shook her head, not daring to breathe.

"That's right you don't, because you weren't there." He rolled another cigarette, in one hand almost as if he wasn't thinking of it. Despite the situation, Sue could not help being impressed by this paltry trick.

"They say they found the body because of the godawful stink rising from that little outhouse. That and the explosion of flies, even more than usual at Miss Tinkler's privy. You see, Tinkler is a big gal, likes her meals, she does. And we all know what that generates . . . in the end."

Mincher chuckled again, a dry, husk of a sound, still no smile on that mouth, and tucked the cigarette between his thin lips. "The constable, one Pervis Bostwick, previously of Kansas City, if I recall the story correctly, rooted around himself down there. But he soon determined the task was beyond anything he was capable of, so he hired a local fellow, ol' crack-minded Carlton Nivers, to fish around. And by God, if Carlton, simple in the head but not in dedication to his task, distasteful as it was, came through in the end. Ha!"

Sue recognized the pause, the stare — the man wanted her response. She tried to force a smile, but anger and fear warred and won out over any false mirth she tried to muster.

He sighed, leaned back, and appeared to take her slight effort as an earnest attempt to participate in his foolish story. "It wasn't but a couple of days later in a different part of town the very same smell was sniffed rising on great clouds of stink powered by bluebottles. And do you know where it was detected?" Again, he looked at her.

She shook her head, but sensed he wanted more than that, words that took all her effort to utter. "No, no, I don't know."

"Why, I will tell you, little miss." He leaned forward once more. Sue heard the soft sound of his trouser fabric and his leather gunbelt creaking. "They found another body wedged deep inside the outhouse of none other than Reverend Whipple. That's right." Mincher nodded. "That pious old man of the cloth had been relieving himself all over the mortal remains of a headless dead man. Now, I ask you, isn't that about the strangest thing you've heard all day?"

Sue closed her eyes a moment and nodded. "Yes, sir. Yes, I can agree with you on that point."

"Good to hear that we come to terms on at least one thing. But I suspect there's something you want to know, isn't there?" He eyed her, squinting, either from the low light or from the smoke, she could not tell.

"Why did you do this? You have no right to kidnap me."

The man sighed. "I have every right to do anything I like in life. You see, whoever in life is the strongest, biggest, and meanest can do whatever he wants. And he will get through his days a whole lot smoother than the meek. They are the ones who must be kept in line."

Sue could think of nothing to say to that. He was crazy in the head, and he was waiting for her to say something more that might rile him. One wrong word and who knows what he'd do.

Sue was tired; she felt the weight of the day, the week, all of it, maybe even the confusing few months that led up to this moment, all of it pressing on her. She wanted to sleep. Nothing more. She wanted to get to her father's house, apologize to him, then fall asleep in a bed, her old bed, big and fluffy and with the thick curtains pulled tight against the bright morning sun.

"I don't think you are being honest with me," said the man. "You have a question you want to ask, something you really want an answer to. Not that other stuff."

Sue stared at him again. She felt drained, dull, and tired beyond measure. She didn't want to play his game any longer, didn't want to listen to his stupid story. But she knew she had to. She licked her lips and forced out more words, hoping they were what he wanted to hear. "What happened to the heads?"

He stared at her, brows pulled together as if he hadn't heard her correctly.

"The heads from the two bodies they found in the latrines? Oh, yes, well . . ." he pulled long on the quirley, then spoke, smoke leaking out, coating the words. "I sold them." He winked. "I mean, our hero, he sold those heads. For a bounty, you see. Because they were wanted men. Bad men who needed killing."

That was not the answer Sue thought she'd hear. And her face must have shown her surprise.

"Oh, come now, you didn't think I was talking about any old soul, did you?" He chuckled once more; this time the sound was accompanied with a smile, slight though it was. "I am a vain man, I admit. And such a deed deserves not to be credited to some faceless, nameless hero but to me — the man who caused it all to happen."

"There's nothing heroic about killing." Sue regretted speaking as soon as she opened her mouth. But as with nearly everything the man did and said, his reaction surprised her.

He leaned back, flicking the stub of his cigarette into the dwindling fire. "Now, see, you may be right about that. You may be right. But then again, I can't think of a single reason why your opinion matters to anyone but yourself. Now," he leaned forward, hands folded between his knees. "The same could be said about me."

Once more the dead black eyes stared at her over the fire. He said nothing for long moments. Sue tried to look away, but this man was unlike any of the other foul men she'd met in her eventful life since leaving home in a foolish huff years before. She thought Al Swearengen, back in Deadwood, had been the picture of man's evil, but this one was far worse, because he was so certain of himself. Not like Rafe who, though also measured and confident, was kind, too. No, this man was evil and happy to be so.

The longer he stared at her, the more frightened Sue became. That fixed line of his mouth that could as easily split into a smile or a hard sneer; the dark eyes unblinking, cold, like those of a snake; the thin puckered scars glowing on his cheeks; the clean shirt and vest and smooth, low-crown hat — didn't the man ever get cold? As she took all this in, Sue felt the beginnings of a thin, birdlike scream clawing up her throat. She felt her neck stiffen, tremble, her jaw muscles tighten. She hadn't felt this frightened in a long time. No, that was not true; she had never felt this way. This scared.

And then the man rose to his feet, barely making a sound. He circled the fire and stood over her, staring down. Oh no, no, no, thought Sue. Not this, not now. Not . . . again.

And that was what it took to yank her from her panic. Sue forgot about the rawhide straps binding her hands and her ankles, and pitched herself to her right, no idea what she was going to do, but knowing she had to do something, anything, even though she knew it would be a futile effort.

CHAPTER TWENTY:
THE MIDNIGHT CALLER

Soft sounds, drawing closer, rose in the night. The rubbery snort of a horse, then the sounds of stamping hooves, the soft chink of traces . . .

Jack woke as if someone had snapped fingers before his face. Someone was there, outside, at the ranch. He reached for his holstered revolver hanging beside his head. The sudden movement twinged a flash of hot pain up his leg.

"Damn," he hissed at the dark, gritting his teeth and sliding the revolver free of leather.

He pushed himself up until he was seated, waiting a moment more for his eyes to adjust to the dark. Scant moonlight shone through the gaps in the drawn shutters. He tugged the latch and nudged the right shutter open with the tip of the gun. The wooden shutter offered the world a slow squawk that made Jack wince inside and out.

He risked a peek outdoors, but saw nothing. Then he heard it again. Footfalls of a horse, maybe another, then a rambling, squeaking sound. Like a wagon. Whoever was here wasn't worried about not disturbing anyone who happened to be sleeping.

Jack pushed himself to his feet, leaning against the wall with one hand. With the other he brushed down to check that his longhandles were buttoned — wouldn't do for an intruder to see him exposed. His crutches leaned beside the bed and he decided on using one so he'd have a hand free to hold the gun. Then he cursed. He wasn't stable enough on one crutch to do much more than fall over.

He grabbed the gunbelt, strapped it on, and then hoisted himself up onto the crutches. He wore a raggedy pair of wool socks, but they would be far less apt to call attention to him than his boots clunking across the floor. As it was, the crutches were louder than he wanted them to be.

If he waked Mala or Arlene, they'd tell him to lay down and curl up like a baby, then they'd go out and face whatever stranger was invading the ranch. No, he'd do it himself or die in the effort. Jack was dog-tired of laying low and healing. Time to prove he was no longer a kept man.

And he almost made it, too. But as he angled through the doorway into the kitchen, stiff-walking his way to the front door, the butt of his gun clunked against the doorframe. He swore it didn't sound any louder than the damned crutch thunking on the plank floor.

He paused, lips pulled tight against his teeth. And heard the soft sound of the straw mattress shifting, then feet touch the floor softly. It was Arlene, whose room was off the far end of the kitchen. He barely made out the light coloring of her nightgown in the doorway.

"Who's there?" she said.

Jack thought her voice sounded forced, as if she were trying to mask fear.

"It's me, Arlene," whispered Jack. "Go on back to bed."

"Jack?"

Then a quick, loud slamming sound reached them from outside.

"Jack — you think that's the soldiers Ferd warned us about?"

"I don't know," he said, but he guessed she was right. "Stay here, get a gun, wake Mala. I'm going to scout." He limped to the door.

"Jack, you're in no state —"

"I appreciate your concern, Arlene, but

now is not the time to argue."

He ignored her as she whispered a flurry of words at him, all, no doubt, intended to keep him inside. He'd be damned.

Jack eased out the door, holding it closed with one hand, nearly dropping the crutch from that hand. He decided he'd be better off with one of the sticks propping him, so he leaned it against the house wall. As he drew his revolver, he heard slight scuffing sounds from behind him, within the house, then the door inched open.

Arlene poked her head out. "Jack?" she whispered.

"Yeah?"

"Mala's not in her room."

"What?"

"That's because I'm right here," said a voice below them at the bottom of the steps. "If you two made any more noise you'd be a circus."

Jack eased over to the top of the steps, "Mala? Go on back in the house. I'll deal with this."

"Jack." Her voice sounded as though she had caught him in a childhood lie. There was a pause, then she said, "We'll both go. You can go first, if that makes you feel better."

"It does," he said, stepping as quietly as

he could down the steps to stand beside her. "But what would make me feel even better is if you'd go on inside with Arlene."

"Not going to happen, Jack. I lost you once, nearly lost you a second time. I'm not going to risk losing my brother again, not without a damn fight."

"Thanks for that," he said, moving ahead of her. "I think."

They heard squeaks — sounded like the double barn doors to Jack — then a sliding sound and a grunt from a man, from the far end of the barn.

"You hear that?"

"Yep." Jack planted the crutch tip and swung with it, feeling better than he thought he would, more alive, bold, even if he was wearing nothing but long johns and wool socks with more hole than wool, as Cookie would say.

They did their best to cat-foot along the north side of the barn; Jack paused at the corner. They were about a dozen feet from the near edge of the big double doors. He peered around quickly once. The closest door was swung wide — he couldn't see the other one. Long shadows conjured by the night's paltry moonlight leached outward onto the gritty, hoof-stomped dirt of the barnyard. Yes, sir, someone was in there.

Jack held up a hand hoping his sister would do as he bid and stay put as he moved forward. She followed. He was about to spin, motion her to go back around the side of the barn where it would be safe, but they heard a man's low voice, mumbling.

The voice was familiar.

Jack edged closer, stopped, and peered around the door. Except for a dark shape in the center aisle, he couldn't make out anything in the dim interior. Mala knocked into him. The top of his crutch hit the door and it squawked and swung inward a foot or so.

Mala whispered, "Oh, no, I'm sorry!"

A man's voice from inside the barn said, "Hello? Who is there?"

Jack regained control of his crutch and cocked the revolver back all the way. "Come out of the shadows with your hands raised high!"

"Oh, God in heaven, why?" And Doc "Deathbed" Jones stumbled out from behind the large dark shape in the center aisle, hands clasped tight atop his head, already squashing his dented bowler. He appeared ready to sob.

"Doc?"

"J-J-Jack? Jack, is that you?"

"Doc!" shouted Mala and pushed past her

brother.

Jack wobbled again and raised his pistol lest it go off in the direction of his reckless sister.

She wrapped her arms about the knock-kneed medical man. "It's good to see you, Doc."

"Oh, Mala, why . . . this sort of homecoming makes a man consider going away more often. Well," he looked at Jack and smiled. "Except for the part with the guns trained on me. Oh, but you almost did me in, my boy!"

"You alone, Doc?" said Jack, walking over as he holstered his revolver.

"Alas, save for these two solid lads here, as well as Ethel, why, yes, I would say I am alone."

Jack wanted to ask, but Mala beat him to it: "We got your telegram. Are Cookie and Mr. Barr okay?" she said.

"Why, yes, I think so. That is to say they were in fine fettle when I left them, but . . ."

"But what, Doc?" said Jack.

"But there will be time enough for that later. Here, you two can make yourselves useful and help me finish with these harnesses. I'll clean them in the morning. I need to rub down these brutes and feed them. They got me here hours sooner than

I anticipated. I had hoped to time my arrival to coincide with whatever heaven-sent breakfast Mrs. Tewksbury will have prepared."

"And what makes you think there will be room for you at the breakfast table, Doctor Jones?"

Doc spun and faced the figure standing in the middle of the door, cradling a double-barrel shotgun.

"Welcome home, Doc." Arlene walked forward and gave him a hug. "As a matter of fact, I was thinking of dishing up breakfast early today."

"I'm always up for one of your fine meals, you know that, Arlene."

Mala and Jack both chuckled as they set about helping Doc with the chores. "Why don't you two head on in. Mala and I will finish up here."

And so, the two senior members walked to the house.

"Jack," said Mala once they were out of hearing range. "You were scared, weren't you?"

He nodded. "Sure. Only a fool wouldn't be."

"I think you ought to teach me how to shoot, Jack. I never had much occasion to use a gun."

He thought a moment, then nodded. "Okay, Mala. We'll start in the morning. Later in the morning, anyway."

Chapter Twenty-One:
Bold as Brass

"Rafe?"

"Yeah, Cook." Rafe turned from the washbasin, drying his freshly shaved face with a tiny towel he found too small by half.

"You might want to see this." Cookie stood looking out the window, a steaming cup of coffee in hand. He'd already been down to the kitchen, capitalizing on Helga's growing fondness for him.

Rafe walked over, draping the little towel over his shoulder and running a hand through his hair. He needed a trim. "You keep toying with that woman's heart, she's liable to —"

"Rafe," interrupted Cookie. "I ain't kidding." He nodded once more at the view downstairs, toward the side yard of the grand home. "He's a hinky-lookin' rig."

Rafe parted the white curtains with a long finger and looked out. He saw a trim man dressed in black wearing a red shirt, riding a black horse dolled up in black leather and silver conchos. The horse stood at the gate, rider mounted atop, smoking a cigarette. He looked relaxed, as if waiting for something to happen. "Cook, that horse look familiar to you?"

His pard narrowed his eyes. "The train!"

"Yep," said Rafe, already crossing the room, setting his hat on his head and strapping on his gunbelt. He didn't look behind him, but spoke as if Cookie were right there. And he was.

"Too much of a coincidence," said Cookie.

"I don't believe in coincidence. But I do believe that man is here because of us. Now, to find out why." Rafe reached the bottom of the grand staircase and strode through the entry room toward the hallway that led to the side yard. Through an open doorway the governor stood from the breakfast table and wiped his mouth on a napkin as he approached them.

"Gentlemen, I —"

"No time, Governor," said Rafe, holding up a big hand to ward off the dapper man. "Stay inside, sir. Away from the windows." And with that, he was out the door, Cookie closing it behind them.

Rafe strode down the long brick walkway to the gate, long steps matched with easy arm swings. He reached the black steel gate and stood inside it, arms loose at his sides. He looked across at the man on the horse, three steps down to the graveled roadway. "Do I know you?" said Rafe.

The man on the horse, who had been looking half at Rafe, then glancing up at the sky as if comparing the two, puffed on his quirley. He sighed and turned his gaze on Rafe. He, too, kept a hand in a casual pose close by a revolver on his hip. "If you don't," he said, "then you aren't half the man your wife said you were."

"You son of a bitch!" Rafe's voice echoed in the still morning air as he lunged like a lion with nothing to lose and clawed his way up the locked steel gate. He had nearly cleared the top of the tall gate when Cookie's iron grip stopped him short. That bony hand was the only thing that kept Rafe from clearing the top.

"Let go of me!"

It was all the older man could do to restrain his partner. "Give it a second, Rafe. Least give him a listen!"

Rafe hung on the gate, one leg over, chest heaving, eyes bulging and focused on the man, his lips pulled wide revealing seething, tight-set teeth.

"Well, now," said the man on horseback,

who hadn't shifted from his casual pose. "Might be your little man there is talking sense."

"Why you . . ." Cookie's eyes sparked like struck flint. "I've a good mind to let go of this bear!"

The man in black raised a finger. "Not yet, little man. I believe I have something you two might find of interest." He plucked a bundle of blue calico cloth from inside his vest and held it up. It unfurled on its own. "Recognize this blouse? No?" He laid it across his saddle horn and reached into the vest once more. "How about this?" He tugged out a length of wide green hair ribbon. He waggled it. "No? Then how about . . ." He reached into his vest once more and retrieved something small and black and heavy. A six-shot pepperbox pistol.

Recognition twitched Rafe's eyebrows. It was the little hideout gun he'd given to Sue. Rafe growled, "No!" and lunged again. Cookie nearly let go of him, but the mounted man was taking great care to show he was not trying to trigger the little gun.

The man in black held his free hand shoulder-height, palm out as if in greeting. With his other hand he held the little gun before him, hanging limp. "I'm guessing from your reaction, Mr. Rafe Barr, that you have seen this here little gun before?"

Rafe bulled forward, lifting Cookie off the ground. His hand slipped free of the big man's gunbelt and Rafe made it over the edge. The big black horse shied back, but settled with a quick warning hiss from the man on his back.

He turned the same attitude on Rafe Barr, holding the little revolver in one hand, clutching the calico and the ribbon in the other. His teeth, too, were gritted, though, unlike Rafe's, were framed with a vicious smile. He canted his head to one side and arched an eyebrow, daring Barr to advance.

The big man restrained himself, his muscles twitching. "Yes, I know that gun," growled Rafe, his entire body a knot of roped muscle, straining to lunge at the man.

"Good. And since you don't seem stupid, can't speak for your little pal, there," he nodded at Cookie, who began his own climb over the gate, teeth bared like a tethered dog. "Then you'll know the little toy belongs to a certain daughter of a certain governor of a certain state named California. Oh!" He held fingers to his lips. "Could it be that we are in that place? And at the home of that man? My my my . . ."

Something happened then to Rafe Barr.

His shoulders slumped and he began to slowly shake his head. "What have you done? Where is she?"

The man sat his horse and smiled, saying nothing.

"Where!" Rafe's shout was not a question but a bellowed demand that caused Cookie to flinch and the man on the horse to lean back, eyes wide.

Any seeming loss of rage Rafe might have shown dissipated with finger-snap speed as he bolted forward, grabbing the big horse's bridle with his left hand and clawing the man in black from his saddle.

The shirt and ribbon slipped to the ground and the pepperbox spun from the stranger's grasp, landing close by on the graveled lane. The man wore a stunned look even as he collapsed in a pile at Rafe's feet. This was not playing out as he anticipated. But he recovered as would a thrown snake, whipping around to try to gain his feet, pawing at his holster.

Rafe was faster, and jammed a big boot hard into the man's chest, flattening him even as he yanked free a Colt and ratcheted back the hammer to half-cock. He trained the snout of the weapon on the man in black's face. "I know it's you. As soon as you spoke. I remember your voice from the

273

alley. You should have killed me then, you bastard."

The man, breathing hard beneath Rafe's boot, smiled. "And miss out on all this fun?"

With more sudden speed, Rafe drove the toe of his boot into the man's chin, raising a welt, then swung the butt of his gun into the stranger's temple. Blood sprayed. From behind Rafe a man's voice, not Cookie's, said, "That's enough, Barr! You'll kill the man!"

It was the governor. Rafe heard him but delivered another blow to the man's leering jaw. "That's the idea." Rafe stood up and held the pistol once more in a steady hand, aimed at the stranger's face.

"You best listen to the man if you want to see the pretty Miss Sue again." The man in black's words were clear enough, wetted as they were with the blood filling his mouth.

"No, Rafe," said Cookie, grabbing his pard's sleeve. "This ain't the way. We have to find out what happened to Sue!"

"Listen to your little friend," said the man on the ground, still smiling, his teeth rimmed with blood.

"You shut up," said Cookie and kicked the man in the ribs. The man's grin drooped as he groaned, but resumed once more.

By then the governor had unlocked the

gate and was now standing beside them, looking down at the man, then left and right. "Rafe, this is not the way. Not in the street like this. I'm the governor, for God's sake."

"He's a killer. And worse," said Rafe, the words grating out of him like steel grinding on rock.

"Oh," said the governor, stepping back a pace, as if standing too close to the supine man might somehow taint him.

"Allow me to make your acquaintance, Governor. I am Turk Mincher." He made to raise a hand but Rafe thumbed the Colt's hammer back all the way. "I would shake your hand, but it seems I am occupied."

"So you're Mincher." Rafe eyed the man.

"Then you have heard of me. All good, I hope."

"No," said Rafe.

"Governor," said Cookie. "This animal wants us to believe he has Sue hostage."

"Oh, I do," said Mincher.

"What? Where?" Now it was the governor's turn to close in on the man, who seemed to be enjoying himself.

"Now, fellas." Cookie stepped close and held a hand to the governor's chest. "I don't like this animal any more than you, but Rafe, the governor's right, we got to get this

275

situation off the street. Then we can decide what's what."

For a long moment, no one spoke. All eyes were on Mincher and Rafe. Rafe's gaze never wavered, nor did his gun barrel. Finally, the governor said, "We're wasting time, man. If he has Sue . . ."

Rafe nodded once, backed up, and jerked the revolver at Mincher. "Stand, hands high."

Cookie darted in and unbuckled the man's gunbelt, which held twin guns, a sheath knife, and bullets in loops. He stepped back, draping the belt over his shoulder.

"Why, thank you for calming the situation, little man," said Mincher, dusting himself off.

"You call me that again, Mincher, and I will peel your hide from bone, slow and with a whole lot of salt."

"Oh, you are a brute." Mincher winked at him. "For such a little man."

"Take him out back to the stable," said the governor. "I don't want him in my house."

"I'll fetch the horse," said Cookie, approaching the black beast with all the caution the big, white-eyed brute seemed to demand.

Rafe prodded the killer in the back, guiding him with hard jabs around the mansion to the barn out back. The governor shouted at the stable boy to go to the house and tell Henry that no one was to leave until he gave them permission.

The wide-eyed youth bolted to the back door of the house where several faces peered through the curtains. The governor shooed them and the curtains closed.

While Cookie led the horse into a box stall and clanged shut the steel door, Rafe guided Mincher into an adjacent empty stall.

"On your face, hands behind your back."

Mincher complied, still smiling, though Cookie fancied the man had had some of the steam taken from him.

"Cook," said Rafe, in a tight voice. "Tie him. Tight."

Cookie nodded and trussed the man with a whole lot of rope.

"My daughter, dammit! Where's my daughter? Has she been harmed?"

"What do you want in exchange for Sue?" said Rafe, ignoring the governor's attempt at discussion with Mincher.

Mincher stretched his chin, then worked his head side to side before he looked back at Rafe. "I thought that would be obvious."

"Well, it ain't," said Cookie.

Mincher sighed and looked at the three men. "You two, of course. Well, not all of you. Just your heads. That way I get the reward money without having to haul your carcasses anywhere. Also, I'll need a substantial grubstake from the governor, here."

Mincher's requests were met with glares. He sighed. "This day did not go as I hoped. You were supposed to be so worked up over my news of Miss Sue that you'd fall over yourselves to save her. What say we put all this unpleasantness behind us and commence with my plans. After all, a woman's life hangs in the balance, eh?"

"What say we don't," said Cookie. "Got you where we want you and that's it. Now tell us where Sue is."

Mincher chuckled. "That's not how this is going to work, little man. Didn't you ever hear about the man who has the upper hand? Why, he's the one who calls the play."

"Not this time, Mincher," said Rafe. "This time you end up dead."

"Fine," said Mincher, leaning back against the puckered, cribbed planking of the stall. "Then so will Miss Sue. Because you will never find her. Oh, you'll try, but you won't be able to track her to the little rocky hidey-hole I have her trussed up in."

The governor dove at the man, stumbling

278

forward on his knees, flailing with open hands, then fists, his teeth gritted. "You bastard! Where's my daughter!"

Mincher ducked and dodged the sloppy blows, giggling as if drunk. "Someone pull this idiot off me."

Rafe stood outside the stall, listening in the dark. He knew Mincher was still in there; he'd seen him when he came out to spell Cookie. Neither of the friends spoke, but Cook had given him a sideways glance as if to say, "You're not going to do anything foolish with Mincher, are you?"

Rafe had merely shaken his head and leaned against the barn. He watched Cookie trudge up to the house to talk with the governor. They had no real solution, but Rafe figured in the morning he and Cook would ride out with Mincher and give him what he wanted. All Rafe cared about was rescuing Sue and then getting Cookie the hell out of there.

As for himself, he didn't care. Let Mincher have him, cut off his head — if he could. Rafe took cold tight comfort in the fact that he'd not give in to Mincher without a hell of a fight. *Let him try to cut off my head and profit from the reward,* he thought, a grim sneer pulling his mouth corners down as he set fire to a fresh cigar.

He wanted to talk with Mincher. Hell, he wanted to kill the man, slowly. But not yet. Never had Rafe so wanted to reach out and wrap his hands around another person's neck. Not since the war had the urge to kill another person so overwhelmed him.

Rafe held his breath and listened. He heard Mincher's breathing — tight, controlled. Was the man asleep? Rafe didn't doubt the bastard knew he was close, outside the stall, within arm's reach. The big man guessed Mincher had the same uncanny ability to sense his surrounds. Mincher, evil though he was, was also a survivor, the same as Rafe. That skill was what had kept Rafe alive in the war and after, and served Mincher in much the same way. It would be foolish to expect Mincher to abandon his instincts and quake in his blunt-toe boots.

Rafe waited, biding his time, trying to figure out some solution, some way to find out where Sue was. He knew, as did Cookie, that torture would likely not work. If Rafe thought so, he would have already begun dismantling the man's body and mind, hacked-off piece by hacked-off piece. But that would not get Sue back alive. And Turk Mincher knew it, damn his hide.

280

If Rafe gave in to his urges and killed him right now, he'd not find Sue. No, there must be a way to force Mincher to give up Sue, provided he hadn't already caused her harm . . . Too much to think about. He pushed vile thoughts from his mind and concentrated on besting Mincher.

A little slipup and he'd have the bastard where he wanted him, the phantom in his dreams all these years. The man was a killer, looked like one, acted like one, smelled like one, if that was even possible, and now that Rafe was face-to-face with him once more, it was all real. All the years of waiting, of grinding his teeth to powder in the dark of his dank cell in Yuma, it was about to happen. He was alone with the killer of his wife and son.

Rafe knew as certain as he had been of anything in his life, even of his love for Maria, that he would kill Turk Mincher. Even if Mincher dealt him a mortal blow as well. And Rafe didn't care. It had to end. Cookie and the others who relied on him would have to live with that. It wasn't as if they were unaware of his all-driving dedication to this end.

Life beyond this moment was not a consideration. And as quickly as he thought that, Sue's smiling face came to him. A future with Sue in it was not something he dared think about, not until this deed was complete. And should he live through it, then there would be time for such thought.

"Come on in, Mr. Rafe Barr. I expect we have much to discuss."

Mincher's cold, knife-blade voice was higher than Rafe expected, thinner than he recalled it from the alley.

Rafe remained outside the door. He would not be summoned. He blew out a cloud of smoke.

"It's time we settle this foolishness," said Turk. "You have been a burr under my saddle blanket and I am tired of the annoyance you are causing in my life."

Mincher was trying to draw him out, rile him even more. But Mincher didn't know there was no way Rafe could be more riled. He'd been this way for years. The next step was death for both of them.

No, Rafe didn't want to converse with the man. He wanted to choke his reedy neck until his fingers crushed whatever held the man's head upright, until he felt popping beneath his fingers, until his thumbs slipped between the cords of the man's neck, gouged into the meat and separated flesh from bone.

"Barr? You hear me? I know you're here.

You're here because you want to kill me. Now that there is a coincidence because right now I'd like to do much the same to you. See? We have something in common. Well, we have a few things in common. But your wife is a topic we already covered. Now this young woman, the offspring of none other than the governor of California, why, she's as pretty as a field of bluebonnets in high bloom! It was all I could do to keep my hands from her. Course, it wasn't my hands that were required, you see."

Rafe knew Mincher's game, but he could keep silent no longer. "You better not have hurt that girl, Mincher." Rafe stepped into the dark barn, close by the stall.

"So there you are," said Mincher.

Rafe didn't think the man could see in the dark any better than he could, but he bet Mincher could sense him, pictured him like a snake, his tongue flicking to guide him. Rafe leaned back against the wall, puffing his cigar. Let the man talk. He would save his strength for the kill.

A scuffing sound, boot on gravel, told Rafe the man was upright, closer than he thought. Had he cut his ropes? Maybe he'd had a hidden knife.

"Barr? I know you're not but there, maybe four feet from me, son. Time we had this out. I swear to you I have kept all my weapons cinched up tight, save for my own two hands."

Did Mincher really have his weapons? How could he have gotten at them — unless they hadn't searched him well enough. No, it was a ploy, nothing more.

A match flared.

Rafe's breath caught — Mincher's hands were free.

The quick flash lit a sharp, bone-featured face, the barest hint of black stubble angling down cheekbones; a line of welted scar ran down along it, as if painted on by a theatrical costumer. But this was no stage play, thought Rafe. And yet . . . Mincher was treating it as such. As an amusement. Was Rafe really that dulled by his accident? By time? By dwelling for so long on his rage and nursing his hatred?

The man was lighting a cigarette, for god's sake!

"You . . ." Rafe gritted his teeth so tight his head trembled as he glared at the captive man.

"Yes. Me." Mincher smiled without taking his eyes from Rafe's eyes, which burned like coals in a hot fire. Mincher sighed, breaking the spell. "You know, Barr. I expected so much . . . more from you. I mean, after all this time?" He gestured at Rafe as he drew on his cigarette. One eye squinted of long practice against the fresh, curling smoke.

Rafe said nothing. His face locked in the same sneer of raw hatred.

"If your looks alone could kill a man, oh, I reckon I'd be gasping my last about now, eh Barr? But what was I saying? Oh, yes, I admit I was the tiniest bit fearful I'd gouged you too deep back in that alley, and thought to myself then that I'd robbed myself, thought I'd not be able to savor the task I'd so long wanted to accomplish. But you're as strong as I hoped you'd be."

Rafe's breathing was full-chested, a bellows working a smithy's heaped coals. When he spoke, his voice drew out raw, gravel ground between boulders. "My wife . . . son . . ."

"Yeah, yeah, your woman and your boy. You go on and on about them, don't you?" Mincher chuckled, drawing on his smoke. "I reckon we all have something that drags us out of our blankets of a morning."

Fast, like a snake strike, Rafe grabbed the bars of the stall door and shook it.

Mincher flinched, despite his usual cool demeanor. One hand snatched for a six-gun, but found no gunbelt there. His smile reappeared. "What's the matter, Rafe Barr?

Can't get at me? You best toddle off and get permission, then we can resume this pleasant little meeting, eh?"

Even as Rafe moved to the stall door, he knew he should pull his gun, force the man facedown, truss him again, then fetch Cookie. As he thought this, he was on the move, tense, keeping the stall door before him, guiding himself around it with a fingertip, his left hand sliding a Colt from the holster and then jamming it back into the worn leather sheath as quickly. No, no guns. This was close-in work, his hip knife's task if bare hands would not do.

Rafe had no time for further thought. A fist drove out of the gloom, skinned the tip of his rangy, square chin, pivoting his head to the right. Instinct jerked Rafe's head back; the blow was a graze, but it confirmed that Turk Mincher was loose. Rafe spun, lashing out with a fist that connected with nothing but dark night air.

Rafe heard fast footsteps in the dark, then a quick, hard blast of pain flowered up the side of his head. Lights brighter than the noonday sun lit up inside, behind his eyes as his head slammed into the bars of the stall. He heard the clang, then felt the hard plank floor rise up to meet him.

He tried to swim against the current as it

closed in, but it pulled him under. *Fool,* he thought. *I'm a fool. I've failed Sue, Cookie, Maria, my son . . . All of them, I have failed all of them.*

"Dammit, Rafe!" barked Cookie, kneeling by the man's head and smacking him none too lightly across the face with the back of his hand. "Should have stayed with you, boy. Should have trusted my gut. I knew you wasn't suited to the task, still too weak from your wounds, too close to the meat of the matter on all counts. Maria, the boy, now Sue. Should have been me here."

"Cook." Rafe's voice was a low, cold croak. He shook his head and bells rung somewhere far off. "Mincher gone?" he said in a whisper.

Cookie nodded. "I reckon. Why would he stick around? Heard a horse pounding on out of here, so I come out."

"How long?" Rafe said, pushing himself up onto an elbow. Even in the dark his sight spun.

Cookie held him firmly by a shoulder. "Not long."

The big man shook his head again. "Have to track him. Help me."

Cookie nodded, letting Rafe lean his bulk against him as they stood together. "Didn't take your guns, anyway. Wonder why?"

"To taunt us, to show us he isn't afraid of us. He'll be back — he wants our heads, and the satisfaction he'll get lopping them off."

"Yeah, well," said Cookie, trying not to think of himself without a head. "If he wants us bad enough, he'll try to get the drop on us."

"Cook," said Rafe, splashing water on his face from a half-filled bucket hanging on the wall. "Get inside, guard the governor and his staff. Lock yourselves in. I have to find Mincher before he kills Sue."

Cookie stared at Rafe. "This mess proves you ain't in no fit shape to track a bear in a bakery, let alone a killer in the near dark!" But Cookie sighed. "I'll set them up, but I ain't playing nursemaid."

Rafe stood still for a moment, reading the situation. Somehow, Mincher had escaped from the stall. Cookie swore the killer had been trussed "tighter than a bull's backside."

Right then, Rafe hated himself, hated that he may have set Turk Mincher off on a killing ride, with Sue as the target.

Given Mincher's long career as an elusive figure throughout the West, a man responsible for more vile deeds, Rafe suspected, than anyone knew, Mincher wasn't about to

288

stick around. Was he?

If I were Mincher, thought Rafe, sneering at the thought, *would I wait here and try to kill the man who most wanted him dead — Rafe himself — or would I go back to my hostage, the kidnapped Sue, and . . . do what?* Cookie was right, Mincher would track them sooner or later. It was more than the reward money now. They had humiliated him, and that made it personal.

Rafe ignored the thudding in his head and, slipping a Colt free of its holster, he stepped deeper into the barn. To his right, the stall with the big black horse was empty, a sure sign the man was gone. It was foolish of Rafe to keep looking, he knew, but . . . what if he wasn't?

Mincher could gut him or shoot him or both and Rafe would never see it coming. But he had to make certain the man wasn't crouched in the dark, fangs dripping his vile venom, waiting. Rafe hoped the bastard was here. That would mean he wasn't back with Sue, doing whatever he would do to her. It meant Rafe could finally kill him, and then find Sue himself. But the thought was a foolish one. Without Mincher, he had no idea where Sue was. The notion that he needed that killer sickened Rafe.

He didn't move save for swiveling his

head, scanning the dark barn for anything — a smell, a feather of sound — that might tell him Mincher was still there. He barely breathed himself, waiting, looking into the darkest corners. It reminded him of a hole in the ground at Yuma, one far less fancy, much smaller, and teeming with creatures, dark, small, stinging, biting beasts that never left a man alone . . . .

A soft sound, maybe the release of a held breath, startled Rafe from his dark musing. "Mincher? If that's you, show yourself and we'll have it out, here and now."

He waited one, two, three heartbeats, then moved swiftly toward the sound, deeper into the dark. The same sound came once more, low, then a squeak as something scurried past.

A sleek shape passed by on the worn plank floor; a brown rat slipped by, disappearing into the dark beyond. Rafe knew then that Mincher was no longer in the barn.

The big man cursed himself for wasting vital moments. He spun, grit grinding beneath his boot soles, and emerged from the barn into the purpling light of predawn. He had no idea which direction he should head. Mincher had been the only clue he'd had to find Sue. *Think,* Rafe told himself. *Track the horse.*

Rafe stood in the stable yard, the mess of the situation pressing down on him as if weighted by stones. "Where are you, Mincher? Where are you keeping her?" Rafe needed a drink of water. Hell, he needed to rest for a year. His head thudded like cannon fire and his thinking was becoming muddled, a sign he was drying out. But there was no time, no time.

Rafe dashed to the house. The rear entry was silent, and he knew Cookie had corralled the governor and his staff into the drawing room. He thundered down the hallway, cursing the governor for having such a big place, and when he reached the door he pounded on it with both fists. "Cook! It's me, Rafe. Open up! You were right — I need your help."

The lock clicked and popped from the other side of the entry, then the big right-side door swung in an inch. Rafe saw an eyeball staring at him. "How do I know it's you, Rafe?"

Rafe pushed open the door, knocking Cookie back a couple of steps. He nodded to the governor and his staff. "No time to explain, sir, but I need Cookie's help. Governor, can you shoot?"

"Of course," said the governor, puffing up a bit. "I'll have you know —"

Rafe interrupted him. "No time, sir. Get weapons and lock yourselves in here. We shouldn't be long. If we don't come back . . . never mind," he said. Pulling a deep breath. "We'll come back. Let's go, Cook." He turned and headed back down the hallway, Cookie close behind.

From the drawing room's entrance, the governor shouted, "Rafe Barr — my daughter? Is she safe?"

"I don't know yet, sir," Rafe shouted over his shoulder. "But the longer I stand here the worse the odds become!" He ran down the hall and out of the house, toward the stable.

"Cook," he said, not turning, trusting Cookie would be right behind him. He was. "You were right, I can't do this alone. Saddle up, I have an idea where Mincher might be holding Sue."

"How big an idea?" said Cookie, tossing a blanket on Stinky's back and flicking a warning finger in her face when she began to fidget.

"Not very big," grunted Rafe, swinging his saddle up onto Horse's back. "Something Mincher said after we caught him. About having Sue tucked away in a rocky place. Some place with rocks no one would ever find her."

292

"Rocks!" said Cookie. "You think he means the ones we camped amongst, few miles east of here?"

"It's the only clue we have."

"Better than nothin'."

"No more questions, not until we get on the trail. Might still be time, but we have to go now!"

"Let's get to it, then," said Cookie. The men finished rigging their horses, then mounted up, and thundered out of the stable, heading east.

Chapter Twenty-Two:
On the Scout

Arlene was the first one to see the riders through the cloud of dust they raised. At least six, maybe eight, skylined along the land rise to the east. She shouted to Doc, Jack, Mala — any of them within hearing distance. "Company's coming in fast! Everybody get to your positions!"

Jack shouted back from the porch. "No time to ride to the ridge to warn Doc. Let's hope he's sober!"

"He'll see them," she said, sounding more hopeful than she felt. They had their parts to play, hopefully it would amount to nothing.

The notion that the place was a secret, hidden location had long-since been given up on. It might never have been, for all Arlene knew. After all, the law had come to the ranch and hauled Rafe off to trial and then Yuma Prison right after he buried his wife and son.

Rafe Barr was a man who valued privacy, but she knew the West was crawling with trackers, bounty men who could locate a wanted man's ranch in their sleepiest moods — especially if the wanted men were Rafe Barr and his sidekick, Cookie McGee; a more famous and infamous pair of war heroes, spies, and double-spies, depending on your side in the fighting, you'd be hard-pressed to find.

Jack looked toward the barn, where Mala had been mucking out stalls. She waved from the far low door with the rifle he'd been teaching her to shoot. She was still pretty green with it, but they'd all agreed none of them would shoot unless it was a real threat from the invaders — they assumed they'd be gunmen sent by President Grant, either privateers or soldiers themselves. All this even though they'd saved Grant's life in Santa Fe.

No, over many cups of coffee and long hours around the kitchen table, spelling each other on round-the-clock guard, from the house and the ridge beyond, they hadn't been able to figure out why Grant would track down members of The Outfit, unless the men Ferd had warned them of weren't sent by the president.

If not, then who? Bounty men, most likely.

Jack didn't think there was a price on his head, nor Mala's, Arlene's, or Doc's, but as they'd been holed up here at Rafe and Cookie's ranch, he guessed that was enough to hang them high.

He didn't have much more time for speculation — thundering hooves coming down the east ridge brought him in from the porch. With a crutch he thunk-walked across the kitchen and peered through the curtains. Two riders, bold as the noonday sun, were headed straight for the ranch house. Jack also saw, from atop the ridge to the southeast, the quick double-flash of the sun's reflection off glass, Doc's insisted-on sign that strangers were coming from the east.

"Better late than never," Jack muttered and checked his sidearm, then hefted his rifle from the table and headed back to the porch. He was in time to see Arlene patting her hair and crossing her arms facing the incoming riders. Jack leaned against a porch upright, his rifle cradled.

The riders were still too far away to hear Arlene speak. She kept her head trained east, but said to Jack, "Two men, no signs yet of uniforms or badges, no guns drawn. I saw at least six of them at the top, maybe more."

"Advance party," said Jack, tensing. "Scouting us out." He looked to the barn, saw the peak hay door had cracked open half a foot, saw the snout of the rifle held in the dark within, and hoped Mala would stay hidden. The riders were close; he didn't dare motion to her. Have to hope for the best, but be prepared for whatever might be the worst these men could do.

"Hello the house!" shouted a voice. Dust clouds taller than Arlene washed over her, but she stood still, arms folded. "Hello yourself," she said. "You in some sort of hurry?"

Jack watched from the shadows of the porch as two horses and their riders walked into view between Arlene and the corner of the house. The rider slightly in the lead nodded toward her and touched his hat brim. "Ma'am, the hill merely gave us momentum, you might say." He nodded toward the watering trough along the barn, shared lengthwise with the corral. "Might we trouble you for water for our mounts?" He asked this even as they continued riding over to the trough.

"If I said no?" she said, turning to watch them.

The man who spoke, a tall fellow, looked somewhat familiar. Jack thought he detected

297

a southern accent. The man barked a laugh and smiled. "Now who would do such a thing?"

No one spoke more as the two men dismounted. The second was stockier and older than the first, graying hair that when he shucked his sweat-brimmed hat surprised Jack with its brevity. The man was bald as a kneecap and the top of his pink head looked as if it rarely saw daylight.

As the horses set to drinking their fill, Arlene said, "Why didn't you bring the rest of your men down with you?"

A quick exchange of glances between the two men read like a book to Jack. The first man canted his head and regarded Arlene. "I'm sure you are mistaken, ma'am. There are but the two of us."

"You are lying, sonny," she said, slipping her hands into the voluminous pockets on her equally voluminous apron. Jack knew she had two, two-shot hideout guns in there, one in each pocket. He also bet the two strangers suspected as much.

"Why, ma'am, I have no idea what you are talking about. My friend here and I are traveling light and alone. We merely wanted nothing more than to refresh our horses."

To Jack's surprise, Arlene backed down. *What was her game?* he wondered. Maybe being closer to the men, she could read something of them they could not see. "My mistake, then," she said.

Instead of mounting up, the taller man, followed by the bald man, led their horses in a circle about the yard, drawing up close by Arlene once more. They still hadn't seen Jack on the porch.

"You have quite a place here, Mrs. . . . ?"

"Yes, I do. It is sizable, and takes much effort to run. Even more so when my chores are interrupted. You've had your water, now I will bid you both good day."

"Now see here," said the first man, taking one step toward Arlene, his arm outstretched as though he intended to shake her hand. That annoying wide smile still rode on his face.

Jack cranked a shell into the chamber. "The lady bid you good day. Where I come from that's a goodbye."

The sound of Jack's rifle spun them both, hands grabbing at their sidearms.

"No, no, sirs. Hands away from the guns."

The man smiled again, looking at Jack but talking to Arlene. "You didn't say you kept slaves."

"I don't."

"Oh," said the bald man, who as yet had not spoken. "I see how it is." His voice sounded thick, clogged.

"No, you do not," said Arlene, whose two palm guns both clicked back, cocked and aimed. The two men swiveled to face her.

"Now, ma'am." The first man raised that hand again.

A hard steel snapping sounded from the barn loft above them, the end of a rifle visible, the holder in shadow. The bold sound carried across the dooryard.

A sharp, familiar ratcheting sound carried down to them from the ridge, followed on its heels with another, then another. Familiar and impressive given their echoes, because they were the throaty, steel clickings of carbines being readied to fire. Jack bit down a grin. So that's why Doc insisted on taking three rifles and Lord knows what else up the ridge with him.

Rafe and Cookie had firepower aplenty about the place, so Jack didn't see any harm in letting ol' Deathbed Jones lug all manner of weapons up to the ridge. But the man had obviously planned making his lone self into an audible presence and Jack would thank him later.

"But," said the man, confusion pulling his brows together.

"I never said I was alone," said Arlene.

For a long moment no one spoke. A gust

carried more dust across the yard, a work horse nickered from the corral. The first man touched his hat brim. "And we bid you good day, ma'am."

Arlene offered a slight nod, her stony face revealing no emotion.

The men mounted and thundered back up the hill. As they emerged at the top, they were joined by six other riders, who all sat skylined once again, as if posing for the folks below at the ranch. Then in a bloom of dust, they were gone.

Arlene let out a burst of held breath. "Well, that was fun."

Jack smiled and shook his head. "You were impressive. Tough on those boys, though."

"Tough?" she said. "That's a taste of what they'll get if they tamper with Arlene Tewksbury. And next time," she eased her pistols off cock. "I'll have my double-gun and not these pocket playthings." She headed for the house. "I'll fix some lunch for you to bring up the ridge when you spell Doc."

"Yes, ma'am," said Jack, smiling as Mala walked out of the barn, eyes wide and rifle held ready. "They're gone."

"For now," she said. "Jack, I was scared."

"Good. That means you won't be as apt to make a mistake should they come again."

She walked up the steps and stood by him.

Jack put an arm around his sister's shoulder. "You did well, Mala."

"We all did," she said, patting his arm. "I'm going to help Arlene."

Jack stepped down to the yard and eyed the empty eastern rise. It was then he remembered where he'd seen the first man, the one who'd talked the most. That man had been one of President Grant's guards, the head of them, if Jack wasn't mistaken. He'd sported beard stubble and no uniform today, but Jack was certain it was that same man. Was he acting on his own? More likely on the president's orders. What had he learned?

Jack sighed and looked to the West. "Where in the hell are you, Rafe Barr and Cookie McGee?"

For hours following the visit, the four defenders kept an eye on that hill and the surrounding landscape, the other directions with longer views. They saw no other riders that day. But for the coming days, they slept in tighter shifts, two on, two off, varied their routines, and learned to rove the perimeter of the ranch proper in the dark, making minimal sound and with eyes wide and ears keen.

CHAPTER TWENTY-THREE:
MISS ME?

Sue's head bobbed; her jaw ached from the spit-soaked bandanna gagged tight about her mouth. A stab of sunlight lanced at her eyes, bothering the one that wasn't swollen shut. She was bone-tired from struggling against the too-tight steel wrist manacles and fending off Mincher's taunting advances of the day before. Or was it earlier the same day? She didn't know any longer. It seemed as if he'd been gone for some time, but it could as well have been minutes.

Shadows in the tumbledown boulder cave had stretched long and leering, receding, then pulling back into spectral shapes for much of the day. Other than the blue-black of night giving way to dawn's stark brightness, Sue was unsure of little else, not of how long she'd been there, stuffed in the crevice like a wad of rags.

Everything about her body and mind ached. It reminded her of life with Al

303

Swearengen. He had been charming . . . for all of a day in his employ. Then when she'd balked at cleaning floors and wiping out thunder-pots he had struck her for the first time. Told her what her real duty was to be there. Not acting, well, not the sort she had dreamed of anyway.

Her stage had been a stained, flea-riddled, horsehair mattress, and she knew she would never forget that nightmare time in her life, or forgive herself for giving up.

The knick of a horseshoe on stone tugged Sue from her dozing reverie. Before she could see him, Sue knew it was Mincher, returned to do God knows what.

At least so far he hadn't touched her, not in that way. She did not fool herself into believing he was any different than all the others. He was crass and foul and disgusting. But he was not crude. It had surprised her to find he behaved according to some unspoken list of rules or standards.

He hadn't told her what he was after, but she sensed he knew more of her than what he found in her bags would have told him.

And then, there he was, astride his horse. But something was different. He sat slouched in the saddle, no jaunty black hat on his head, no grim, knowing smile on his face. And that face — it looked as if he'd been on the bad end of a beating. No gun-belt rode about his waist. What had happened?

He rode closer, then drew to a standstill and looked down at her.

"Well now," he said. "Looks like you are still right where I left you. Excellent choice, missy."

She could do nothing but glare at him, though she knew the effort was a waste. He dismounted, quickly, and looked once or twice toward the direction he'd come. He stalked the campsite, rummaging in his own belongings, and pulled out a spare revolver and knife. "I have been," he said as he worked, "to a place you will be most interested in." He checked the revolver, stuffed in bullets from the depths of a saddlebag, then slid the gun and the knife in his waistband. He looked at her, smiling. "That would be your pappy's not-so-humble abode."

Her eyes widened.

"Oh, yes, yes, but don't look so surprised, my dear. After all, I am a man of the world. Well, at least of the wide, woolly, and wild west. What? Tongue tied? More like tongue tied up, eh?" Mincher chuckled, the sound dry and raspy. "You see, I had a special reason to visit there, two of them, actually.

305

And they were there, lucky me. And do you know what?" He looked at her, no sign of mirth on his swollen, dirt-smudged face.

He bent down, repeating the question.

Sue shook her head stiffly.

"I will tell you, then. Finding you gave me a whole other reason to visit your pappy's fine home."

Sue stared at him, confusion plain on her face.

"First, I get to settle with Barr and McGee, then collect the bounty on their sorry heads, and now I get to play your father for the fool he is. Milk him of great stacks of cash." Mincher looked down at her. "For your safe return, of course."

He bent closer and, with his nose an inch from hers, said, "Unless, of course, you'd like to visit Old Mexico with Turk. Hmm? You are a fine-looking piece of flesh. A fellow could get right comfortable saddled with you."

He pulled his head back. "Do I take your lack of negative reaction to mean you are considering my generous offer?"

Sue couldn't help the tears filling her eyes. She barely heard what Mincher had said, something about Mexico. Little of it came to her after he said Barr and McGee. Had he . . . had he killed them? And her father?

What of him?

Mincher's voice cut into her thoughts. It was softer than it had been, smoother, but still cold. Dangerous. "Now, now, darlin', don't carry on so. You have found ol' Turk's weak spot, you see. A teary woman, why, it's a sinful thing to behold. Here," he reached behind her neck and worked the double-knots loose of the tight bandanna in her mouth. He tugged it free, leaving her lips puckered and reddened. She gently moved her mouth, flexing her cheeks, never once taking her eyes from his cold, gray-black eyes.

"Did . . ." Sue's voice was raw, her throat felt burred like a hoof-trimmer's rasp.

"Here now." He uncorked a canteen and tipped it to her lips. She trembled with confusion, anger, and shame at being dependent on this vicious bastard, but the coolness of the water felt good in her mouth and down her parched throat. It came faster than she could swallow, each attempt a painful task. The water spilled down her chin and neck and still he dumped it in her mouth.

She opened her eyes and he was watching her, a sneer lifting one corner of his mouth, anger and mirth warring in his eyes. He chuckled, then yanked the canteen away.

"You liked that a little too much, me-thinks. Remind you of the old days, did it? Back in Deadwood?"

This man knew more about her than she suspected, so much more. If he knew that, then . . . "You said the names Barr and McGee . . ."

"So I did."

Her eyes began to fill once more with tears and she didn't care. "Did you . . ."

"Did I what, darlin'?"

She swallowed and said, "Did you kill them?"

He looked up, as if trying to recall some-thing someone once told him. "No," he shook his head. "No, not yet." He looked at her and wagged a finger in her face. "And that's the gospel truth, that is. You see, ol' Turk Mincher, he does get up to a whole lot of things, but the one thing he doesn't do is lie. No, sir, he's as straight as an Apache war lance on that score."

"Then they're alive. And my father . . ."

He nodded his head with vigor. "Yep, all of them, last I saw. Though that will not be the case in the very near future. You see, I aim to collect twice on the heads of those two rascals. Once by way of barter for a sack brimming with money. Oh, but you should see the carpetbag of money Warden Talbot

Timmons had himself when he left Santa Fe. Betwixt you and me, I don't believe he earned it fair and square, but that's the way of things nowadays, a fellow can't trust the law any more than he can his own kin."

"You said twice, you would collect twice . . . on their heads."

"Oh, yeah, the next stop, after I relieve Timmons of his money and liberate his head from his lying body, is a law office, somewhere east of Yuma. Not sure where yet, but that task will work itself out."

Sue didn't dare ask her next questions, but Mincher seemed to know what was on her mind. "As to your father, well, let's say if he plays his cards as a good gambler ought, he'll live. Oh, he'll be lighter in the coin purse and missing one daughter, but that right there is life. We can't win all the hands we are dealt. Trick is to come out with more than anyone else at the end of the big game."

They sat in silence for a few long moments. Mincher rolled a quirley and lit it, pulled the smoke in deep, then pushed it out again.

Sue spoke, "Why do you hate Rafe and Cookie so much?"

"Oh, hate's not the right word." He licked his lips and faced her, sitting cross-legged

309

and smoking, a thoughtful look on his face. "I detest loose ends, you see. And those two are threads that I have been trying to snip clean for a long while now. When Turk Mincher is hired to do a job, he sees it through, elsewise, I had best find a new line of work. I had the opportunity to snip them clean a couple of different times, only managed to do for Barr's wife and little boy." He looked up and smiled, as if recalling a fond memory.

For a moment Sue was not certain of what he had told her. Then the truth of it clanged like a cracked bell in her head and she screamed, "You bastard!"

He looked at her, surprise drawing his mouth corners down. "Oh, not quite. A whore's child, yes. But not a bastard. I had me a daddy. Knew him, too. Until I gutted him like a trout. Sold his head to a marshal in Dodge City. For a tidy sum, too."

"You . . . you sick, murdering bastard!"

"Ahh," he stood, stubbed out the cigarette end under his boot, and stretched his back. "Seems to me," he looked down at her. "You are not ever going to be agreeable to a trip to Mexico with me. So," he grinned and slid his long, gleaming skinning knife from that black leather sheath on his belt. "Best to part ways here and now. While we're both so happy with each other." He chuckled and thumbed the keen edge of the big knife's blade.

A sudden sound came to them, the rubbery snort of a horse somewhere not far from their camp. Sue's eyes grew wide and she wriggled against the tight bonds. Then she opened her mouth to scream.

Mincher bent low and, quick as a snake strike, wrapped a hand around her mouth, but not tight enough. She felt the thick flesh at the base of his thumb push between her teeth. She bit down hard and drew blood.

"Ahh! Jesus and Mother Mary, too!" Mincher rammed the hand between his knees and danced in a tight circle before her.

Sue wasted no time, but screamed as loud as she was able. He'd not yet gutted her, but that knife was seconds from sliding across her throat. As he'd promised.

He growled and lunged at her. Sue jerked her head to the side but he caught her by the neck, slapped her hard with the thick knuckles of his left hand, then reached for the knife. "Get set to meet your maker, missy. I am done with you and so is this world." He knelt, snatched at her forehead, snagging his blunt fingers in her blond hair and jerking her head backward, exposing her thin neck.

The stark, throaty click of a hammer ratcheting back for the kill stilled his hand.

"I was you, I'd think twice about that, Mincher."

Sue and Turk both looked up toward the narrow entrance in the rocks.

Sue recognized the voice — Cookie.

For the first time in days, she felt the warmth of hope bloom in her chest. She was about to scream again, fear and joy filling her throat, her mouth. Then she saw that Mincher had shifted his brief attentions from the shout back to Sue. He doesn't care, she thought. This crazy man does not care if he gets shot. And Sue realized that was the most frightening thing about Turk Mincher.

"Don't be a fool!" the killer shouted, loud enough for Cookie to hear.

"I see one fool here, and it's not Cookie, and not Sue." Rafe Barr rose up behind a boulder to Mincher's right. "And not me." The killing snout of his rifle stared straight at Mincher's head.

Sue looked from Rafe to Mincher, swallowing out of reflex as she felt the slick blade touching the sweat-grimed skin of her throat.

"Now," said Mincher, staring once more

into Sue's eyes, and smiling wider than he had the entire time she'd been his captive. "What's about to happen here is entirely in your control, Mr. Rafe Barr. Seeing as how you view yourself, and rightly so, I might add, as one tough son of a bitch, I suspect you are about to do something that I can guarantee will result in the bloody slow death of this here pretty woman with the corn-silk hair. Oh, maybe when it's washed and clean. But trust me, she's a fine piece of flesh. Course, you would know that already, wouldn't you, Barr?"

Rafe said nothing, never took his eyes from Mincher, aligned perfectly beyond the end of his rifle's barrel. One squeeze of the trigger. Time seized, hushed, soundless. The moment when he should have done it, needed to do it, passed.

Mincher knew. Sue saw the one moment die, saw smugness bloom on his scarred face. Why hadn't Rafe fired?

The killer whipped the knife backward, then stood up with catlike speed, the knife pinched between thumb and forefinger. He turned to face Rafe, hands spread, knife raised high. "I tell you what, Mr. Rafe Barr. I will make you a deal." He waited for a response, but Rafe didn't move. "You put down your rifle and your revolver and we'll go at each other with our knives, fight like devils right here in the dirt. One of us will win, one will lose. Of course, I will win, so that leaves you . . . the loser. But I am willing to grant you this favor, as I am a gentleman."

"Two things you should know." Rafe's voice was level, cold.

"Oh, and what are they, Mr. Rafe Barr?"

"One: You talk too much."

Mincher's one-sided grin was not matched by his eyes. "And?"

"Two," said Rafe, as if he were not interrupted. "I was only waiting for you to move away from Sue."

Mincher's eyebrows pulled together and he cocked his head to the side, as if he hadn't heard correctly. And then his eyes widened and his scarred jaw dropped. He was about to speak when Rafe's rifle barked once and a bullet cored a tight hole between Turk Mincher's eyes, leaving behind a third unblinking eye.

Mincher stood still, balanced on his dusty, black, square-toe boots. His long knife was the first thing to drop. It slipped from his weakened grasp and clattered on the rocks at his feet. A high-pitched whimper squeezed out of his mouth, pushed out by a bubble of blood that popped, itself chased by a wheeze. Mincher weaved, then dropped to his knees, facing Rafe, staring at the one man who'd done the thing no one else had.

Then Mincher pitched forward and slammed his face into the dirt.

Rafe held his pose for long moments. Everyone did. Then Cookie stepped into the little clearing. He toed the dead man. " 'Bout time," he said.

As a precaution, he slid the man's replacement revolver from its sheath, and shoved away the knife. "Defanged," he said, winking at Sue and bending down beside her.

"How you been keeping yourself, girly?" Cookie gently touched her cheek with his big knuckles. He winced at what he saw. "All over now, Sue. Let's get those limbs of yours freed up."

Cookie pulled his knife out gently, considering she'd been accosted by a man with a knife, and sliced through her bonds. He looked at her and saw she was staring toward Rafe.

Cookie followed her gaze. Rafe still stood, rifle lowered to chest level. He stared not at them but at the dead man on the ground as if hypnotized.

"Rafe." Cookie waited, then repeated himself. "Rafe! Come around, boy!"

That did it. Rafe blinked, turning his attention to them, and his face softened. "Are you okay, Sue?"

She knew it was a foolish question. She did not feel okay. Not close at all. If she looked as bad as she felt, she suspected they'd want to bury her right there. "I'm so happy to see you . . . both." She smiled and Cookie helped her to her feet, but she nearly fell over. He caught her and helped her hobble to a sizable boulder, where she leaned and slowly massaged her arms and legs with trembling hands.

Rafe clambered over the smaller rocks separating them. "Sue," he said, resting a big hand on her shoulder. "What did that beast do to you?" He reached for her face, but changed his mind and lightly stroked her hair.

"That bad, huh?" she said, forcing a smile. She knew she looked rough and felt even worse, but it didn't matter. She held his hand on her shoulder with a trembling hand and laid her cheek against it, then reached for Cookie and held one of his hands in hers.

Cookie's lip trembled and he looked away, snuffled a bit as he inspected the skyline. Sue smiled and let them go. "We have to stop meeting this way," she said in a raspy voice.

"Good thing Mincher screamed," said Cookie. "Then you, too. Gave me a direction. I was close already, being a natural tracker. Course, I didn't expect to hear him yelpin'."

"I bit him," said Sue, rubbing her wrists.

Cookie and Rafe exchanged glances.

"Remind me never to cross you, girly," said Cookie. "I'll fetch the horses."

Rafe dragged Mincher's body over to nearby rocks and flopped him atop them with a sloppy clunk. Then he helped Sue regain the feeling in her limbs, rubbing her arms and ankles, then walking with her around the little rocky campsite.

She stopped, grabbed his arms, and said, "My father! What's happened? Mincher said . . ."

"Calm down, your father is fine. We were here looking for help from him and he ended up needing our help."

"Why, what's happening?"

"He's being blackmailed."

Sue nodded, "Mincher told me he was going to use me as the bait."

"No, well, yes, Mincher had designs to blackmail your father for your safe return, but there's someone else, Timmons, the warden from Yuma Prison."

"What does he want with my father?"

"Everything. Money, power, he wants everything. He's a greedy man. And your father is not, so we're going to do something about it."

"What?"

Rafe smiled. "I'm not sure yet, but I'm beginning to have an idea. Cookie, too."

"It's because of me, isn't it?" said Sue, looking as forlorn as he'd seen her when Turk had the knife to her throat.

"Some of it, yes. But a man like Timmons, he'd find some other way to get at what he wants. The sad thing is, he'll never get it all. Because he's never satisfied."

"And you?" said Sue. "Are you satisfied?"

Rafe glanced toward Mincher's body. "Closer every day. One more thing to do and I'll be as close as I'll ever get." He sighed. "Come on, let's get your things together. I know somebody who will be mighty happy to see you, Sue."

"Are you, Rafe?"

"Am I what?" he said, lifting her gear from where Mincher had tossed it on the ground.

"Happy . . . to see me, I mean?"

"Sue, I —"

"Course he is," said Cookie, ambling back into camp. "He's too foolish to know it." He shook his head and mumbled as he

318

walked by Rafe. "I worry about you, boy, I honestly do."

CHAPTER TWENTY-FOUR:
SO CLOSE, YET . . .

Later that night, Cookie and Rafe were sitting on the broad veranda of the governor's mansion, sipping whiskey and discussing the day's events. Or rather Cookie was talking and Rafe was half-listening.

"Governor sure was happy to see his little girl," said Cookie.

"Yep."

"And that doctor said she was going to be fine. Bumps and bruises."

"Yep."

"She's a tough girl, that Sue."

"Yep."

"You reckon we should get word to the ranch on what we're up to?"

Rafe nodded. "Talked about that with the governor. He's going to send a telegram to President Grant that will clear us. And then he's going to explain it in a formal, detailed letter. And then he's going to send a telegram to Ferd to let the rest of The Outfit know we're on level ground again."

"Mighty trusting of him," said Cookie, rocking back in his chair. "Considerin' we ain't really done with things yet."

Rafe nodded. "Can't let him down now."

"No," said Cookie, letting out a deep breath. "Say, what was all that palaver betwixt you and the governor about a letter? Have to do with Timmons?"

"Yep. The governor signed a confession written by Mincher implicating Timmons as the man behind . . . behind Maria's and my son's murders."

"Oh, good." Cookie was silent a moment, then said, "When'd you get Mincher to write out such a thing?"

"Didn't."

Cookie almost spoke, then nodded. "Ah, I see. Okay then."

A few moments of quiet passed, then Cookie sighed. "Well, I reckon we should stuff him in a pauper's section of some burial ground hereabouts."

"Mincher?" said Rafe, eyeing Cookie as if he smelled something off. "Like hell. I intend to claim whatever bounty money is offered on his head." He shifted his gaze back to the setting sun. "He owes me."

"You mean you want to lug his mangy hide to wherever it is you're fixing to go?"

"Nope."

Cookie raised his arms and let them flop. "Now I really don't know what you're talking about. One thing one minute, another the next! You wear me out, Rafe Barr. I swear it."

"Just his head." He looked at Cookie again and a slow smile spread across his face. "You're going to need it."

"Me? Why would I —"

"I have a plan." Rafe tapped his temple.

"Oh, no. Is it one of those plans where I have to stir up a distraction? Or is it a real plan?"

"Real. But we'll need dynamite."

Cookie's eyes widened and he rubbed his hands together. "Hoo-boy! I got the very thing — been saving these two sticks for the right time." He patted the worn, brown leather holster riding on his right hip. "So, what's the plan?"

Rafe stuck a half-cigar in his mouth and scratched a match alight. When the stub glowed orange, he puffed out a blue cloud and eyed Cookie through the smoke with one squinting eye. "We're going to break into Yuma Prison."

Before Cookie's wide eyes gave over to a tirade of questions peppered with the word "crazy," Helga clanged the brass dinner bell and called them in to supper.

Rafe was relieved, as he hadn't thought any further than that. He made for the door, with Cookie following in his wake, sputtering. Rafe was smiling.

CHAPTER TWENTY-FIVE:
PROMISES TO KEEP

"You two wouldn't ride off without saying goodbye, now, would you?"

Rafe looked over at the broad side steps of the mansion. Sue stood on the top step, arms crossed. She was still bruised, maybe even more so than the day before, her eye still mostly swollen shut, but she was smiling.

Rafe left off fiddling with the buckle on his saddlebag and walked to the steps. She met him at the bottom.

"Sue, there's something I should tell you." He rubbed his clean-shaven jaw. "I need to know you're going to be okay now."

Sue looked up at Rafe, her good eye squinting in the sunlight. She shifted so that his hat brim shaded her face and her eyes relaxed. "Rafe," she smiled, choosing her words with care. "I can't promise you that. No one can. And there's nothing you can do to protect me or anyone else from all the things that can happen in life. I'm speaking of the bad things. No one needs protection from all the good things, because they happen, too, Rafe."

He looked away, but felt gentle hands on his cheeks guiding him. "Rafe, look at me. If you decide I am someone who you'd like to be part of your life, then you should know that I would like that, too."

"Sue, I —"

She held a finger gently to his lips, shushing him, then said, "Cookie once told me to be good to myself. At the time, I didn't think much of it, but his simple words stayed with me and they helped me."

"He's a wise man," said Rafe.

"That's why I think, right now, we have to be good to ourselves." She rested her hands on his chest. "We each have things we need to do apart from each other. I need to get to know my father again, and yes, God help me, my stepmother, all over again. And you . . . you need to go back to the ranch . . . and spend time with your wife and son."

She felt his chest tense beneath her hand, but she continued. "You have done what you set out to do, Rafe. You found out the horrible truth and you made it as right as you could. That is noble and final, and you should be with them. For as long as it takes."

"Sue, I don't think I can ever leave them."

"I would never ask you to. That ranch is your home, their home. And it's the only place I've ever felt at home, and safe."

He wrapped his big arms around her shoulders and pulled her to his chest, resting his cheek gently on her head. "But when . . . ?"

"We'll know, Rafe. We'll both know. Trust in that."

He looked down at her, this feisty young woman with a battered eye, a split lip, and more courage and grit than anyone he'd ever met, save perhaps for Cookie. And Rafe smiled.

"May I . . . may I kiss you, Sue?"

"You damn well better!" shouted Cookie from a dozen feet away, shaking his head. "Else I will!"

"You said he was wise," said Sue, smiling.

And so, Rafe kissed her, once, gently. And he didn't take his eyes from her for long moments as he mounted up on Horse, side by side with Cookie astride Stinky. In one hand, Rafe held a lead rope to Mincher's black stallion, on which rode a thickly wrapped burlap bundle, roughly the size of a man's head. It was tied to the stallion's load, bumping in counterpoint to the horse's steps. They walked through the wide side-yard gate.

A shout from the house pulled them to a stop. Helga, the burly German cook, barreled down the walk toward them, a linen-wrapped bundle held high before her ample bosom.

"Coo-kee! Coo-kee!" she shouted.

"What have you done now?" said Rafe.

"Rafe, let's go! We can outrun her!"

"No," said the big man. "We wait here and see what she wants. It's the gentlemanly thing to do."

"Oh, Lordy."

The burly woman panted up to them, her chest heaving, her face bright red. She walked over to Cookie's horse.

"Ma'am," he said, doffing his cap and looking more frightened than Rafe had seen him in many years. Maybe since the war.

"You would leave mit-out saying goodbyes?" The woman looked ready to cry.

"No, ma'am, I mean, no, ma'am . . ." Cookie looked at his pard and whispered, "Rafe?"

Rafe pretended not to hear as he smiled back at Sue, who still stood on the steps, her arms folded, a smile on her face as she watched the proceedings.

Helga curled a finger and Cookie bent low, sensing there was food in the white bundle she held. She wrapped a big arm around his neck and mashed her lips against his for so long he began to whimper and thrash and nearly fell out of the saddle. Stinky stood as still as a rock and stared straight ahead.

Just as Rafe thought he might have to intervene, Helga let go of Cookie, handed him the bundle, and ran back to the gate. Blubbering, she dabbed at her eyes with a tiny handkerchief, and waved. "Goodbyes, my Coo-kee! Goodbyes! Come back to me someday!"

As they rode away, and Cookie's breathing returned to a regular rhythm, he rubbed his chin. "You see, Rafe," he said. "Some men can't help it. And I am one of 'em. Why, I'll wager I've left a trail of crying women all over these here United States."

"I don't doubt it, Cook."

Cookie nodded. "That's right. And the sad thing is, I ain't half through yet! No sir, some men can't help it."

While Cookie marveled at himself and tugged free the twine wrappings on his bundle of surprise treats, Rafe puffed a cigar to keep from chuckling as they rode southeast toward Yuma.

CHAPTER TWENTY-SIX:
BACK TO HELL . . .

One train trek and three days of hard riding found the two trail pards closing in on Yuma, Arizona. Rafe shook out his match and puffed up a blue cloud and a glowing end on a fresh half-cigar. "You ready for this, Cook?" When he didn't hear his old trail mate, he looked to his left.

Cookie rode atop Turk Mincher's black stallion, straight-backed in the fancy black saddle, his jaw thrust out, his eyes hidden beneath the low-pulled black brim of the killer's hat. After a few moments he said, "You sure we have to do this? I feel . . . disgusting wearing that bastard's togs, Rafe."

"I know, Cook, and if it weren't so important, I'd not ask. If I could, I'd do it myself. But you're closer to Mincher in size."

Cookie nodded, saying nothing.

Rafe continued, "We need to get inside and I don't know any other way."

"Told you what we ought to have done," Cookie turned to face his friend. "Should have drug along Governor Pendleton. He'd have got us in right enough."

Rafe nodded. "He's been through enough, I wouldn't want to sully his reputation any further. I have a feeling if this country has any hope of getting a leg up and over the blown-out mess the war left behind, it's men like Pendleton who'll be able to do it. And like it or not, politics is a powerful way to go about it."

"I reckon," said Cookie. "Like using a net instead of a hook when you're fishing."

Rafe smiled, puffed the cigar. "Cook, sometimes I think you are a poet at heart."

"Now don't go insulting me. I'm right on the edge, Rafe. I tell ya. One little thing and I might cut loose!"

"You keep shouting like that and that horse will do it for you." Rafe nodded.

Cookie looked down at the gleaming black, a barely controlled brute quivering in pent-up power, flexing his nostrils and tossing his head. "I don't trust this beast," muttered Cookie. He glanced to his right. "How can you be so calm? Here we are, wanted men, the pair of us, riding straight back into the place you most don't want to be!"

The big man shrugged. "The only part I

330

feel bad about is bringing you here."

"What?" said Cookie, reining the horse to a stop.

Rafe followed suit. "I meant that I have nothing to lose. I'm the one with the argument with Timmons, not you."

"That's a hell of a thing to say to your oldest friend on the earth, Rafe Barr! I knowed Maria, too, you know. Like to think I'd have made a decent uncle to your boy. Damn hard thing, all this. I want to see that bastard squirm as much as you do, Rafe."

Rafe stared at the smoking cigar jutting from his knotted fist resting atop his saddle horn. "Appreciate it, Cook."

"Good. Yonder's the prison. Let's get to it."

They rode in silence a few moments longer, then Cookie said, "So what's the plan, again?"

Rafe puffed out a great blue cloud of cigar smoke. "Same as last night and this morning at camp."

"Good," said Cookie, sneering at the red shirt and doing his best to keep from tearing off the dead man's clothes. "Now tell me again."

"If Mincher was correct, the warden will be expecting him. So, we play that up. You ride up to the front gate. The guards will likely recognize you and let you pass."

"If they don't?"

"Then shout something about being Turk Mincher. Spend his name as though it were gold coins and you have an endless supply."

"I like that idea. Might be that vicious bastard had one good trait. We'll see." He looked once more at Rafe. "Where you going to be?"

"See that bend in the road ahead?"

"Yep."

"When we reach it, I'm going to cut wide and come up on the east wall. That should give you time enough inside."

"To do what?"

Rafe drew the last long puff from his cigar, blowing out the smoke. "To get through the front gate, up to Timmons's office, convince him you're Mincher, then when he gets a look at you, draw down on him."

"Oh, is that all?" said Cookie, shaking his head and looking wide-eyed ahead at the looming bulk of Yuma Territorial Prison.

"Nope," said Rafe. "Then you have to somehow get him to open up the side gate for me. I'll take him off your hands then. Oh, and don't trust him for a second. He's wily."

"Any idea how I'm going to do all this?"

Rafe swigged from his canteen, then

handed it over to Cookie, who licked his lips and gulped back a couple of swallows. Earlier in camp they'd streaked Cookie's face once on each side, down the jawbone to the chin, with a thin line of pink face paint Cookie had produced from his saddlebag.

Rafe had raised his eyebrows but Cookie gave him the hard eye. "You ain't forgetting I dressed up as a grieving widow on your account, are you?" He held up the little glass vial of face paint. "Had to look the part, didn't I?"

Rafe had nodded and done his best to hide the smirk that threatened to spread over his face. Now he looked at his friend and thought perhaps he'd pass, from a distance at least, as Mincher. "Keep your hat low."

"Yeah, I know. How about the plan? Or did you forget more of the details?"

"You'll be fine. You'll think of something." Rafe smiled. "Don't worry. I'll have Stinky ready for you." At the mention of her name, Cookie's mustang let loose with a chesty rumble and followed along, the lead line preventing her from riding ahead. She was not used to being led anywhere.

"How bad would it be if I was to use a little bit of the boom-boom stick?" Cookie looked with hopeful eyes at Rafe.

"Not good at all. That'll be my job, if it needs doing. You do it and you'll bring every guard down on you. Keep it as quiet as you can and get that door open. I'll do the rest."

Cookie swallowed and nodded, but said nothing.

"Okay then, here's where we part." Rafe halted Horse, with Stinky walking up alongside. Cookie stopped the black, holding the reins tight. The horse pranced and pawed in place. "Be glad to get offa this brute."

"Looks like the feeling's mutual," said Rafe, smiling. "Got the bundle, that's good." He nodded toward the awkward burlap sack cinched atop and lashed behind the cantle. "That should be the only calling card you'll need. But keep those six-guns at the ready, in case."

"Hell, I know that. Don't you think I don't know that? Ain't my first day at the ball, Rafe."

The big man smiled again at his friend, then lost the smile. "Look, Cook, say the word and I'll figure out a different way. You don't have to do this, you know."

"Yeah, I do. You're my family, boy, I got nothing else. We're in this side by side, no backing out. Now get along and you best be at that door or I'll track you down and don't

334

you think I won't, mister." Cookie tried to fill his threat with menace but it came out quiet.

Rafe laid a hand atop Cookie's shoulder, thinner than Mincher's. The red shirt hung off him like loose skin. A snag of regret grabbed him, but he knew there was no way he could alter their plans now. "Thanks, Cookie."

"You bet. Now get the hell gone. I got work to do and nerve to build up and a better plan to conjure, no thanks to you." Cookie grinned and nudged the black into a lope without looking back.

Rafe sat at the road's fork and watched his friend a moment. "There goes the bravest man I've ever known," he said to his horse. Cookie's mount, Stinky, whickered and walked forward, trying to follow Cookie. "Soon enough," said Rafe, urging Horse eastward to loop wide back toward the prison. "I hope."

CHAPTER TWENTY-SEVEN: INTO THE GAPING MAW

Cookie swallowed back a hard knot of dust and fear all but blocking his airway. He didn't want to let Rafe down, but lord-a-mighty this was shaping up to be the biggest challenge he'd faced in a good many years. Trying to break Rafe out of jail in Denver had been easier than this.

Here he was riding straight into the lion's mouth, decked out in a dead man's clothes and riding the killer's ornery mount, which at that moment chose to kick up a fuss. "Simmer down, you rank beast!" Cookie snapped a light backhand at the horse's neck and was rewarded with a smoother ride.

"Well now ain't that about something? Guess I had to show you who's ramrod of this here outfit." Cookie sat taller in the saddle. "Besides, I reckon, no matter how foul a human that bastard Mincher was, you got a right to be worked up. I am wearing

336

his clothes, riding on you, and toting his head in a sack." He glanced down at the burlap bag, noting the second lump beside the first, stained a dark near-black color along the bottom corner where inside the killer's head rested. "Gruesome, but I don't feel a twinge of nothing but glad that he's dead and Rafe and me ain't." Cookie looked up at the rising edifice of the jail, closer than he expected. "At least not yet."

Even the horse seemed daunted by the place. It felt to Cookie as if the dry, hot air of the foreboding place was stained with anger and hate and skinned with sadness. He felt it as if it were a dark cloud settling over him. "Easy boy," he said, patting the horse where he'd smacked it minutes before.

They rode forward; Cookie tugged the hat brim even lower and did his best to sit tall and solid-seeming. He wasn't certain how Mincher carried himself in the saddle but he figured it wasn't slouched and sloppy.

They were within fifty feet of the main gate when he heard, "Ho there!" A man's voice called from above. Cookie looked up and spied a guard cradling a carbine and staring down at him. "You there! Halt and report yourself!"

Cookie was tempted to call the fool an insolent pup but that would likely give him away and end the escapade right there and then.

The guard shouted again: "Dismount, hand over your guns, and advance to the gate."

Cookie kept his eyes on his saddle horn and did his best to bellow in a deep southern voice, "I think I will do the first and the last but not the middle."

"Huh?"

Cookie sighed. Keeping his hat brim tugged down, he shouted, "Go fetch your boss, boy. Tell him Turk is here."

The man shifted, then spat a long stream of tobacco juice that ribboned outward and spattered on the parched earth outside the wall. "Like hell . . . boy."

That did it. Cookie poked a long finger upward. "Look, you. One more remark like that and you'll be . . ." Come on, now, Cookie, he told himself. Tamp it down and push past it. You can't let Rafe down. "I said you best go tell Warden Timmons his old buddy Turk is here."

"Turk who?"

Cookie sighed. No reason he couldn't use the dead man's full name, was there? After all, Rafe said to dole it out aplenty. "Turk Mincher," he said, hoping he sounded and looked the part.

The change that came over the guard was impressive and quick. "Oh, oh . . ." The man ran his straw hat back and forth atop his head as if in deep consideration. He mumbled something to someone behind him and another man walked over. "How do, sir, you —"

Cookie didn't let him finish. *Like the horse,* he told himself. *Have to keep the upper hand or you'll fall off this situation right quick.* "Listen here," he bellowed, trying to keep his voice low and mean. "You tell the warden Mincher's here." He reached around and hoisted the grimy sack he'd loosened on his way forward. "And I have been on official prison business, tracking miscreants, and if you do not want a taste of this yourselves, you will tell the warden I am here and I got something for him!"

"Yes, sir!" The two men conferred briefly, then the second shouted again, "Yes, sir!" The first disappeared from Cookie's sight, but he heard the man's boots clunking quick down unseen stairs. Now that was more like it, he thought.

He realized he'd been riding for nearly two hours, from their campsite of the evening before. He was prone to being stiff if he spent longer than twenty minutes at a time in the saddle without stretching his legs. He slipped down, careful to angle the horse so he'd be out of view of the peeking tower guard. Didn't want the man to see a stiff old broke-down trail hound working out the kinks from his legs and aching back and numb backside. He wanted to be fit and mean-looking, able to shuck Mincher's guns should the need present itself. This was getting dicier than he'd reckoned, and nothing much yet had happened.

"Steady," he told himself. "You been through a hell of a lot worse than this before."

He had no more opportunity for pep talking, as muffled clanking and sliding sounds reached him from the other side of the big wood-and-strap-steel door. Then one half of it squawked and slowly swung inward. He didn't see who'd done the hauling on that thing, but too soon he found himself walking inside.

He'd wished he could have tugged the fool black hat even lower on his forehead. And he wished he could stop sweating. Felt like all his life juices were draining out from under that damn hat. Then he had a terrible thought — what if his sweat was smearing away the fake scar lines they'd painted down his jaws? Too late to worry about it now, he told himself and tugged on the reins, he led the big black horse on through the entrance to Yuma Territorial Prison.

He gulped and hoped the rest wouldn't be too much more difficult. Then he heard the door squawk in the dry desert air and slam shut. He jerked, feeling like a small skeleton of a man inside the killer's clothes. The sound of chains and clanking and steel-on-steel slamming as the door was locked again from the inside nearly made him turn around and make a run for the door. And then, unbidden, a vision of Rafe and Maria and their young boy sitting atop Rafe's shoulder came to him. The three of them, smiling, something Rafe had not truly done since . . . since Timmons had ordered Mincher to kill Rafe and his family.

That had been the last time Cookie had seen his friend's family alive and well. It was as he rode on out of there after spending a week. Rafe had begged him to stay. Maria, too. And the boy, he'd been sweet. The only child ever to make Cookie consider he'd maybe made a mistake all those years before in not settling down himself and having a brood of little monsters.

"Mr. Mincher. Mr. Mincher?"

The voice from a dozen feet away yanked him from his reverie. The guard he'd first seen was staring at him. *Dang it, Cookie Mc-Gee,* he scolded himself. *Tighten the hell up!*

"Yes, what?"

"Your horse, sir. You best tie it up here. Can't rightly take it on into the warden's office, can you?" The guard chuckled. Cookie did not.

The guard, Cookie now saw, was a young man, maybe in his early twenties, with peach fuzz for whiskers. He wanted to tell him to get the hell out of there, that being trapped in this place, guard or no, steady pay or no, was no way to spend any amount of time in your life.

"I'll see it gets watered."

"Damn right you will."

"Yes, sir."

Cookie was led down a long, cool, dark corridor of stone block, and he recalled hearing that the first prisoners there had built the jail that was to house them. Some of them might still be there, he thought, wincing inside at the thought of being housed there. And then it occurred to him it could well happen should he fail. He suppressed a groan and the guard walking before him half-turned. "You okay, sir?"

"You never mind, boy." Then Cookie had a thought and as so often happened, it popped right out of his mouth before he could stop it. "Been poorly lately, more ornery than usual. Got me a case of the pox."

That hitched the guard's step for a moment, then in a sudden move, he dashed ahead, keeping an eye on Cookie as he ran. He headed toward a lit end of the corridor and pointed. "That's the warden's office door yonder, Mister Mincher. You go right in there. I . . . I got to go . . ."

He fairly whimpered the last of those words and left them hanging like a bad odor in the hot, still air before he disappeared. But not out of hearing. By the time Cookie made it to the door the kid had pointed to, he heard the young guard's voice receding down the stone walkway beyond, shouting, "Pox! Pox!"

Cookie indulged in a quick grin. If that don't shake up the guards, what will? Rafe didn't say not to cause a jail-wide ruckus, now, did he? On the other hand, this could go the other way quick, with all those guards and cooks and staff; however many weren't inmates. Why, they might take it into their heads to corner him in the warden's office and lay him low in the name of self-preservation. Maybe the pox idea wasn't so good.

"Ah well," he said, "In for a penny," reciting one of Maria's favorite sayings. And with that, and the last lingering taste of a smile on his mouth, Cookie rapped on the door to Timmons's office.

Nothing. He rapped harder and heard shoes of some sort clunk across a floor. Sounded wooden, like planking. Then a deadbolt slid to one side and the door parted a few inches. "Yes?" said a woman's voice from within. The sound startled him. What was a woman doing in this dank place? Before he could reply, the door parted wider and she said, "Oh, Mr. Mincher, I didn't recognize you."

Cookie stepped backward, bending his neck lower so he was nearly gazing at his toes. The grimy burlap sack bounced against his right boot. "Oh, been poorly lately. Pox or some such."

"Pox?"

Before she could scream and slam the door, Cookie jammed a boot in the gap and shoved with his shoulder. "Out of my way, lady. Here to see the warden. He's expecting me. Got a delivery."

He kept his voice low, growly, and swaggered as he stepped into a brighter small stone room that served as her office. Stacks of leather-covered ledger books rose up in piles atop a sagging table along the far wall beneath a high-up window allowing in a blocky shaft of mote-filled sunlight. An equally stacked roll-top desk sat angled in a back corner as if placed there by someone who wasn't very good at making decisions. Ink pens and quills and all manner of loose papers looked to be awaiting attention. As did the woman.

The room wore its gloom like a mothy old shawl and Cookie felt a stab of pity for the homely old stick of a woman who regarded him as one might a rat emerging from shadow. She stood beside a closed door, Cookie hoped that led to the damnable warden's office; he was growing weary of tarrying with one door after another.

He reckoned that's what life in prisons was like — doors and doors and tiny windows set up high and dark cold stones and stale air with no tang of hope, nor freshness at all. Had to wear a body down.

"This way, Mr. Mincher." She pointed at the door to her right, but kept one hand over her sunken bird chest, her tired eyes wide. She pulled her face back, mouth a tight-closed slit, not daring to breathe.

Cookie stepped forward, the bag feeling heavier with each moment. Sweat slid from his hairline down his backbone and into his trousers. Felt like bugs crawling down his spine. The woman whimpered, a small sound, then clipped it off as if she'd not intended it to leak out. Cookie stopped.

"I should go in first," she said in a whisper.

"Good," he said. "Yes."

She was afraid of him, that much was plain. Was it Mincher she'd been afraid of or his comment about pox? Or a mix of the two? He didn't much care, but he thought he should tell her to skedaddle, warn her that unpleasantness would soon take place hereabouts.

She turned her back to him briefly to open the door and before the door swung open he said, "When you're done in there you ought to leave. Got important matters to discuss. Get outside, take a long walk."

Her eyes widened and she nodded twice, then rushed ahead through the doorway.

Cookie was beginning to get the feel for this new, low voice. Didn't much sound like himself, and though he didn't think it sounded much like Turk Mincher, he didn't much care. As long as it worked and kept people away from him.

He looked ahead at twenty feet or so of stone corridor. Might explain why Timmons hadn't come out, might be he didn't hear them. Good. Cookie wanted this to be a surprise. He kept himself a dozen feet behind the woman and slowed when she stopped once more at yet another door.

This time she knocked, put an ear to the door, knocked again, louder, and Cookie heard a muffled, irritated voice from within. She shoved open the door, another heavy affair, and it squeaked lightly. A wedge of gold light widened about her. She stepped in and stood to one side, an arm pointed in Cookie's direction.

"Mr. Mincher to see you, sir."

"What? What? Why in hell wasn't I told?"

Cookie heard a squawking sound, like a chair scraping floorboards, papers rustled, and a man's voice growled and mumbled. The woman edged toward the doorway, stopping when she was still six feet from Cookie, stiff and uncertain.

Timmons looked up from the desk he was standing behind, pushing papers into sloppy piles, running a hand along the side of his head, smoothing his bristly graying hair. The room had two curtained windows, both closed and the curtains drawn. Two oil lamps with matching green glass shades glowed at the front corners of the massive mahogany desk. To the left sat a long, worn leather sofa.

Cookie kept his head down, tugged the hat's brim lower, and advanced through the doorway. The woman still looked at him with closed-mouth desperation.

Cookie stepped to his right, and she whispered past him, not once taking her eyes from him. She is worried I'm going to reach out and grab her with my poxy hands, thought Cookie. He wanted to giggle, despite the situation, but tamped it down.

She slid the door closed behind her; the sound seemed final to Cookie.

"Turk Mincher," said Timmons.

Cookie angled his head, not looking over at the man. Timmons was rounding the desk, head angled forward, a look of confusion on his face. "Turk? You . . . you look rough, my friend. Yes, rough."

"Stop right there, damn you!" Cookie stopped short of holding up a hand. The warden complied, but didn't lose his curious stare.

"Been poorly. Turn down those wicks, dammit. What I have to show won't take long."

"Now, Turk." The warden cocked a head to the side. Cookie saw a slight smile beginning to show on his face.

"Turn down those lamps, I said." With his free right hand, Cookie shucked one of the revolvers. He was surprised at the speed with which he did so. Usually it was a slow affair for him to slick one free of the holster. Now, a stick of dynamite, he'd have that fuse sparking and sizzling in finger-snap speed.

"You don't, you'll feel the sting of crossing Turk Mincher, you hear?"

"All right, all right, Turk, don't get riled. I will do as you say," said the warden, even as he hurried to lessen the light in the room.

"That's better," said Cookie, growling a bit more than he thought he ought to. "Pox has me at odds with myself."

"Pox?" Timmons straightened and backed around behind the desk once more. "Did you say pox?"

"Don't quiz me, you worm. I got a whole lot of reason to pull this trigger. Now," Cookie jerked the pistol and wagged it like a nodding dog, the snout pointing at Timmons. "Stand where you are and raise your hands so I can see them."

Timmons complied, his sneering smile beginning to droop. "I . . . I'm sure whatever you're facing, Turk, I can help you . . ."

"Help? You pathetic whelp." Cookie watched Timmons's face sag further, his eyes widen, unsure what to do. Can't push this longer, thought Cookie. He suspected right off that something was amiss, but the pox notion bought him time. Cookie cleared his throat and before his nerve drizzled, he swung the burlap sack upward, released it at the top of its swing, and let go. It arced high.

Cookie watched Timmons's face as if the hands on the clock had slowed. The pendulous sack landed with a clunk atop the desk and skidded across the surface, sliding to a stop directly before the staring warden.

"God, no, not . . ."

"Told you I had a present for you. At least I told the damn fools who welcomed me in here. You ought to look into hiring smarter guards. Told them you wanted to see me, said I had a gift for you."

"Gift?" said Timmons.

"Yep. Take a look. Then we'll talk."

Cookie wagged the pistol side to side.

Timmons swallowed hard, looked from Cookie to the sack, squinted down at it, then tweezered his fingers and parted the loose top. It didn't give.

"Untie the damn rawhide, fool."

So help me I am beginning to enjoy this, thought Cookie. He suppressed a smile and watched Timmons struggle with the wrappings.

"It's . . . it's another one, isn't it?" said Timmons.

"Another what, Warden?" said Cookie, allowing himself the beginnings of a smirk.

"Head, damn you. It's another head. I told you I don't want —"

"This you'll want to see. But you have it all wrong. It's not a head."

"No?"

"No," said Cookie shaking his head. "It's two heads."

"Oh, God."

"But two heads you have wanted for a long, long time."

Timmons squinted once more, hands poised on the rawhide wrappings. He stared at Cookie. Then his eyes widened. "Can't be. You don't mean you've . . ." He smiled, then lost it as quickly. "No, I wanted him here, to serve out the remainder of his sentence, his life, that son of a bitch bested me too many times!" Timmons clenched a pasty white fist before him as if he were holding a prize from a fair.

"Now, now, Warden. You can't do a thing about it. Except pay me for the task completed."

"I don't recall hiring you to do anything." Timmons looked sidelong at Cookie, doubt beginning to creep back onto his face. At the same time, his fingers worked loose the rawhide wrappings cinching the top of the sack. He parted the top, his nose wrinkling

351

at the scent drifting up from it.

"Really, Mincher, I'm not so certain your methods of . . . disposal are something I care to . . . what's this?" Timmons looked up at Cookie, who hadn't shifted from his spot, save for flexing his thumb to rest atop the revolver's hammer.

"But there's only one head in here. This other thing . . . it's . . . what is it?"

"Oh, that? That there's a gourd. You see, Mincher worked alone. I wanted you to think that was my head in there, too. Vain of me, I know. And gruesome, don't you think?"

"No, I . . . don't understand, unless . . . who are you?"

The look on the warden's face dragged up a quick bubble of laughter from Cookie. He couldn't help it.

"But . . ." the warden looked down into the bag again, then back up to Cookie.

"I will say, Timmons, for a mastermind of all manner of evil doings, you are slower on the draw than I expected. You worked it out yet?"

"You! You're . . ." the warden stalked out from behind the desk, teeth gritted and eyes stony.

"Easy now, Warden. You take one step

352

closer and this here six-gun is liable to go off."

"Then that's not Barr?"

"Nope."

"That means . . ." Timmons looked around the darkened room as if Rafe might leap at him from a corner.

"Yep, he's here. And he's itchin' to chat with you, Warden. First, we'd better settle that little matter of payment."

"Payment? What are you talking about?"

"Oh, a little birdy told me about a carpetbag somebody looking a whole lot like you lugged all the way from Santa Fe to Yuma. And do you know what was rumored to be in that ol' bag. No? Well, I'll tell you, I heard tell it was a-brimmin' with poker winnings." Cookie nodded.

"Yep, I know, I found it hard to believe, too. But that Mincher, right up until we liberated his yammering head from his trembling body, he was one chatty and persuasive fella.

"So, I started to thinking, and I said to Rafe, I said, 'Rafe? What say we pay ol' Warden Timmons a visit down Yuma way? Might be he could shed some thought on this puzzling matter.' "

"Don't condescend to me, you stupid little man. You . . . you bluebelly!"

Cookie smiled, shaking his head. "Warden, you are going to have to work a whole lot harder than that if you want to insult ol' Cookie McGee. I'm proud to be a bluebelly. Wasn't that the same war you and your Phoenix chums was dipping into both buckets, north and south, making all manner of profit from one and the other?"

"You have to be as deluded as I thought. There is no way you'll get away with this."

"Oh, give me the money, Timmons. I have a powerful urge to shoot you and that would not please Rafe. Did I mention he's anxious to see you again? You should be flattered, really. Rafe Barr, he's a busy man these days. Seems everybody wants to bend his ear."

"More like lock him up for the murdering savage he is."

"Careful, Warden. My good humor only stretches so far. Now, here's what we're going to do next — after you hand over the carpetbag, that is."

Chapter Twenty-Eight:
It's Now or Never

Rafe eyed the flat plain before him, the heat-conjured wavering lines rising from the burnt ground, proving once more to him that this was indeed the foulest place on earth. At least the prison was. And here he was back again, and of his own will. Not only that, but he'd wrangled his best friend into accompanying him.

The sooner he was out of here the better. But first he would make what amends he could among the living, lay blame and mete out retribution. And, so help him, he would take pleasure in it. Then he would make his peace with the dead.

"What have we done, eh, Horse?"

The mount gave a chesty rumble and kept up his brisk pace. Soon the east entrance came into view.

Rafe stopped a few hundred yards from the double doors, close enough to see a man in the south tower staring toward him. Rafe waved a wide-armed halloo. The man didn't reply for a moment, then offered a tentative wave.

Rafe smiled and nodded and walked the horse closer. He plucked out a cigar from his left breast pocket, sniffed its length, and sighed. "Never gets old, that smell." He stuck the end in his mouth and patted himself for a match, pulled it out of another pocket, and held it while they sauntered forward, eyes on the guard.

"I do believe," Rafe said in a low voice, "our presence is making that guard nervous." He made straight for the end of the long stone enclosure beneath where the tower stood.

"What are you doing?" shouted the guard.

Rafe looked up, as if surprised to be addressed. He pointed a thumb at his chest. "Me?"

"Yeah, you. This here's Yuma Territorial Prison. You aren't allowed to be here."

"If you only knew," mumbled Rafe. Keeping an eye on the guard, Rafe halted the horses twenty or so feet from the wall and made a show of setting fire to the tip of his cigar. He puffed up a bold, blue cloud, held out the cigar, admired the glowing tip, then stuck it back in his mouth.

"Hey, you!" the guard shouted down.

"Yeah, you. I warned you once. I am authorized to shoot to kill should you not heed my words."

Rafe sighed slowly, his big chest letting out a lungful of air. He nudged his hat brim back with an index finger and looked up slowly at the man above. "Now why would you do that, son? Could be I am here on official business."

"Then why ain't you at the front gate."

"You mean this isn't the front gate?"

"No, sir, no, it ain't."

"Well, no matter. As I said, it's possible I am here on official business. It's also possible I am here on other business."

"You are confusing me, mister."

"I don't doubt that, son." As Rafe spoke he reached around and lifted the flap on his right-side saddlebag. He pulled out a quarter-stick of dynamite and stuck the tip of his cigar to the end of the short fuse. It hissed and sparked. "If ever there was a time to shoot a man, son, it's before he lights the fuse on one of these things. Believe me, I've seen the mess they make."

"Hey! Hey, you can't . . ."

"Better run, son, I only have a few seconds before I have to do something with this thing."

"Ohhh!"

That was the last Rafe heard from the guard, except for the pounding of boots on stairs. Rafe lobbed the little stick of dynamite up high. It left a trail of smoke and sparks as it rose, end over end, into the sky before disappearing into the tower, right where the guard had been standing moments before.

Rafe had enough time to turn away. With his fingers in his ears he urged Horse forward toward the double doors to his right. The blast rattled unseen timbers, blowing hunks of wood and rock up and outward. It wasn't enough to knock down the tower, he knew, but it would be enough to do what he wanted — cause a ruckus within the walls.

Rafe knew every inch of the place in his mind. Well, at least the parts prisoners saw. Five years of seeing, of taking in every inch of the grounds, the walls, the towers, the strap-steel cell doors, how blistering and untouchable they were in the sizzling heat of midsummer. How sunlight lit the rock walls and puckered your entire body, withering your brain as small as a bean inside your bone gourd of a head.

The blast did as he hoped — someone was manning the clanking alarm bell, the frenzied shouts of prisoners and guards nearly drowning it out.

Rafe had another stick of dynamite, but he didn't want to use it yet. He wanted to give Cookie more time to appear with Timmons. But the door was closed tighter than a bull's backside.

"Come on, Cook, they'll be out here any second." He slid from the saddle, snugged the mounts close by the wall, and looped Horse's reins through an iron ring hanging from the mortar work between blocks of stone.

Rafe pulled a Colt, thumbed back the hammer, and hugged the wall as he worked his way to the edge of the doors. They were inset enough to provide scant cover from any guards daring enough to rain lead down on him from above.

Then he heard a shout shriller and more insistent than the others, and it was drawing closer. It was a voice he knew well, and it wasn't Cookie's. "Timmons," said Rafe, shifting the cigar to the other side of his mouth. He tilted his hat, then jammed an ear to the door. Yep, it was the warden, and he was drawing closer.

Why wasn't Cookie hushing him? He had no more time to wonder because a grinding, rattling sound reached him from the other side of the doors. Clanks of dropped chains as they slammed against the thick wooden doors, then one side of the seldom-opened doors swung slowly inward. Rafe raised his gun and peered through the widening gap, ready to kill.

Cookie nudged the warden's gray suitcoat square in the back with the sniffer of the revolver.

"Stop that, damn you." The warden growled his words.

"I will when you stop lollygagging. I have an appointment to keep and you are testing my patience."

"Where are all my men?" The warden looked up toward the guard tower, but saw nobody where two guards should be standing, scanning the yard.

"Likely they are riled about the pox, didn't want to be anywhere near here should my afflicted old self, or should I say Turk Mincher, carry a foul disease that could wipe them all out. I can't hardly blame them. Risk my skin protecting a bunch of killers and thieves or skedaddle and live?"

"My men would do no such thing."

"No, no, you're right. Not only your men. That woman, I believe she's your secretary? She looks to have scampered on out of here, too."

That was when they heard an explosion from a far corner of the compound. "What was that?" The warden tried to turn but Cookie poked him in the back. "Do you know what you're doing? This place is packed full of humanity's worst!"

"Don't I know it," said Cookie, ramming the man forward once more. "And I'm standing behind the worst of them all."

"You know nothing, you insignificant fool!"

"Keep that up, Warden, and I'm liable to take offense. Now get walking and head to the doors on the east side. I daresay you know where that's at. If not, I will gladly give you some more persuading."

They reached the end of the long, dim hallway Cookie had taken on his way in. Cookie reckoned they were headed somewhat due east; that felt right. And then he spied the double doors ahead. Had to be the ones. The explosion meant Rafe would be there, hopefully not dodging shots from on high. But from the looks of things the prison guards were clustering at the far corner, near the crippled tower.

They made it to the side doors without being seen by the guards and Cookie prodded Timmons once more. "Open the doors, Warden. And if you make any sort of noise to bring those rascals on over here, you will regret it."

"See here, I've had about enough from you, McGee. You and Barr will pay for this, mark my words. There is no way this will stand!"

"Yammer all you want, but hurry up with that door."

Timmons growled and whined, but fumbled with the steel sliding latch and chains, then swung the doors inward. And as the gap widened, the outline of a tall, lean form emerged.

"Why, Warden," said Rafe Barr, a grim grin on his face. "Fancy meeting you here."

Talbot Timmons straightened his stance and smiled. "Glad to see you're coming to your senses, Barr. I knew you would return in time."

"Shut up, Timmons. You will speak when I say so, and not before."

"But —"

Rafe held up a finger between his hard face and the warden's sagging features. "Not one word."

"Cook," Rafe handed his chum the second stick of dynamite. "Take this and do the same thing to the southwest corner. That should keep them busy for a while."

"That and the pox," said Cookie, rubbing

his hands together as he slid the dynamite into his vest.

"What?" said Rafe, then shook his head. "Never mind. Tell me later."

"There will be no later for you fools!"

Rafe's big hand lashed out with the speed of a striking diamondback and caught the gray flesh of Timmons's cheek with a tight smack. The blow whipped the man's head to the side. Even in the dim light Cookie saw the imprint of Rafe's fingers blazing pink on the man's cheek.

"Not another word until I say so," said Rafe. They headed back in.

Rafe looked up and down the corridor, satisfied no guard was descending on them. Then he pulled out a tri-folded sheet of vellum from an inside vest pocket and shoved the warden into an alcove beneath a low window. Using the sill as a makeshift desk, Rafe spread the paper and jammed a finger at the bottom, opposite a signature. "Sign this, now."

"I will not," said Timmons. "I have no idea what it is, but I can guess. And you'll not get me to sign it."

"You certain about that?"

The warden nodded.

"Fine," said Rafe, leaving one hand pinning down the paper. "Then give me the key."

"What key?" said Timmons.

"The one key you have that no one else has." He watched the warden's eyes widen. Rafe nodded. "Yep, that one."

"No, no, I won't do it. I . . . I don't have it any longer."

"That's a lie. You'd never give up using the hell cell." He held out his other hand. "The key."

"All right, I'll sign your damned paper. It won't mean a thing you know. In a court of law, my word against yours will —"

"Who said anything about a courtroom, or the law for that matter?"

"I have friends in high places."

"So do I, Timmons. So do I. Now sign." He thrust the tip of a meaty finger on the page.

"I'll read it first, if you don't mind."

"I do mind, as it happens, but as I'm feeling indulgent, and as Cookie's about to buy us more time, I think I will let you read it. Aloud, though, if you don't mind. I'd like to hear the words fall out of your mouth."

The warden cleared his throat and picked up the page. He squinted at it, and made a quick movement, but Rafe's huge clamplike hand lashed out and encircled the man's neck, crushing his suit collar into the thin skin and Adam's apple bobbing like a little bird in the man's neck.

"Don't tear up that paper, Warden. That won't do."

The warden nodded slightly and stretched his neck as Rafe let go.

"Now read."

And so the warden read: "I, Turk Mincher, being of my own mind and not coerced by anyone, do swear and attest on this page that I was hired by a private party six years ago to kill Rafe Barr and his family. I rode to his ranch, but, as Mr. Barr was away on business, I made myself at home with Mr. Barr's wife and young son. Then I killed them.

"Other duties required my presence, but I figured at some point in the near future I would track down Mr. Barr and finish the job. Before I could, Mr. Barr was arrested, charged with the murder of his family, and sent to Yuma Territorial Prison for life. Odd, that. Especially as it was the warden of Yuma Territorial Prison, Talbot Timmons, who hired me to kill Barr and his family. By my own hand and free will, I do swear this."

Timmons barely finished reading the note signed by Mincher. By the end he was talking through gritted teeth. He finished and stared at the sheet.

Rafe lifted it from the man's fingers. "You'll have noticed," he said, tapping the page once more. "There's a blank line at the bottom, across from Mincher's signature."

"So?"

"So, sign your name on it."

Timmons crossed his arms. "I won't do that." He tried to smile. His left eyelid twitched.

Rafe sighed. "Fine. Then give me the key to the hell cell. I'm done with your games."

Timmons didn't move, but his smile slipped from his face. "No, I . . . all right, all right." He reached into his jacket.

Rafe tensed, thumbing the hammer back all the way.

"My fountain pen," said Timmons, shaking his head. He unscrewed the cap and signed it with a flourish, taking ample space. "It won't matter, you know. There isn't a jury, a judge, or a court in this country that would consider this as anything less than laughable evidence." He screwed the top back on his tortoiseshell pen and slid it into his inner pocket. "Besides, I know important people who hold positions of high authority."

Rafe gently waved the sheet as if to dry

366

the ink. "As I said before, so do I." Then he looked at the sheet. "Oh, how silly of me. You didn't see those other signatures? No? There, below Mincher's?" Rafe lifted the page and looked at it critically. "In my haste, I see I had the bottom folded over." He unfolded the bottom of the long sheet to reveal more signatures. "There now, see? Here's my signature, of course, as well as Cookie's. And below ours? You might recall that rather fancy-sounding name there, as it belongs to none other than your old friend, or perhaps that's too strong a word. He's more likely an acquaintance of yours . . ."

Timmons leaned forward, squinting. Rafe watched his eyes as recognition overcame them. "Cuthbert Pendleton?"

"None other," said Rafe. "Seems he felt like we'd done him a favor, bringing his daughter home to him. Oh, and there's that little matter of him being blackmailed. We told him we'd take care of that, too. After all, what are friends for?" He grinned. "I'd say you're not the only one with chums in, what was that you called it? 'Positions of high authority'? Did I mention Governor Pendleton's name is being bandied about for the Senate? There's even talk of him taking up residence in the White House. High authority, indeed."

Timmons said nothing, but his narrowed eyes and clenched jaw spoke volumes.

Rafe continued: "And as for your winnings from Santa Fe, I'd say there will be a whole lot of folks eager to talk with you about how you got so darned lucky at that poker tournament. Lucky enough that you walked away with every cent in the place. Why, if I didn't know better, I'd swear it was almost criminal. I know there will be a bunch of fat southern gents in fancy white suits who are wondering where their investments in the Brotherhood of the Phoenix have gone. Looks to me like you'll be a popular fellow before long. Don't worry, Cookie and I will make certain everybody knows where to find you."

Timmons balled his thin gray hands until his knuckles whitened, the fingers ready to snap. "You . . ." he seethed through gritted teeth. "You bastard."

Rafe shrugged. "I've been called worse. There's nothing you can do to me that hasn't been done, Timmons. In fact, let that be a lesson: Never tangle with a man who has nothing left to lose. Especially if you're the one who put him in that position." He held out a hand, palm up. "Now, the key, if you please."

"But . . . but you said . . . you promised!"

368

"I promised nothing." The big man's voice was suddenly low and cold. "The key."

Timmons's hand shook as if he were freezing to death. Rafe took grim pleasure in every palsied twitch.

"That's him!"

Cookie heard the shout from behind him, somewhere near the front entrance. He glanced over his shoulder and spied the two tower guards he'd seen when he first rode up. They were standing before three other men with long guns; none of them looked sure what to do. Cookie knew they were confused because Mincher had obviously been there in the past and was known as someone in Timmons's confidence. Fine with Cookie — he'd play on that fear for as long as he was able.

Right now, he had to work up another distraction so Rafe could get Timmons to sign the paper. Trouble was, there were guards and prisoners — unarmed and shuffling along with ankle chains hindering their quick movement from one place to another. All of them looked confused, trying to rummage through the few planks and loose stone blocks Rafe's lobbed charge had caused. None of them looked too frantic, however. Cookie hoped that meant no one had been harmed.

He decided to change his plans in mid-stride. One minor blast was enough. He'd cause a distraction in a more refined manner. If these fools were convinced he had the pox, on top of the fact they had no idea what was going on with the warden, why not play it up? He turned and waved to the staring men. Then he limped toward them. Limped because the heavy carpetbag filled with the Santa Fe cash bumped against his leg.

He hoped Rafe would hurry up with the warden. Cookie would hold on to the cash for as long as he needed to, but loading it onto a horse sure would feel good.

"Gentlemen," said Cookie walking toward the clot of men. They backed from him, eyes wider with each step forward he took.

"The warden asked me to make certain all you good men had the situation well in hand. Seems he doesn't like all this ruckus. I expect he'll be along any minute."

Chapter Twenty-Nine: Welcome to Hell, Sir

Rafe prodded the warden toward the hell cell.

"I'll have you both in chains for this!" Timmons howled.

"On the contrary, Timmons. I think we will get away with this. And we'll have our day in court, too."

"I don't know what you mean."

"It's a little late to claim innocence, Timmons. You have committed, and are responsible for, more crimes than those committed by most of your inmates here in Yuma."

"I'll see you are hunted to the ends of the earth and beyond for the rest of your mortal days!"

"Suits me fine, Timmons. And in return I'll see to it that you are haunted far beyond the borders of this mortal world."

"I don't know what that means. You're making no sense."

371

"On the contrary, I'm making all manner of sense. I'm talking about hell, and it's a place I know well. You sent me there, after all."

Timmons shook his head.

"Warden, I will never leave you be. Never. But then, again, we have all of eternity to frolic together. For now, I'll leave you to ponder your situation. This time it will be a different sort of hell. The one you created. It's hell on earth."

They slowed before a gaping black hole of a doorway. "There she be," said Rafe, one corner of his mouth raised in a sneer, as if he were a hydrophobic dog set to lunge.

"We . . ." Timmons spun from Rafe's grasp and backed away, hands up before him. "We can work this out, Mr. Barr. I have money. And more! Why, the safe in my office is full of assorted promising documents and cash, not that silly Confederate kind, I assure you!"

His eyes shone with promise, with the belief that what he was saying would convince Barr of the error of his ways. Timmons nodded, "Yes, yes, you see what I mean. Why, I can even let you in on a secret." He shook, his head twitching as if he were afflicted with some bizarre disease. "The safe in my office, behind my desk? You know the one," he leaned forward, a small smile playing at his lips. "It's not even locked," he nodded, smiling wider. "What do you say? Partners?" He nodded again as if this were the best offer anyone had ever given or received.

Rafe stared at him, pooching out his lips in consideration.

A single bead of sweat jellied between Timmons's eyes, slid down the center of his nose, then hung, quivering, at the tip as if awaiting Rafe's response.

"Well, now, Timmons. I do believe you have told me something of worth. Something, if you will permit me to say so, I can chew on."

Timmons nodded and squared his shoulders. He tugged down the bottom of his blue brocade vest, his smile settling into its accustomed half-sneer. "Very well then, Barr. Let us retire to my office and we can draw up the particulars." He advanced a step. "Oh, one thing, I would like to have that little piece of paper I so recently signed. You understand, don't you?" He held out a steady hand, eyes hooded, nearly squinting.

"Why, Timmons, I do believe you have misunderstood me. And for that I take full blame." Rafe nodded.

Timmons's smile slumped.

"Now, let's go." Rafe nodded toward the darkened doorway. "After you."

"But . . . but the money! I told you about the safe!"

"Yes, and I'm grateful. It will go a long way toward soothing some of the financial hardships you put me through while I was in here. Now, let's go."

Timmons leaned against the stone wall behind him, his shoulders slumping once more. "No, no, no! There has to be a way to resolve this."

"There is. You either get in there or I will drag you. Now, so far no one has seen you rumple like the delicate flower you are, but that's all about to change, judging by the way you are handling yourself."

Timmons shook his head, refusing to budge.

Rafe sighed. Quick as a rifle shot, his big left fist, a solid mass of bone and tendon, slammed the man's chin. It hit with a smack, and Timmons's head caromed off the stone wall. His knees unlocked and he slipped forward. Rafe caught him by the chest, balling the man's shirt, tie, and vest in his punching hand. He ducked into the dark doorway, dragging the man behind him.

The shaded corridor was welcome to his

squinting eyes. He reached the end, a couple of dozen feet in, and paused. He holstered the revolver and smacked Timmons's face. "Wake up, Talbot. Time to rise and greet your future."

"Huh?" Timmons's head bobbed as he came back to his senses. "Barr, no, I . . . has to be a way to make this right."

"There is." Rafe looked a few feet in toward the center of the low, domed room. The ceiling itself was carved from rock, stubbly and raw and perfectly suited to the task of directing any sounds in the chamber back into the chamber. "Ah, there's the spot." He bent low, the revolver drawn once more as Timmons propped himself on an elbow and regarded him, rubbing his addled head.

Rafe felt the dark spot with his left hand, felt the rough lip of the hole in the middle of the floor. "There now, won't this be fun?" He lifted out a match, scratched it alight, and tossed it down into the hole before him.

It shone enough to reveal the scuttling shapes of large hairy spiders, the curved menace of a handful of scorpions, something resembling a many-legged worm, and that was followed with a quick, stabbing form several feet long that wound and slithered across the raw stone floor of the chamber below. The unmistakable, random squeaks of rats greeted their ears as the match winked out.

"Like old times," said Rafe. "Well, almost. This time, Timmons, you'll be the guest of honor. Now, in you go."

"No!" The man's shout echoed in the dim, close hollow of stone.

"Yes," said Rafe, in a casual tone. He snatched the warden's shirt front once more and dragged the flailing man to the hole in the floor, barely wide enough to accommodate Rafe's broad shoulders, but wide enough to stuff down the thrashing, screaming man.

Timmons dropped the ten feet, his hands clawing the dry stone wall on the way down. He hit hard, on his back and shoulder, quickly righted himself and stood, weaving at the bottom of the hole.

Rafe looked down at him. "I can never take away from you everything you took from me. But I will die trying."

The space Timmons now occupied, Rafe recalled, was roughly seven feet wide at the base, uneven, and riddled with crevices and cracks that leaked unseen crawling, slithering, clawing critters that bit, stung, stabbed, poked, and choked.

"A little advice, Timmons. Down there it's

kill or be killed. Course, that part will come slowly. Might take those critters a long time to finish feasting on you. By then you may or may not have died. In body, anyway. So my advice is to kill as many as you can before they get to you. But don't forget where you put the bodies. They'll come in mighty handy when you get hungry. Goodbye for now, Talbot Timmons. See you in hell."

The man's screams rose in pitch and volume, any words he may have been screaming became guttural sounds indecipherable by anyone but madmen. Even before Rafe slid the massive flat stone, which took all his considerable strength to move over the hole, Timmons's voice had become a raw, hoarse sound, blown out as if hot flame and searing wind raced through a steel pipe.

The stone slid, and covered the last of the hole. The sound of Timmons's raw screeches all but pinched out.

"Hmm," said Rafe as he tapped the rock with a boot toe. "Too bad you lost your voice, now you won't have anybody to listen to."

He walked from the chamber toward the sunlit prison yard, lighting a cigar and letting a genuine smile stretch across his face.

His satisfaction was clipped short by the cackling of a familiar voice. "You rank bastards best back away! I am Turk Mincher and I am riddled with the pox, I tell you! Riddled! Why, I might start shedding my parts as we speak. This here type of pox sort of chews away at a man's limbs. My ears have been feeling a mite touchy lately, and these thumbs of mine, why, I don't doubt but they might drop clean off, too. No telling with the pox."

"If you are as infected as you say, that might well account for the fact that you don't much look like Mr. Mincher, at all." The man who said this, a tall, thin guard, laid his head to one side, regarding Cookie through narrowed eyes.

Rafe strode up. "Cookie, what in tarnation are you up to?"

Cookie turned to Rafe, eyes wide.

"Hey," said a pudgy guard from beneath the sagging broken brim of a stained straw hat. "What'd you call him? Cookie? Said he was Turk Mincher. Who's who here, anyway?"

Another man stepped forward, tall, thin with gray-blue eyes and a neatly trimmed sandy moustache that bristled like the feet of a dead bug atop his upper lip. "I tell you who that one is," he jerked his chin at Rafe and held his rifle across his chest as though he was about to use it to push the world back a pace. "That big fellow is an old resident, long escaped from this place."

The other guards mumbled, eyes narrowed, brows drawn tight as they craned their heads forward. They regarded the big man before them, casually puffing a cigar, arms folded across his chest, no weapon in his hands.

"That," said the thin man. "Is none other than Rafe Barr."

"What?" said several men at once, mitts grasping their rifles tighter.

"Now, now boys, he ain't nothing of the sort. He's a . . ." Cookie looked at Rafe for a bit of help, but received a grin in reply as Rafe kept puffing that damnable cigar, a blue cloud of smoke boiling up above his head into the clear desert sky.

Cookie swallowed and nodded, "Why, he's an emissary from the federal government, name of Rupert Ball, yeah," he nodded with vigor as he agreed with himself. "Rupert Ball."

The tall man shook his head slowly, not smiling, and not taking his eyes from Rafe. "No, no, he isn't. He's Rafe Barr, all right."

Rafe pulled the cigar from his mouth. The movement caused several of the armed guards to tense, their weapons jostling in steely unison.

"How do, Monte. Miss me?" said Rafe.

"Rafe," hissed Cookie. "I had 'em right where I wanted 'em!"

"No need anymore, Cook," said Rafe. "But Rupert Ball thanks you."

The men pressed forward and drew down on the pair, most of the rifles aimed at Rafe. The big man did nothing to defend himself, save for speaking slow and even.

"Whoa now, boys. I'll have you know I am fully exonerated." Rafe held up a thumb and forefinger and showed them to the group. "Don't shoot me yet. I'm going to reach into my inner pocket for a piece of paper."

He slipped the signed sheet of paper from his inner pocket and unfolded it. A swarthy guard stepped around Monte, reached out a pudgy hand, dark crescents of dirt griming his fingernails. The tang of stale sweat wafted off him in a cloud. He made a grab for the paper but Rafe tugged it back gently.

Monte stepped forward, directing a hard, quick stare at the swarthy man, who scowled down at his boots and stepped backward.

"May I?" said Monte.

Rafe nodded once, handing the trim guard the paper. The man read it top to bottom, then nodded slowly. "Okay then, that appears in order." He handed the paper back to Rafe. "Good for you, Barr. I hoped you weren't what they said you were. I saw you," he nodded at Cookie, "and you, Mr. Mc-Gee, on the battlefield at Dawe Ridge." He raised his voice, half-turning so the other guards could hear him. "Any men that valiant don't deserve to die forgotten in this place."

"Thanks, Monte. I appreciate that."

"Where's Warden Timmons?" said a man from the back of the group.

"Well, now," Rafe puffed on the cigar. "That's a good question. He signed this paper, we exchanged pleasantries, of sorts, and then he sort of disappeared from my sight. Said something about seeing us all in hell. Or maybe it was me he was talking to."

Monte chewed the inside of his cheek, regarding Rafe and Cookie alternately. "Okay boys, we'd better tend to the damage some irresponsible soul wrought on our tower yonder."

Rafe looked at the light rubble. "I hope no one was hurt."

"No, no injuries. The no-account made work for us, that's all."

Rafe nodded. "Good to hear. I'll see you around, Monte."

"I hope not, Rafe." The man smiled. "If

you know what I mean."

"I do. Thanks. I have one last thing to do before we hit the trail."

"Okay then, I expect you know your way around the place." Monte touched his hat brim and headed toward the group of guards he'd sent toward the far corner of the compound.

Cookie whistled long and low. "That was bold of you, Rafe. I don't mind saying. Did the warden really take off on you?"

"He had a long overdue appointment to keep." Rafe nodded toward the bulging but closed carpetbag at Cookie's feet. "You have room in that thing for more?"

"Money?" Cookie's eyes shone like diamonds in sunlight. "Why, there's always room for such as that, Rafe. Don't you know nothing?"

"A few things, but that's all. The safe in Timmons's office is unlocked. We should clean it out — he hinted there might be papers, too, something we can use to expose the rest of the Brotherhood of the Phoenix."

"That trash. Good. Anything we can do to topple that big bird off its roost. Let's go. Then let's get on out of here."

"One more thing before that, though."

Cookie's shoulders slumped. "Always is with you, ain't there?"

"Follow me. And keep your voice down, I don't want to push Monte's good graces any more than we have. There's a man I need to see, Cookie. In fact, I'd like you to meet him, Cookie. I hope he's still . . . here."

Rafe led the way along the western wall to a strap-steel door like all the rest. He paused, not looking in, then walked to the next door. Cookie squinted in through the flat steel of the first door at the dark, gloomy space. Then his eyes softened and he nodded and followed Rafe to the next door.

"Mossback. Mossback?"

No sound came from within. Rafe tried again. "Mossy?"

A rustling, then scuffing as though soft-soled shoes dragged along stone. Cookie peered in from behind Rafe. He saw a dim figure, small and hunched, shuffle forward.

"Mossy? How are you?"

"Who is there?" the voice was that of an old man, tremulous and suspicious.

"It's me, Rafe. Rafe Barr."

"Oh, no. Boy, they didn't get you again, did they? Not back here." The disappointment in the man's voice was obvious to Cookie. Then the man shuffled into view.

"No, Mossy. I'm free. For now." He glanced briefly at Cookie.

"Rafe!" The man's old face widened into a smile.

Cookie was shocked to see that the man didn't appear any older than himself.

"Good to see you," said Rafe, smiling and reaching through the strapping to take the man's hand in his.

"You mean good to see me still alive, eh?" the old man chuckled. "You should go, Rafe. Don't get caught, not tossed back in here."

"No, really, I'm free now. And you'll be too. As soon as I open this lock."

"No need," said Cookie, patting his dynamite holster. "Got one right here, best key there is!"

"Cook, I appreciate the sentiment, but you'll bring the whole place down on us."

"What do you take me for? I won't make it a hot batch!"

"I believe you, but as it happens, I have Timmons's key." Rafe held up a skeleton key on a ring from which several others dangled. "Besides, I think we made enough ruckus for one day, don't you?"

Cookie nodded, scuffing the dirt with his boot. "I reckon."

Mossy cleared his throat. "You are the famous Cookie McGee?"

Cookie perked up. "You bet I am. Heard

384

of me, have you?"

"All about you, from my friend, Rafe, here." The old man's eyes shone above his gap-toothed smile.

"Uh-oh," said Cookie. "Sounds like I'm in trouble."

"All good, I can promise you that."

"Yeah, Cook," said Rafe, clicking the lock open and swinging the door wide. "All good." He extended a hand to help his old friend into the sunlight. "Mostly."

Once his friend was outside the cell, Rafe said, "Is there anything in there you would like to bring with you?"

"I leave behind nothing in there but memories, memories of grief and misery. No, I move forward." He began to walk across the open yard.

Rafe hurried after him. "Um, Mossy, you'd better stick to the wall, follow me. We're leaving this way."

"Ah, yes, that's good." He ambled along after Rafe, Cookie bringing up the rear, the big carpetbag softly thudding against his legs. Mincher's boots were a pinch too large for him and his feet slopped inside them. "I do believe I'm growing blisters on my toes, my hands, all over, in fact."

"Better them than the bites of the little night bugs." Mossback said this as if he were reporting the weather. "Oh, they are a torment."

Cookie reddened and said nothing for a time. The two men followed Rafe, who walked quickly along the west wall, then along the north wall. They slipped unseen past the entry gate and continued on.

"Mossback, if you don't mind my askin'," said Cookie in a whisper. "What'd you do to land yourself in here, anyway?"

Mossy stopped and faced Cookie. Rafe stood behind him and glared wide-eyed at Cookie over the old man's shoulder. Mossy stood erect, his back no longer hunched. The one action seemed, now that he was in sunlight, to peel away ten years of the old-man look that clung to him. "My real name is Marcello. I am Italian."

Cookie rasped his hand across his chin. "Well now, that's fine, fine."

Rafe touched his old chum on the elbow, gently guiding him back on their route. "We'll have plenty of time to chat once we hit the trail, as I'm sure Cookie will agree." Rafe cast a hard gaze over his shoulder at Cookie. "Right now, I have to go to Timmons's office for a few items. I'll meet you outside. Mossy, maybe you'd better come with me." He nodded at Cookie. "He's liable to talk you to sleep."

"Why, you whelp!" Cookie shook, then simmered down. "Okay, okay, while you fellas are busy in there, I'll go fetch Mincher's horse."

Rafe eyed him. "You think that's a good idea?"

"Well, it ain't a bad idea," said Cookie. "We need a third horse and I'm damn sure not about to steal one, especially not from a prison. Besides, me and that rascal come to an agreement, so to speak. We respect each other. I think."

"Fine," said Rafe. "But we're selling or trading that man's horse and his traps once we reach a decent town."

Cookie didn't agree right away, then said, "Okay, then." He turned and mumbled, "We'll see."

Rafe and Mossback headed for the passageway leading to the warden's office. Cookie made for where he'd seen the first guard lead the horse. It turned out to be a small stable, two stalls, inside the entry gate. Cookie suspected it was reserved for visitors' mounts. He was relieved to find the horse still saddled and standing, ears perked, waiting in the near stall.

He approached the horse with caution. He'd been a chum of Stinky for far too long to trust a horse. They could be sweet as a fall apple one minute, viperlike the next. "How's it going to be, Blackie? You going to treat me right or are we going to have a set-to?"

He approached with a palm outstretched, wishing he had a carrot or some such sweet treat to tempt the horse into behaving himself. But the horse nickered low and bobbed his head once.

"Okay, boy, let's get you out of here. We'll slip through the front gate and make our way around to the east side, slick as goose grease on a hot day. But first," he said. "We have a little something to take care of. And you're going to help me, ain't you?" Cookie kept his voice low and friendly and soothing. Or what he hoped was a soothing tone. Any horse that belonged to a devil such as Turk Mincher, why, you never could tell.

He hoisted the big loop handles of the carpetbag up, hoping to snag them around the saddle horn. It took him three tries and he almost fell over on the third attempt, but the handles caught and the heavy bag of cash sagged and stayed put on the right side of the horse, resting against the beast's shoulder.

He led the beast to the front gate, glancing about himself so often he feared getting a crick in his neck. No one about. But he didn't think that would last long. The gate proved more of a challenge than he anticipated, and then he saw why — it was chained and locked. A clot of panic snagged in his throat.

But then as he scanned the gate for some solution, his eye caught the low, single-door cut in the side of the entry. It was big enough for a wide-shouldered man to pass through — barely. "You think so?" He asked out loud, and shrugged. "Nothing going to happen if I stand here not trying." He led the horse to the door.

It was unlocked and creaked open when he shoved the crude steel handle. "My God, Blackie. This might well be our day. Provided you can squeeze your bulk through there." He swung the door wide and stepped through, scanning each side once more. The horse balked, planted its feet at the threshold, and stood stiff-legged.

Cookie sighed and tugged harder. Nothing worked. He felt himself getting worked up, and knew that wasn't something most horses reacted well to. But he couldn't stop himself and barked a loud, quick oath at the horse. It did the trick. The horse's front knees unlocked and it started through the door. Never mind that its shoulder, then belly, were too wide to squeak through the narrow portal.

And then, when they finally did, the bulging carpetbag wedged tight between horse and doorframe.

"Oh, Lord have mercy," said Cookie. The situation looked grimmer by the second. The horse was growing fidgety, starting to roll his eyes and shake his head. This was one animal that did not like to be confined.

"Well, horse, that cash bag is the holdup. But there ain't a snowball's chance in the hereafter I'm about to let that go." What Cookie needed was to get behind the horse and whomp on its thrashing backside. But he was at the wrong end for that. There wasn't enough space atop the horse to climb over him, even if he could manage the odd body manipulations that would require. The only way back there was under the horse.

He'd been under horses before, on the battlefield, chucked out of barrooms and into the street, and a few other tight spots, never of his choosing, and they only resulted in quick flashes of slashing hooves, broken ribs, and a bruised belly. He'd seen plenty of men take hooves to the head and it never ended well. At best, they'd be addle-pated for days, maybe weeks, sometimes months. And then they'd up and die. Best thing for them was when they died right away.

Stomped to death. The thought made Cookie shudder.

As if it had sensed Cookie's thoughts, the big black horse shoved himself upward, slashing with both forelegs, and pawing with all the fury his muscled body could muster. It worked. The timbered doorframe shuddered, but held, and the horse cracked his own head once, twice, against the low top frame of stone and wood. It didn't matter. That horse had convinced himself he was going to be free of this strange, squeezing spot, no matter the cost.

Cookie stood back and watched this sudden thrashing black devil, for all of three seconds before he realized he was about to be raked to the ground. He leapt backward, feeling the breeze from a flailing hoof, far too close to his sweat-reddened face. Still, he held the reins, looped twice about his hand, his arm jerking skyward as the big beast leapt. Then it was free, and it lunged forward, a quivering black mass of hair and hooves and scraped flanks and saddle and flopping carpetbag.

"Whoa, now, damn your hide!" Cookie loped as the horse plowed ahead. But the big black mount paid him no heed. It was soon free of the doorway and bucking as though it was afire. Cookie scissored his lean legs and took off after it, barely keeping abreast of the lunging head, foam trailing from its mouth, eyes wide and head working up and down with each long step gained.

Cookie saw this would not end well or any time soon. He grunted and doubled his efforts at keeping up. But it was a losing battle. He took to cursing it, then even his spat words dissipated. The horse was not interested in slowing, let alone listening to a ranting old man.

The carpetbag jounced and slid and slammed in counterpoint with the horse's bucking. The reins began to slide out of Cookie's fingers at the same time he reached out with his left arm and felt the taut leather loops of the bag's handles. He muckled on with his old horned left hand as the reins jerked free from his right hand.

"Gaaah!" he shouted as his legs flailed, his boots hitting the ground once every two or three steps in an increasing effort to keep up with the bolting horse. He wrapped the fingers of his cramping left hand tight around the carpetbag's handles, vowing to himself to never let go, even if the fool horse ran all the way to Montana.

The right stirrup had been whacking him in the thigh and had shifted so that it clacked and whapped right between his legs. The sensation was as if he were being pounded in the crotch by a blacksmith's hammer, over and over and over.

His right arm whipped out and up, out and up, under no control by himself. His right boot, or rather Mincher's right boot, slid free and sailed in a clean arc right past the side of his face. Then Mincher's hat spun from his head. Still Cookie ran, bounding like an old, bald, two-legged deer.

He knew he couldn't keep this up more than a minute or so before his arm ripped free. It was that image of a bloodied stump waving goodbye to him as he tumbled to the desert floor that brought his skinning knife to mind. It rode as always on his right hip.

It took Cookie three tries with his flailing right arm before he was able to snatch at the knife, another two tries before his fingers closed around the jigged bone handle. He slid it free and nearly lost it to the flailing, but managed to arc it around.

The knife's impressive steel blade found its way right before his face, sinking into the looped leather of the bag's handles. But it didn't cut in so well because he couldn't muster the strength, given his awkward galloping pose. It was a race he was quickly losing, sagging every few seconds, his left arm stretched beyond belief, feeling as if it might separate in the middle at the elbow. It also didn't help that he was notoriously lax about keeping a keen edge on the blade. He knew he should, and Rafe commented on it each time he borrowed the knife for some minor task, but it was one of those annoying chores he was forever forgetting to tend to. Now it was paying him back, and not in a way he liked.

Cookie did his best to saw through the strap, and his efforts were enough to weaken the leather. The stress of his weight hanging on the well-used handles persuaded one to snap right before Cookie's eyes, as he felt certain he was about to drop free without his prize and be kicked into the dust by the black demon of a horse. The second handle, though it did not break, did pull free from its stitching where it met the thick brocade of the bag.

One more jounce and the bag and the man pinwheeled to the pricker-laden, stony ground.

Dust boiled high about him — breathing wasn't a possibility. Cookie lay on his side, half expecting the devil horse to swing wide, and return to stomp his head like an old melon left in a field. But that didn't happen.

The dust broke apart, powdered away on an unseen breeze, and breath returned in shallow gasping sips between his battered lips.

"Gaaaah . . ." was all Cookie could say for long minutes, the same wordy sound over and over. He sensed a heavy weight to his left, something pressing on his arm. Maybe if he was lucky, he thought, it was a rattlesnake, a big old bull of a rattler, come to sink fang in his neck and finish him off.

If only it was that easy.

He parted his dust-filled, red-circled eyes and looked to his left. Saw nothing but sky. He forced his head to the side, not so bad. *Tomorrow,* he thought. *My body will be in hell itself. If I live that long.*

But what he saw to his left heartened him — the bulging bulk of the carpetbag sitting on his arm like a fat child.

"Hello there," he croaked. "Glad to see you." He wanted to smile, but couldn't remember how. Maybe his face was froze forever. Like those soldiers who lost all feeling in their bodies. He'd seen such horrible sights, enough to convince him if he ever was worked over so bad that he lost touch with his own body, why he'd be best off to die. But then how do you go about that?

The sun, now that he could see straight upward, was a brutal, blazing thing. He felt like an egg in a pan and knew he had to get up. Somehow.

Curse that Rafe for getting him into this shenanigan. For every shenanigan they'd ever been in. But he knew he was being crabby, nothing more. Rafe wasn't any more to blame than the horse was. Still, he hoped he'd seen the last of that brute horse.

Cookie's breathing was almost normal, and it took him half a minute to prop himself up on an elbow. He surveyed his lean body, the once-somewhat tidy clothes belonging to Mincher now torn, more dusty than color to them. His right boot was gone, the left looked chewed by wolverines along the front, and the leather had worn through along his second and third toes.

He wiggled his toes and saw the tips in there, sock free. Now how did that happen, he wondered. He looked to the right boot-less foot and that sock was gone. His toes were red, bloodied here and there from scratches and scrapes.

He tried to sit up and groaned once more. If I move now it will be far better than if I lay here and moan, mortifying and seizing up like a fresh-killed man. So, with such thoughts guiding him, Cookie McGee, after long minutes of odd sounds and gouts of breath that under normal circumstances would have been rich, colorful curse words, managed to stand.

He tried to say, "Aah," as though he were sinking into a hot tub of water at a Chinese bathhouse. But it came out sounding like he was gargling gravel. He spat, spat again, and toed the bag of money.

"Okay friend. It's you and me."

He looked to the south, back from the direction they'd bolted, and saw Yuma Prison much closer than it should be. He thought for certain that fool horse had dragged him at least twenty miles. But no, maybe a mile off, maybe even less.

And was that a dark shape emerging from the shimmering bone-dry desert? Growing larger and larger? Cookie looked down at the money bag, shuffling over in front of it. Between the sun and the grit in his eyes, he couldn't make out who or what it was until the shape was nearly on him. If it was the devil horse, he was prepared to kill it somehow. Maybe bite it to death. That reminded him he needed to look for his knife. He scanned the earth close by where he stood but saw no sign of the dull blade. So much for that. Have to chew his way through whatever fight was coming. He had gone through far too much to rescue that cash. No way was he giving it up easy.

"Cook?" A dark shape looked down at him.

Cookie squinted up. "Rafe? That you?"

"Yep. You look like hell." The big man slid down from his horse. "What have you been up to?"

"Oh," Cookie spat a wad of phlegmy grit. "You know me, I been out riding in this godawful scalding desert for the pure pleasure of it. I been taking the air and lounging."

"Ahh," said Rafe. "Well, I see you still have your magic bag. Do I dare ask the whereabouts of the horse?"

"You can ask anything you please." Cookie spat again. "Don't mean I aim to tell you."

"Okay, then. Mossy can ride with me on Horse and you can climb aboard Stinky. If you can manage it. You look like you've been dragged a spell."

"You never mind what I been up to!" He bent over in a coughing spasm. Rafe laid a hand on his friend's bony shoulder. Cookie shook it off and ambled over to his horse. "Tell you when I'm good and ready, I said!"

He hesitated before reaching up to the saddle, as though it lay in wait ready to strike. "You want to make yourself useful, you rummage around hereabouts and look for my long knife. Lost it in a recent fracas."

Rafe nodded, and toed the churned dirt. He found the dusty knife a few moments later and handed it to Cookie, who still stood by the horse, leaning against it. Rafe bent low and laced his big hands together. Cookie looked at them, looked away, and nodded. Then he hoisted his stiffening left leg and placed his one booted foot in his pard's hands and allowed himself to be hoisted up into the saddle.

Cookie motioned to Rafe to lash the battered carpetbag to the mustang's saddle horn.

Rafe said nothing, kept his hat pulled down low, and retrieved his canteen from his saddle. He offered it to Cookie, who drank deeply, his reedy throat working like a bird's.

The entire time, Mossback stood quietly beside Horse, glancing back now and again at the prison.

After a few silent minutes, Rafe mounted up, leaned down, and hoisted his old prison friend up behind him in the saddle. Then they rode east at a slow gait.

"Is Cookie okay?" said Mossy quietly to Rafe.

Rafe nodded and offered his old prison friend a cigar. "He's fine. Not much different than usual, to be honest. They don't come any tougher." He smiled and struck a match.

For an hour, Cookie thought only of how he was going to spend all the money on himself and no one else. Not even Stinky. Because at that moment, a horse was a horse, all were the same, he thought, coughing up desert dust.

Why, he might even buy himself decent boots and give up on horses altogether. The very thought of it made him smile. Then his dried lips cracked and he resumed his scowl once more.

CHAPTER THIRTY: HOME AGAIN, HOME AGAIN . . .

For the rest of that day, Cookie rode stiff-backed, wincing as they jostled eastward along the trail toward Colorado. They all agreed it would be wise to put distance between them and Yuma, in case someone came to their senses and found fault with their shenanigans there.

Cookie found the trip tolerable with the help of frequent nips off the bottle of the surprisingly fine whiskey Rafe produced from out of his saddlebag.

"Compliments of the warden." He winked and all three men knocked back a few swallows, but it was Cookie who cradled the bottle. By the time they made camp that night, he was convinced he'd been worried over nothing, that he was still a tough enough man that the encounter with Mincher's horse had been little more than an annoying jostling.

But at dawn the next morning, his body

401

told him differently. He was battered and stiffened beneath his blanket. He woke and found he was able to move his eyelids, but little else. "Rafe," he wheezed. "Need a hand here."

The big man knelt by his pard's side. "What can I do, Cook?"

"Hoist me up. I'm a mite stiff."

Cookie spent a few minutes on his hands and knees, then crab-walked about the campsite before he was able to straighten up to his full height. He rubbed his back. "So this is what rigor mortis feels like."

Mossback looked years younger than he had when he stepped from his cell back in Yuma. He also proved himself a fair hand at campfire cookery. Though they had meager provisions — bacon, hard tack, a sack of dried apple slices, coffee, spices — Mossy was able to make the combination taste like more than it was. The coffee was ample and strong, helped by the dollops of whiskey Cookie drizzled into his cup. The other men declined, but Cookie didn't feel any guilt. He had, after all, and he finally admitted it to himself, grappled with Satan's own steed and lived to tell of it, though not in any animated way for a few days yet.

An hour into their ride that second day, Cookie clucked Stinky up beside Rafe and

Mossy. "Back in Yuma you said you was Italian."

"Yes," said Mossback, smiling as if the word gave him pleasure.

Rafe pulled the cigar from his mouth. "You'll have to excuse Cookie, Mossy. He likes to know things."

"You don't have to go makin' excuses for me! I'm my own man, right enough."

"What you really want to know," said Mossy, as if Cookie hadn't spoken, "is what was my crime."

"Yes. You see, Rafe? Can a man help it if he is the curious sort?"

"Oh, you're curious, all right," said Rafe, puffing on his cigar and watching the trail ahead.

Mossback cut in before Cookie could respond. "I replied honestly yesterday. I am an Italian. And my real name is Marcello, which somehow in prison became Mossback, which I do not mind. But being Italian, that is my crime. You see, Warden Timmons and some of his men did not like an Italian, and one from the north, well." He shrugged. "They set me up for a crime, far from here." He quieted a moment, lost in his thoughts, then said, "It was bread. A loaf of bread. They said I stole it from a bakery in Dodge City. But I had already

403

paid for it." He looked at Cookie and smiled. "It proves no matter how good you try to be in life, you cannot change how people feel in their blackest heart. That is where these men dwelt. And because I wasn't like them, I caused them fear."

Cookie scratched his chin and finally said, "That don't make no sense at all. But then again, I have found the more you stick around in this old life, the more odd things you come upon. I'm glad we were able to spring you from that leg-hold trap of a place."

"Me, too, Mr. McGee."

"It's Cookie, Mossy. Nothin' but. We're pards, now."

"What say we head on home, chums," said Rafe.

"I'd like that," said Cookie.

"Mossy," said Rafe. "I seem to recall you telling me you have family up Minnesota way. Is that still the case?"

"Yes, I believe so. A daughter, Vanessa. And maybe grandbabies by now, too." He shrugged. "But they think I am dead. Timmons saw to that."

"Bah," said Cookie. "We'll let them know the score."

"I would like that very much. Grand-babies? A man dreams of such things."

"Well, we got us a right fine place for you to rest up, get your strength back before your journey northward to meet with your family. You like to eat?"

"Oh, yes," said Mossy.

"Good, 'cause we got mighty fine food at the ranch. Say, you like biscuits? Cause I know a woman who's . . . no, no, I ain't going to talk her up too much lest you take a shine to her. Already got my hands full with Doc, that rascal."

Mossy said nothing, but looked at Cookie with raised eyebrows.

Rafe puffed up a blue cloud, exhaling. "Oh, you mean Doc Jones? The man who's been back at the ranch with Arlene for weeks now without you? That Doc?"

"Now you look here!" said Cookie, twisting in his saddle. The movement unleashed a fresh wave of aches and throbs. "Oh, you wait, you big lummox!"

Rafe pulled ahead slightly, puffing his cigar. He uncorked a fresh flask of whiskey and handed it to his old trail pard. "Don't ever change, Cookie McGee."

Cookie gurgled back a few swallows and smacked his lips. "What makes you think I can, boy?"

And they rode northeastward toward

Colorado and the ranch, heading home to friends and family.

The end.

The Outfit will return . . .

ABOUT THE AUTHOR

Matthew P. Mayo is an award-winning author of more than thirty books and dozens of short stories. His novel, *Stranded: A Story of Frontier Survival,* won the prestigious Western Heritage Award for Outstanding Western Novel by the National Cowboy & Western Heritage Museum, as well as the Spur Award for Best Western Juvenile Fiction by the Western Writers of America, and the Peacemaker Award by Western Fictioneers. His novel, *Tucker's Reckoning,* won the Western Writers of America's Spur Award for Best Western Novel, and his short stories have been Spur Award and Peacemaker Award finalists.

Matthew and his wife, videographer Jennifer Smith-Mayo, run Gritty Press (www.GrittyPress.com) and rove the byways of North America in search of hot coffee, tasty whiskey, and high adventure. For more information, drop by Matthew's website at www.MatthewMayo.com.

The employees of Thorndike Press hope you have enjoyed this Large Print book. All our Thorndike, Wheeler, and Kennebec Large Print titles are designed for easy reading, and all our books are made to last. Other Thorndike Press Large Print books are available at your library, through selected bookstores, or directly from us.

For information about titles, please call:
(800) 223-1244

or visit our Web site at:
http://gale.com/thorndike

To share your comments, please write:
Publisher
Thorndike Press
10 Water St., Suite 310
Waterville, ME 04901